ADVANCE PRAISE FOR
CARRY YOURSELF BACK TO ME

"Deborah Reed's novel, *Carry Yourself Back to Me*, tells the compelling story of long-held family secrets, romantic entanglements, and a small-town murder that starts it all unraveling. With deft humor and insight and a marvelous sense of pacing, Reed explores the limits of trust and loyalty, the enduring nature of family bonds, and the clash between illusions and truth in the quest for lasting love."

—Jim Tomlinson, author of *Things Kept, Things Left Behind*
(Iowa Short Fiction Award)

"*Carry Yourself Back to Me* is a beautifully written, thoroughly engaging novel. Deborah Reed's prose is lyrical, elegant, and vivid—she is a standout among new American novelists."

—Jessica Anya Blau, author of *The Summer of Naked Swim Parties* and *Drinking Closer to Home*

"Deborah Reed has written here a novel peopled with real, flesh-and-bone characters—men and women both as good and delightfully flawed as our best friends, our spouses, ourselves. And the icing on this cake is Reed's lucid, lovely prose. *Carry Yourself Back to Me* is, simply, a pleasure to read."

—Kirsten Sundberg Lunstrum, author of
This Life She's Chosen and *Swimming with Strangers*

"*Carry Yourself Back to Me* marries gorgeous and wise prose with a can't-help-but-read-one-more-chapter plot. In it, Reed weaves a complex story of love and longing that's mysterious, intelligent, and full of heart. She had me from page one."

—Cheryl Strayed, author of the novel *Torch*, and *Wild,* a memoir

"Deborah Reed writes beautifully about the interlocking puzzles of romantic and family love and the patterns that play out from generation to generation. While her protagonist is a master of the sad song, Reed achieves a symphonic effect—rich, intense, and surprisingly joyful.

—Dawn Raffel, author of *Carrying the Body* and *Further Adventures in the Restless Universe*

CARRY
YOURSELF
BACK
TO
ME

CARRY YOURSELF BACK TO ME

A NOVEL BY
DEBORAH REED

PUBLISHED BY

amazon encore

The characters and events portrayed in this book are fictitious. Any similarity to real persons, living or dead, is coincidental and not intended by the author.

Published by AmazonEncore
P.O. Box 400818
Las Vegas, NV 89140

ISBN-13: 9781935597674
ISBN-10: 1935597671

For my parents

There's nothin' you can send me, my own true love,
There's nothin' I wish to be ownin'.
Just carry yourself back to me unspoiled,
From across that lonesome ocean.

—Bob Dylan, "Boots of Spanish Leather"

PART ONE

PART ONE

ONE

Annie lifts her father's old binoculars off the porch. Out past the cornfield a lime-colored pickup idles in the fog of Mrs. Lanie's tangelo grove next door. The driver's side hangs open, but no one is behind the wheel. Clutter juts from the truck bed, vapor rises from the tailpipe. Annie knows most of Mrs. Lanie's pickers, but she doesn't know this truck.

A ridiculous thought occurs to her. Owen's come back. He's sneaking through the grove and coming around the back of the house to surprise her. He'll cup her eyes from behind and say something stupid like, "Guess who needs glasses?" Or "Who turned out the lights?"

It's early. She hasn't brushed her teeth or concealed her dark circles. She hasn't washed her hair or even pulled it back. The ropey ends catch on her mouth as she sips her coffee. She scans the grove for the shape of a person stealing tangelos. There's no one she can see.

The last thing Annie wants to do is think about Owen. But it's like one foot tumbling over a slippery edge of earth the way she unexpectedly falls again and again into the same opening. Her thoughts have become flimsy, sentimental, throwaway songs. Nursery rhymes. *Where oh where have you gone?*

Steam rises to her lashes from the coffee stalled at her lips. She lowers the cup and presses its warmth into her chest, into the pocket of chilled bare skin above the zipper of her fleece.

It's not as if their five years together were perfect. They were riddled with rough patches, cruel things slipping from their mouths. She watches the fog shift over the field and remembers all those brassy, merciless words. No doubt she'd use them again, given the chance.

The problem is the nights she couldn't sleep for all the pleasure rushing through her. The malty scent of his skin, like freshly cut grain, something meant to be eaten. The feel of his cuff brushing her wrist made her greedy for sex and food and music to be played even louder. She'd spent years floundering in smoky, mediocre venues hoping for a crowd to show, and suddenly, here was her muse, her good luck charm, making her old hopes seem puny, amateurish in comparison to what she had with him.

She can't forget this is the porch where most of the songs for *Gull on a Steeple* were written. Detour the same old dog that howled at the harmonica. These Adirondack chairs the ones whose red paint Annie and Owen wore away from so much use. Annie circles the rings of coffee and wine with her finger, the oily bug spray sealed into the arms like evidence of mornings, evenings, late nights spent trying to get it right. He made an honest-to-God singer-songwriter out of her. She made a sought-after music producer out of him. *Rolling Stone* declared *Gull on a Steeple* "An instant classic filled with vivid tales of love and loss without the slightest hint of sentimentality." *Depression* magazine claimed, "Annie Walsh's painful, clear-eyed, storied songs are woven with a voice reminiscent of the great Patsy Cline, Lucinda Williams, and Aimee Mann, all spun into one." The comparisons flattered her for the first few minutes, but after that and ever since she's done nothing but worry about measuring up. Even when *Entertainment Weekly* came along and knocked her down to something of a Disney production. "A sprightly, nearly elfin frame that charms its way across the stage and into your heart."

Now it's hard to even listen to music, let alone play it.

Cold fog quiets the birds and shifts like hot steam above Lake Winsor to the east. Minutes earlier hailstones sliced past Annie's bedroom window and skipped off the ground like pearls on concrete, escaping in all directions. The timer on the coffee pot had already gone off, and Annie dressed quickly in a fleece and jeans, her red rubber boots with the knobby black soles. She emerged onto the porch as if from a cave, coffee sloshing down her wrist, Detour stumbling at her heels the way old dogs do, scared old dogs, with no direction. Annie wanted the hail to prick her skin, to shake loose the stubborn reveries pinned behind her eyes. But in the time it took to pour coffee, the hail had already moved on.

She flips on the small radio she keeps on the porch. It's set to a station she found by accident at the end of the dial, thinking she was turning up the news. It runs crackly old serials where salesmen and seamstresses make their way through hard times—characters who do things that don't always make sense. But then you hear the backstory the next day, something to do with an aunt's dying wish, or an orphan on the side of the road whose true identity is just becoming clear. Today it's a butcher in New York and a young boy, his nephew, the son of a brother the man hates. He seems to love the boy in spite of this. "You remind me of me at your age," the butcher says. The accents are a little overplayed.

Backstory. A word she's been trying to think of. She ought to write a song called *Backstory*. Some days it feels as if every cup in the kitchen, every tree in the yard, patch of crabgrass, anthill, the pine planks beneath her feet, even the sky itself is buzzing with backstory, existing for the sole purpose of reminding her of Owen. The songs, the jokes, the curious observations resonate like a tuning fork to the head.

Detour heaves himself up and lets loose a sharp, single bark at a chase of squirrels in the live oak tree. Acorns tumble and click in their wake. The bark pierces the quiet like a gunshot.

"You're a big man when it comes to little squirrels," Annie says. He'd trembled when hail struck the cedar roof. But he's a good dog. Bulky and older than he has a right to be.

It takes her a moment to realize he wasn't barking at the squirrels. At least one of his senses is still keen. Annie barely sees the man in the grove. He quickly hops into the truck and shuts the door as if he's gone out there to relieve himself and doesn't want anyone to know.

The truck starts on the road toward to her driveway. Annie knocks the binoculars into the spongy grass, hops off the porch and snatches them up. It's hard to focus on a moving target. She quits trying when the truck reaches her gate. Her driveway is at least an eighth of a mile long. But the far-off, tinny sound of music reaches her ears.

Detour lumbers down the steps as if each leg is made of a wooden cane. He strains his hips in the muddy driveway. "Stay here, boy," Annie says. "Over here."

All at once the sun bores a hole through the fog and glares off the filmy windshield, hiding whoever's behind the wheel.

But she can see that the clutter sticking out of the back of the truck is rakes, shovels, a mower, and a mess of brown clippings, and she knows just who it is.

Detour knows too. He escorts the truck toward Annie, so closely his tail thumps the door. Her brother hangs his hand through the open window and touches the tip of Detour's nose.

The music on the stereo is The Beautiful South doing a cover of "Dream a Little Dream of Me." "They're the cheeriest bunch of sad songs you'll ever hear," she'd said when she gave it to him years ago.

The truck comes to a jerky stop. Walsh Landscaping is spelled out in bold, cursive script beneath an outline of a live oak tree on the door.

My name is Annie Walsh. She used to say this, gently, after walking on stage. Then came the applause. The swirling whistles. The screams.

The music dies down in the truck, and the engine rattles off in stages. The air smells like french fries.

Her heart pulses against the thin wall of her chest, her brain, her ears, her hands. She's not prepared to see her own brother, no matter how many times she's imagined him showing up like this.

He steps out in a T-shirt and canvas shorts. He isn't wearing a jacket. A sure sign it's going to be warmer than Annie has hoped.

He isn't smiling so much as grinning, just slightly, to one side as if to say, "What do you make of this? Here I am after six whole months, showing up like it's nothing to nobody." He has a habit of running his hand through his floppy hair, and when he gets within fifteen feet he stops and does exactly that.

"Did you see me in the binoculars?" he asks.

Detour slides his ribs along Calder's legs like a cat.

"Detour, come," Annie says.

"I was making the pig face you used to laugh at."

"Detour, now."

"I guess not." He scratches Detour's back. "Christ almighty. You're an old man." He flings loose fur from his fingers and gently pats Detour's stiff hip.

Mrs. Lanie's house is close enough to see her eyes go wide when she pulls the curtain back in her kitchen window. Her hair is an early morning tangle of gray.

Calder turns and lifts a meek hand as if he's embarrassed, as if he's remembering all that went on the last time he was here, Annie screaming until her voice gave way. *How long? At least tell me that! How long did you know he was seeing her?*

Mrs. Lanie waves against the glass, and then the curtain drops and she's gone.

Calder sighs and studies Annie's house up somewhere along the trim of the low-slung roof. The gutters obviously need cleaning, and she expects this is what he'll say. "Looks like you had the place painted," he says.

Annie turns toward the Buttery Cream siding and Dove White trim. Her pale creamsicle of a bungalow, more cabin than house, cloaked by overgrown trees. Maple, tupelo, sweet gum, willow.

"Looks good," he says. "Looks new again. Amazing what a little paint can do."

He doesn't say Owen's name, but it's there in the air, the thing missing from this house, this picture. It seems to touch Calder's face, his eyes, which he rubs.

"What are you listening to?" He gestures to the radio on the porch.

"You're too young to understand, son," the butcher says.

"Nothing," Annie says.

He nods as if he's just agreed not to ask any more questions. "Well. The hail did a number on that tupelo. It's hunkering down like a kid getting pelted with rocks."

Annie glances at the tree. The limbs are twisted at odd angles, their ends horned and jerking, barbed wire claws.

"Anyway, I'm doing a job right up the road," Calder says. "I figured it was like some kind of sign or something, being this close, and being on your birthday and all. Happy birthday. You don't look a minute past thirty."

She's forty years old today. She thinks of her chaffed hands and clasps them to the binoculars at her back.

"I swear, Annie. You're pretty as ever."

She's well aware that another year, one half-filled with a mountain of stress, has changed the way she looks.

"I heard one of your songs on that Chevy commercial. and someone said another was in that movie with what's her name, Jessica Lange."

"It's been six months," she says, keeping her voice in check. "This probably isn't the first time you've been within a few miles of here."

Calder chews the inside of his cheek, something he's done since they were kids. "No. I can't say it is."

Detour hobbles over and leans against her leg.

"It's been a long time," Calder says. "I thought maybe it was OK to come and see you—it's your birthday. And Christmas less than two weeks away. How have you been?"

She tucks the binoculars under her arm and shoves her hands into her pockets. "Fine."

Calder turns his head as if wishing he could take back the question. He studies her yard. She follows his line of sight, sure he's taking stock of broken branches and anthills and the fact that the soil doesn't drain quite right with the tree roots exposed like that. "It's been a while since you've seen Uncle Calder," he says.

It's not what she expects. He's caught her off guard. Her mind tunnels backwards to the first time she lost someone she loved. She and Calder are twelve and eleven, Uncle Calder is wiping her tears, patting the top of her head with his oversized palm after setting flowers on her father's grave. "It's going to be all right, squirt," he'll tell her more than once. A far off ringing pricks her ears.

"He's not getting any younger," Calder says.

It takes a moment to clear.

"You mind if we sit down on the porch for a minute?" Calder asks.

She looks at the porch, now drenched in sun, the empty chair where she had planned to eat breakfast. Granola, fresh yogurt, and blackberries from the farmer's market. More than enough for two, but she doesn't offer, not that or anything else. Not even the chair.

Detour drags himself onto the porch, lies down between the chairs, and sighs.

It's clear that the boy on the radio is being played by a man. He raises his voice in some kind of anguish and the switch gives him away.

The sooner Calder says whatever he's come to say, the sooner he'll leave. Annie throws her arm out as a signal for him to head up the steps. "They're slippery," she says, and immediately regrets the impression that she cares.

Calder steps onto the porch but doesn't sit in a chair. He sits on the railing and grips it near his hips. He's already talking a blue streak about work before she joins him on the porch. "So anyway, I'm pulling these thorny sonsabitches out while Jerry's gone off somewhere with my gloves. You remember Jerry..."

Annie shuts off the radio. She feels outside of herself, leaning against the doorframe, studying the two of them, the dailiness of their chitchat, the ordinary scene. He's still so good at conversation, hard won from a childhood marked by tics. Blinking, jumping, swinging legs beneath a chair. He learned to switch conversations from one thing to the next, drawing attention from his jerky body to anything from a USDA Textural Triangle for measuring sandy loam to singing a Hank Williams tune to predicting sinkholes in parking lots. He's doing it now, even though he hasn't had tics in years—going from old houses to cutting back thorny scrub plums, from his third pickup in five years to their mother's inability to grow anything aside from weeds, from Uncle Calder's paid participation in medical studies to a woman Calder met downtown while landscaping the law office next door, "and well, I'll get to her in a minute, but first," he says, and the ebb and flow of his voice is so familiar that Annie begins to move with him, her nods, her half smiles, signaling him on.

His laugh lines have deepened. Especially when he gets back to talking about the woman downtown.

"She owns a Danish bakery on Church Street," he says. "Got all these raspberry and pecan Kringles and bread pudding that sweetens the whole block by seven every morning. I swear she's got eyes the color of limes. Her name's Sidsel Jørgenson. A slash through the first O." He slices the air diagonally with his finger. "That's how you spell her last name in Danish."

Annie nods, just a little, in reply.

"The only problem is, Sidsel has a husband named Magnus. A big ol' Dane." He opens his arms to the sides, and then he hesitates as if he's thinking something else about the man that he'd rather not say. "And meaner than a skillet full of rattlesnakes."

This sounds funnier than he seems to have intended. He sounds like their father, and the soft, thrown-back cadence of his laughter is so familiar, so suddenly missed that she can't help herself. She laughs with him, still conscious of her every move, every sound that comes from her mouth like a token she grudgingly hands him in exchange for another minute in her world.

When the laughter runs its course, Calder shakes his head at the porch and smiles a taut, self-conscious smile she's sure isn't meant for her to see.

It's getting warm on the porch. Annie slips off her boots, unzips her fleece, and goes inside for something to drink. She comes back with two glasses of tangerine juice and finds Calder whistling a tune at the yard. She barely reaches his shoulders. Other than that, they look more alike than any siblings she knows. Heads full of dark wavy hair, light blue eyes, and a mess of summer freckles they inherited from Grandad Walsh. She follows the fine, curvy line of his brow down to the blotchy Irish red in his cheeks. He appears happy. Relaxed. Unquestionably sober.

She takes a seat next to him on the railing and places the juice in his hand like a peace offering. Sandy soil smells drift from his skin. No alcohol. Not even the acrid kind that could seep from his pores and give away recent days of drinking. Six months ago she'd found him at Hal's roadside bar, red-faced and yeasty, slung onto the counter with red- and yellow-tinged eyes. He could barely utter the sloppy, sour words in her ear. "You don't want to know how young she is. I should have told you. I wanted to tell you." Before he passed out he called Owen an asshole. Owen had been his best friend.

Several days after that he stopped by to pick up his Bobcat loader still sitting in Annie's backyard from the landscaping he'd done. He smelled like whiskey and days of unwashed skin.

Then came the screaming, the cursing. "How could you do this to me!" She must have yelled that at least ten times. When he refused to answer, refused to even look her in the eye, she realized there was more. She thought of the times he and Owen had gone off to buy sound equipment, fish the St. John's, and haul trees. She realized they hadn't gone off at all. "You covered for him, didn't you?" He shielded his eyes from the sun, and then massaged what must have been a nasty hangover in his forehead. "Answer me!" He didn't know the half of all she'd been through in those three days after Owen left. She would have given anything to have the one saving grace be that her own brother, the one person she had counted on her whole life, hadn't helped the man she loved cheat on her. But her brother flinched and stammered, and that was all the answer she needed. "Don't you come back here again," she'd said. "I mean it. Not ever." The sickest kind of betrayal she'd ever felt, sicker even, than Owen's betrayal days before, had wormed its way inside her.

Now, here he is six months later, smelling fresh like the earth. Like strong coffee and cinnamon.

The breeze is warm and moist. The birds have started up again in a sky that's practically clear.

"I'm in love with her, Annie," Calder says. Then softer, "And she's in love with me." He swallows a gulp of air. His hands shake. He looks off to the side when he speaks. "I've never known in all my life what it is to love like this."

All she can do is stare. She almost laughs. Then she does laugh, but it's awkward, too close to a cry. "*What?*" Her voice breaks. She looks down at her cracked hands, at the tiny lotus tattoo inside her wrist, remembering how Calder had gone first and told her it wasn't so bad, no worse than a shot in the arm. But it was, it was much worse, and she thinks of the needle dipping in and out of the thin, tender skin of her wrist.

"Tell me you didn't come here to say how happy in love you are."

Calder knocks a rusty cowbell to the porch when he comes to his feet. Detour jerks his head at the clang.

"It's bad enough what you did. It's bad enough," she says, and catches herself before adding—*that I was at the supermarket buying chicken, cheddar cheese, and a pregnancy test when he left me.* "That for months," she continues, "I've been waking up wondering if there's something wrong with me for someone to leave me the way he did, but now you want to rub all your happiness—with a woman who belongs to someone else by the way—in my face?"

Detour thumps his tail but doesn't get up.

Calder places a hand on her shoulder. "I'm sorry. I'm sorry about what happened between you and Owen. I can't imagine being without Sidsel, and I just—"

She knocks his hand off. "Are you *kidding* me? She's *married*, Calder! I'm beginning to think the world is made up of nothing but liars and cheats."

"You don't understand. I've known her for a long time."

"And just what is that supposed to mean? You two setting some kind of record? See how long you can go before someone finds out, or better yet, runs off and leaves a goddamn letter in his place?"

"I'm sorry. This was such a bad idea."

"You think?"

"Hold on." He catches her eye and she quickly turns away. "What letter?"

She holds her bottom lip between her teeth and focuses on a heron's nest across the lake.

"He left you a *letter*? You mean in place of saying *good-bye*?"

It's too far away to tell if the heron is in there.

"He didn't explain things to you himself?"

Annie meets his eyes. "What was there to explain?"

Calder flexes his fists. He looks as if he means to say more, but instead shakes his head at the lake and turns and steps off the porch.

"Explain *what*, Calder?"

But he's already started the truck and is pulling it around in the circular driveway with the shovels and rakes clanging at his back. His bumper sticker reads, POWERED BY VEGETABLE OIL. The smell of french fries fills the air again.

From the stereo comes, "Say nightie-night and kiss me. Just hold me tight and tell me you'll miss me."

He shuts the truck off and it rattles like before. He gets out and climbs into the bed where he slides out a piece of plywood for a ramp. He jumps down and pulls the mower to the ground.

"What the hell are you doing?"

"This here's a lawn mower."

"Stop it, Calder."

"It's your birthday," he says.

"Put it back. I don't want you here. I don't want you doing this. The grass is wet, asshole."

"I'm trying to do something nice. I'll be the judge of wet grass."

"You'll be the judge of bullshit," she says.

"You shouldn't be alone."

"You should have thought about that before you decided to cover for him."

"Annie, please."

"He might still be here if I'd known what was going on. Maybe I could have stopped it."

He pulls the mower to the edge of the lawn. The grass is higher than the wheels. He stares at her as if to say no one could have stopped it. "This whole thing has eaten me alive," he says. "It's a wonder I'm standing here sober." He picks up the larger branches and tosses them into the driveway.

"Well, thank goodness for that girlfriend of yours. It comes in handy to have someone around when you need them."

He walks back to the mower.

"Where is he, Calder?"

"I don't know."

"No one has heard from him. Where is he?"

"Maybe they're just not saying." He reaches for the ripcord on the mower. He holds it between his fingers without looking at her. "I honestly don't know." He yanks the cord and the blade rips through the overgrown grass.

Annie scoops up the scratched aviator sunglasses off the oak stump side-table. Were they hers or Owen's? She snaps them against her eyes and lowers herself into the Adirondack chair. It could be spring for all this weather. Sunshine and cut grass, the buzz of a mower growing distant. Detour sprawls sideways in the sun at her feet. Within seconds his paws twitch in his sleep. *He dreams of running,* Owen used to say. *With you, at the beach.*

TWO

The ocean looks like a frothy cocktail out there. Owen pulls on his ear at the kitchen table and sighs, half expecting to see his breath turn white. It's thirty-seven degrees outside and near impossible to heat the open plan of a mid-century modern with its concrete floor, high ceilings, and glass walls seeping with the windy outdoors.

"What's wrong?" Tess plugs in the Christmas lights across from him in the living room. She tucks the tangle of cords behind the scooped woven chair with the sheepskin. Her bare feet shuffle across the waxy concrete toward him. He knows if he touched them they'd feel as warm as sand in summertime. *Ship, ship*, they go, like the sound of brushing crumbs off paper. She plods into the kitchen in her pajamas—no robe—with the white lights flickering behind her.

Owen drops his hand from his ear. "Good morning." He's been looking out the glass doors at the Gulf of Mexico for the last hour, the waves curling and smacking the sugar-white sand. The rhythmic trance has pulled him miles and years away, but now he's looking at the curve of his wife's belly as it reaches toward him, closer it seems, than yesterday. "Sleep well?" he asks. He finds her most beautiful in the morning. Maybe it's just seeing her for the first time of the day. Her blond hair is thrown behind her shoulders. Thick lashes rim her sleepy brown eyes.

She rubs her round belly and *ship, ships* toward the coffee pot on the counter. Her breasts have ballooned even more overnight. "I'm still tired," she says. "Little Caroline played soccer with my spleen all night."

Caroline is the name Tess has picked out for the baby. Owen doesn't have a problem with the name. In fact he likes the classic sound of it, the small pink face it conjures in his mind. He just can't bring himself to call her *Caroline*. She's hardly a real person yet. At least that's how he feels. But he doesn't say this to Tess. He doesn't know if she's noticed his references to *baby, her,* and *she*.

Tess manages herself into the armless chair across from him. She glances outside toward the waves. "Something on your mind?" she asks.

"Does the coffee taste all right? I made it over an hour ago."

She takes a sip. "It isn't bad."

The blue strap of her top reminds him of the middle of the night when he watched her sleep. She never seemed to be aware of his eyes on her or the fact that he was wide awake, and this had made him think of Annie. The nights he'd done the very same thing with her, except Annie always woke, suddenly with a smile in the dark, and she would pull him close and say, "Doodle bug" or "Sweet baby" or "Give me that honey," silly, mocking things she never said in the daytime. She'd laugh and within moments her breath was slow and steady against his shoulder. Her capacity to feel him next to her was unnatural, he knew that, and yet he craved the way it filled him with relief.

"Is it the baby? Are you nervous?" Tess asks.

"Of course not. A little." He grins and touches her hand. Warm, always warm, an oven for the bun inside her.

Tess tilts her head to the side and smiles the way she does when she thinks something is cute. A big-eyed kitten. A toddler in pigtails. She quickly moves on, taking a long, solid breath before pulling the morning paper from its plastic sheath. She picks through the folds and then settles back on the front page.

She is twenty-eight years old. Smart and decent and painfully beautiful. Plenty to place her in a category by herself.

He turns back to the water. Pelicans form a V above the waves. Several at the back switch and fall in line again. He wonders about their ability to do this, to know exactly where to go, and when.

Tess yawns behind the paper. She moans softly toward the end and gently shakes her head of sleep.

Annie turned forty a week ago. He still hasn't recovered from thinking on her so hard that day. The clichés exhausted him. He couldn't stop the vision of them hoisting into the air, message-filled balloons heading south until they popped and filled the sky above Annie's house with all the tired expressions that could have been meant for anyone, everyone.

I didn't mean for this to happen.

I never meant to hurt you.

I still love you.

Will you ever take me back?

"It's not going to get above thirty-eight degrees today," Tess says from behind the paper.

"Is that normal for this time of year up here?" he asks.

"Not really. I don't remember it being cold like this when I was growing up."

Owen can't help but think that at twenty-eight "growing up" wasn't really that long ago. But in just a few weeks their own little girl will begin growing up here, too. Within months she'll be kicking her legs and squealing with excitement when she's lifted into his arms like babies he's seen in restaurants and parks and movies. He'll breathe in layers of baby powder and her own sweet honey smell that'll have a way of stirring the fibrous, primal love, which, according to the stories in the new edition of *First Time Father* that Tess gave him, is buried somewhere deep inside his chest.

"We've got to get Caroline's room ready," Tess says. "I still don't have a changing table figured out."

"Maybe this weekend."

"I thought you were working."

"I'll make the time."

"Thank you, sweetie," she says from behind the paper.

There's something duplicitous in the way she calls him *sweetie*. Maybe it is just the way he hears it. He needs to get more sleep. He still wakes from dreams of Annie laughing, her mouth close enough for him to touch her wet tongue, and he finds himself hard beneath the sheet where the real live flesh of his pregnant wife's leg is pressing against him.

"What were you thinking about when I came in?" The paper still hasn't moved from her face.

"What?"

"It's the pulling-on-the-earlobe thing. I can tell something was bothering you."

"Why do you keep asking me that?" He caresses the side of her arm and feels a rush of love and desire toward her for all the wrong reasons. He clears the small scratch in his throat.

"I don't know. Sometimes I worry about you." She lays the paper down and keeps her gaze on it.

"I don't remember pulling on my ear," he says with more emotion than is called for.

"You were."

"Hmn." He brings it down a notch. "I was just thinking about what I've got to do today. And that song I've been working on with Danny Williams."

Tess flips the page. "And what's bothering you about all that?"

"I wouldn't really say it's *bothering* me. Maybe my ear was itching or something. I don't know. I'm not *bothered* by anything really."

He looks out at the stream of icy cold water flowing flatly over the limestone slab. Getty Images owns twenty stock photos of this house. Tess has included some in her articles for home and garden magazines—the supposedly serene view through the glass doors, the blinding white sand, the small Japanese garden complete with a slab stone water feature. The first time he saw Tess she stood alone taking notes in the lobby of the historic building that housed a studio he worked in. She was studying sconces on the fourteen-foot ceiling, her head thrown back as sun streamed the long windows and hit her bare neck like spotlight cones. The image hollowed his insides. Then it turned right around and filled him with a burning curiosity. A craving. A relentless itch. To this day clichés are all he has for an explanation.

"I'm sorry. But I'm not stupid, you know." Tess finally looks up.

"What?"

"You were thinking about her, weren't you?"

"What?"

"Come on, Owen."

A pathetic laugh bursts from his mouth. "I was just thinking about the first time I saw you, the way the sun came through those long windows—"

Her head drops to the side. "Please."

"*What?*" He throws his hands in the air. "Please don't start that again. I'm here aren't I? My God, we're having a *baby* together. We're *married.*"

"And all of that is proof that you weren't thinking about her?" She pitches several pages before looking down.

The smell of burnt coffee seeps from the coffeemaker. He looks at the red button she forgot to switch off. He turns to her with his best incredulous look. "Listen. I was just sitting here minding my own business, enjoying the view outside—"

Tess raises her head. "What the hell."

"No, let me finish," he says, but her eyes have the rounded look of deep, penetrating shock.

She gapes at the paper with the same twisted expression and he realizes this is no longer about him. She holds her finger up to say, *Just a sec and I'll tell you.*

His raised voice lingers in the air, and he thinks of his big-eyed daughter smacking her chubby hands on her highchair to cut through her parent's squabbling. Guilt fills his lungs like smog.

"There couldn't be more than one Calder Walsh in the Orlando area, could there?" Tess asks.

Blood rushes to his skin. His cheeks burn. His legs feel full. How is it possible that she's saying Calder's name, here, now, in their kitchen, four hundred miles and six months away from his past? He jumps up to grab the Cheerios as if seized by hunger. He slows, reaches for the box, and then holds it to his chest. "I wouldn't think so. Why? What is it?"

"It says here that a man named Calder Walsh has been arrested for murder."

There isn't enough time to put this right in his mind before Tess adds, "It *is* him! It says, 'brother of singer/songwriter Annie Walsh.'" She's gaping now, her lower jaw sliding to the side, just enough to betray the satisfaction she's trying to hide. *Look at your old life*, her jaw says. *Thank God you're here with me.*

Owen has stopped midway to the table. She's saying *her* name now. He opens his mouth to speak, and then closes it, tightly, so nothing can escape.

Tess reads from the middle of the article. "…a brutal murder a week ago today at a roadside bar…Clues that led homicide detectives to Walsh, brother of singer/songwriter Annie Walsh…Wait," she says. "Let me read the whole thing from the start."

He sets the box of Cheerios onto the highchair tray and reaches for his earlobe then lets go, watching through the glass doors as a squall of gulls fly in a mess of angles, swooping at a man alone on a Sunday morning, eating his pastry on the beach.

Owen's going to be sick. He lowers himself into his chair. His skin feels warm and prickly. He tries to think of the right words. Words that won't give away too much. A line from one of Annie's songs runs through his head. *This feels like falling. Falling off the edge of the world.* His arms begin to itch. Now his scalp. Someone is dead. Calder is to blame.

"Who the hell are they saying he killed?" he yells.

"Just a second," she says, softer now, in a tone that stops him from ripping the paper from her warm hands.

"Someone named Magnus Jørgenson. A man from Denmark. Where have I heard that name?"

Owen pops up and hits the red button on the coffee maker with the side of his fist. He reaches for his ear and accidentally knocks the Cheerios from the tray. A river of round oats spills across the floor.

Tess watches him without comment. "I think I wrote about that guy's house last year," she finally says. She leans back in her chair and clutches her arms across her belly as if it's a kickball she is daring someone, anyone, to try and take. "I'm pretty sure it's him. Was him," she corrects.

Owen releases his ear and snatches the paper from the table.

"It says he was beaten beyond recognition," she says, before Owen has a chance to read it for himself.

THREE

Annie starts a fire so the warmth will greet her when she returns from the grove. She bundles in layers of wool and steps out onto the porch. What a relief to look out this time of year and find the haze of mosquitoes finally hidden away in logs and burrows, menacing snakes and gophers instead of Annie. The days are altered in a way that make her feel as if she's made other choices, as if she lives somewhere other than Central Florida.

Lake Winsor ripples and slaps its soggy banks. A blue heron strolls along the water's edge and spears a frog in its bill. He swallows it whole then leaps into the air, disappearing behind a wall of white, in the direction of the bowed stick nest across the lake.

Annie holds her throat, imagining a frog in there, legs thrashing, the panicked thumping of a racing, miniature heart. Does the frog know what's happening? Does he just give in? Or go on thinking there's still a chance to claw his way out?

For some reason this has her tracing, once again, Owen's steps in their last days together. He'd bought a new belt to fit his shrinking waist. He mentioned how the crooked crown molding in the kitchen needed straightening. He pointed his finger, asked her to gaze upward as if it were important for her to see exactly where it bothered him to look. And then he came down with a fever. "I love you," he mumbled through chills in the night. Who? Who did he love while she covered him with blankets? While she wiped his forehead with a cold cloth and pressed ice water into his red, burning lips?

Somewhere between the crooked molding and the fever, he'd drawn her into him at the kitchen sink and held her there without a word. A gray chest hair she'd never noticed twisted its way above the neckline of his T-shirt and quivered beneath her breath. His holding her that way was nothing he hadn't done before. Nothing the faithful wouldn't do. And yet she returns to that quiet embrace, the chest hair, the counter pressing into her hip as if they're all part of some defining moment. Hints to a larger narrative. Fragments that need only be brought together to make sense.

She heads for the grove. Haze, thick as smoke, engulfs the trees. It isn't until she gets within fifty yards that the red fruit begin to pop through.

She removes her glove and plucks down a tangelo. Sweet and juicy and surprisingly ripe. The low-hanging ones need to be picked right away. Bitter cold is seeping across the state. There's even been talk of snow.

She hears the sound of a car approaching her driveway. She can't see through the fog but can tell by the gentle hum that it isn't Calder's truck. She jogs across the field. The fog is just lifting over her house. The red chairs appear at the edge of the porch. Then Detour's golden face in the window.

Her mother's creamy sedan pulls in next to the house. It is nine o'clock in the morning. This doesn't make sense. For decades—ever since Annie's father died—her mother has rarely begun a day before noon.

She steps out in a butter-colored dress and matching jacket that stops at her waist, making her waist look even smaller than it already is. She darts in thin heels from one clump of grass to the next. Her hair is clasped into a tight arrangement at the back of her head. She doesn't attend church, but if she did this is how Annie imagines she'd look.

"You're sure out early this morning!" Annie yells as she lopes across Mrs. Lanie's yard. "What's with the church dress?"

Her mother turns and nearly slips down the steps.

Annie sees now that she's chosen the wrong words to greet her with. Tears have rolled through her mother's blush and dried.

"What's wrong?"

"You haven't heard, have you?"

"Heard what?"

"Dear God," her mother says. "You ought to answer your phone."

"What is it?"

"Can we sit down out here on the porch?" She takes a seat. "I need some fresh air."

Annie pulls the door open and Detour hobbles onto the porch. He sniffs her mother's bare knees. She gives his head a single pat.

"You painted the place," her mother says, looking around.

"What happened?" Annie sits next to her.

Her mother gathers her purse beneath her breasts. "It's brightened up a little."

"Is it Uncle Calder?" Annie braces for the words—*passed away, no longer with us, died in his sleep*—

"It's your brother."

At first Annie thinks she's saying that Calder is dead.

"He was arrested last night."

The tension built in Annie's throat releases through a squeaky laugh. *"What?"*

Her mother's eyes lock onto Annie's. The whites are splintered red, haunted with the look of terrible news. "They're saying he killed some man named Magnus."

Annie turns her ear toward her. She needs to hear these words again to make sure she's getting them right, only the words used to make such a request are lost on her.

The only problem is, Sidsel has a husband named Magnus.

Her mind switches to the grove. She has to tell Mrs. Lanie that the pickers need to get out there. She has no words for the feeling in her chest. Only an image of a soft rind punctured.

Her mother pulls a tissue from her purse and blows her nose. "I just came from seeing him. His tics are back in full swing. He could barely get a word out."

"Well, he must have said *something.*"

"He said he had nothing to do with it. Of course he had nothing to do with it. He just needed to say it, I guess."

Annie leans forward, rests her elbows on her thighs, and clasps her hands as if she's about to say grace over a plate of food. She pats her closed lips and thinks she doesn't know what to think.

"He also said he needs to talk to you," her mother adds. "He asked if I could get you to come down there."

The maple logs release a smoky sweetness she can taste. Her living room will be warm and quiet, and she wants nothing more than to go inside and close the door on all of this. Her thoughts feel erratic, beyond her control. She needs to lug another cord of wood in from the shed. She imagines the chipped feel of bark in her hands, and it's then that a fragment of old memory rushes in from nowhere. Long before Lakeview Road was paved, back when her father was still a living man, Annie had picked up a giant branch and nearly killed Josh and Gabe Pinckney when they wouldn't leave Calder alone.

Her mother leans forward and lifts the cowbell Calder knocked to the porch. She sets it on the railing. "I've never known a single person in my life to get arrested." She swallows in a clear attempt not to cry.

Annie can't believe she was ever capable of such a thing. Even more impossible is all that came later when she thinks of how she left those boys in the road with bloody pulps for heads. She thinks of Josh. Then Calder. Her hands shake.

"Are you sure he didn't do it?" The words are said before she catches them.

Her mother digs her nails into her purse. "Your brother didn't kill this Magnus—whatever his name is—any more than you or I did."

Jørgenson, Annie thinks. A slash through the first *o*.

"How can you even think such a thing?"

"I'm just saying."

"You're just *say-ing*? My God, if your father had lived to hear this."

Detour thumps his tail against the porch.

"What do you do all day? When was the last time you picked up your guitar?"

Annie glances at her hands.

"Have you put up a Christmas tree yet?" Her mother strains to look through the front window. She catches Annie looking at her hands. "Why are your hands so rough?"

"It's nothing."

"Something caused all that chaffing."

"Sandpaper."

"What in hell are you doing with sandpaper?"

"Didn't you come here to talk about Calder?"

At the mention of Calder's name her mother appears struck with the news all over again. Her mouth falls into a soft *o* and she dabs the corners of her eyes with a tissue. "It's worse than you think. Calder was seeing the man's wife."

Annie blinks slowly, only half deciding to open her eyes again.

"I asked him if he knew the man that was killed and he told me he knew *of* him," her mother says. "Then he told me how."

"When was he killed?"

"A week ago. Your birthday, in fact."

"Calder was here that morning."

"I know. I was glad to hear you two were patching up your monkey business." She shakes her head as if to say, "And now *this*."

"What time was the man killed?"

"I don't know. Evening, I think. Why?"

"Just trying to get the whole story."

"It was in the parking lot of some roadside bar."

"Hal's?"

"Yes, Hal's. So you *did* hear about it?"

"No. Just a lucky guess."

"Well, it's been all over the papers and in the news this week. Blunt force to the man's face." She swipes the air back and forth in front of her face and scowls. "Calling for dental records to see who he even was. Like something out of a movie. Are you still not getting the paper?"

Annie lifts an eyebrow. She's been told her father used to make the same face, and she regrets not being able to remember.

"What about the Internet?"

"Don't have it."

"Why haven't you replaced the computer he ran off with?"

"He ran off with a woman."

Her mother doesn't even crack a smile.

"It was *his* computer," Annie says.

Her mother sighs through her nose. "You need to make some connection with the outside world."

Annie's face tightens. She thinks of all the years her mother spent in the den with the drapes drawn and her father's old Marvin Gaye record set on repeat, the static interlude the only quiet for hours as she sluggishly pitched through past issues of *Life* and *Good Housekeeping*, baking imaginary pies, decorating imaginary windows, throwing imaginary parties that were certain to include her long-departed husband.

"I've got a copy of the paper in the car," her mother says.

"Fantastic." Annie pictures a man's crushed skull on the front page. Wavy chestnut hair plastered to the sides of a bloody face. A brown eye turned out like a dead deer's. But it isn't some Dane's face she imagines. It's Owen's.

She rubs her eyes and groans. Her whole body feels heavy, exhausted, unable to sit a moment longer.

"There's already talk of them going for the death penalty," her mother says.

A wave of nausea washes over Annie. Her teeth ache. "OK. This is about as much as I can stand to know."

"This isn't about you."

"I need to get inside. I'm sorry." She rises, feeling light-headed and confused, thinking of a grapefruit on the counter.

"Annie. You could afford to hire him a good lawyer. He's got a court-appointed one right now, and they won't even set bail. The judge claims he's a flight risk because his girlfriend is Danish."

"I'll see what I can do," Annie says, but she doesn't know if she means this or if she's just trying to get her mother to leave. She wants her to leave.

Annie heads for the door. She rests her hand on the latch and turns. "I don't really know how to say this, but has it even occurred to you that maybe, just maybe, I mean he *is* the most likely suspect."

Her mother comes to her feet. She's taller than Annie even without those heels. "You've known him your whole life. He's not capable of such a thing."

"It could have been an accident. Maybe he was drinking. Maybe they got into a fight."

"They needed dental records to figure out who the man was."

Annie shivers from the cold. "I need to go inside."

"This is still about Calder not telling you Owen was cheating on you, isn't it?"

"What?"

"You're still holding it against him."

"That's ridiculous."

"Calder is in *jail*, accused of *murder*, Annie, and if that's not ridiculous enough, you know what he says to me? He says, 'Tell Annie I need to see her. I need to tell her that I found Owen.'"

Annie drops her hand from the latch.

Her mother stares in a way that makes it clear she's thinking one thing while forcing herself to say another. "He lives in Destin."

Destin. What's in Destin? She never would have thought of *Destin*. How many miles north is that? Four hundred? Five hundred?

"There's more."

"What?"

"Calder wants to tell you himself."

"*What?*" Annie can't hide the urgency in her voice.

Her mother hesitates. "Calder said he got some cousin's number and got a hold of Owen's aunt and she said she'd heard from her niece that that was where he lived."

"And?"

She suddenly knows what's coming. Knows it like it's already been said. And yet for some reason she thinks of the gauzy light. Owen has no way of knowing it's returned. This time of year it filters through low morning clouds and mutes the orangey red of the grove, the rows of young corn, Annie's muddy driveway, the Dove White columns of the porch. Everything turns into a filtered portrait of a place. It's no longer just the place itself.

You could have been a painter, babe. You're a great songwriter, but you could have been a painter the way you notice the world like that.

"He *married* her, Annie. It's over now. Listen to me. It's done."

34

FOUR

"I'm sorry to have to call you over," Mrs. Lanie says. "And the day already half gone."

Annie finishes buttoning her jacket on Mrs. Lanie's porch.

"I wasn't sure what else to do," she continues. "The pickers can't get here for another two days. They weren't scheduled for another week."

"It's no trouble," Annie tells her, slipping on her leather gloves. "I was headed over before you called."

"Do you think we can use the smudge pots?" Mrs. Lanie asks. "I haven't used them in years."

"I'm afraid the fruit can't stay on the trees either way. It's already ripe," Annie says, squeezing her stiff gloves into fists while her mother's voice runs through her head—*Why are your hands so rough? When was the last time you picked up your guitar?*

Something no one knows about Annie is that she's spent months sanding down nearly everything in her house. Its rooms smell of her father's old workshop, fused with resin, wood pulp, sweet and bitter dust. The pine armoire in her bedroom with *Made in Mexico* stamped on the back was whitewashed when she and Owen first bought it from the flea market, and it's stood against the wall, holding winter clothes and blankets, virtually invisible for years. But after Owen left she couldn't stand the way the evening sun lit the deeper streaks of paint, the ones absorbed into the long, slender cracks like narrow bands of fat in a slice of meat. She was filled with an overwhelming urge to strip it lean.

It took weeks of going through the grits before every last trace of paint had been ground away and the wood restored to a brightened, velvety finish. But it didn't stop there. As the days passed Annie felt a certain irritation when the light in the house was at its fullest and the brassy patina was laid bare across the buffet. Then the mahogany chest in the mudroom, the end tables, a headboard on the guestroom bed. The fireplace mantel where Owen had left the note proved the most difficult with its hand-carved vertical drops, scrolling urn, and fluting and oval rosettes in the corners. She had to use a chemical compound to boil away the stain and then scrub the tiny crevasses clean with the toothbrush Owen had left behind. She scraped and scrubbed until her right shoulder locked in pain, and still she got up at four in the morning to begin again. Foot and paw prints have dotted the dusted floors for months. She finally exhausted all the furniture by her birthday and swiped every surface clean. The only wood left untouched is the instruments. Guitar, dulcimer, bongos in the corner, tambourine on the mantel, and a violin she'd just begun learning to play.

"I don't have any fuel for them anyway," Mrs. Lanie says.

"What's that?"

"The smudge pots."

"Yes."

"It's a lot of work," Mrs. Lanie says.

"I'm happy to do it," Annie says.

Mrs. Lanie plucks the keys to her late husband's old Ford pickup from the tiny hook near the door. She squeezes them inside Annie's hand. The television blares the local news jingle in the living room behind her. Annie sees the look of recognition in Mrs. Lanie's eyes and is certain the woman has seen the same mugshot of Calder that's plastered on the front of the paper Annie's mother left on the porch.

"I saw your mom was here earlier," Mrs. Lanie says.

"Do you have enough canned goods?" Annie asks. "The storm might knock out the power."

"It's going to be all right," Mrs. Lanie says.

"Yes," Annie replies. "Yes it is."

In the barn Annie heaves the wooden crates into the truck bed and drives to the grove, taking care not to bore deep tracks into the wet grass and loose soil as she parks between the trees.

She hops from the cab with a lantern from the barn and balances her knobby soles in the ribbed bed of the pickup. The lantern reminds her of fireflies, which remind her of Mrs. Lanie stopping by on that first evening without Owen. Annie was floating in a dreary daze, on the verge of unexplained laughter as if everything could only be explained by an elaborate joke. She was sitting on the front porch, watching fireflies, when Mrs. Lanie joined her. For the longest time they just sat there, listening to frogs and crickets pulsing along the lake and beneath the dark edges of the porch. Detour lay behind them in the light of the front door. "I know just how you feel, sweetheart," Mrs. Lanie finally said. "Everybody knows I lost my husband to the Lord. But what most don't know is that I had someone else before he came along." She caressed Annie's hand with the papery tips of her fingers. "He left me of his own free will," she said. "And I don't know what's worse, this is the God's honest truth, I don't know what's worse. A final good-bye at the hands of the Lord, or a lifetime spent wondering if he's ever coming back."

Giant hailstones have beaten some of the upper fruit. Bruised tangelos litter the ground between broken branches and melting balls of ice. Annie knows she needs to get the low-hanging ones first, the ones more vulnerable to frost, but she can't help trying to include as many as she can grab above her head, the ones hit by the hail. For having such a thick rind tangelos are surprisingly fragile.

Tiny hailstones needle her upturned face. She quickens her reach, snatching the bells of fruit into her gloved hand, alternately, meticulously, plucking the wire picker above her head in the other, then releasing them all into the crate. Reaching, dipping, turning herself around. The crates begin to fill, and yet there are still so many trees. After twenty minutes her hands are already stiff and achy from the cold. Maybe the frost will hold off for a couple more days. Long enough for her to haul the bulk of the crop safely into Mrs. Lanie's barn.

He married her, Annie. It's over now. It's done.

"Calder got himself into this mess," she suddenly tells the trees. "I beat those boys senseless over him," she adds, as if the incidents are somehow connected. She examines a tangelo, trying to decide its fate. *"Josh."* Her voice strains like the man's on the radio did that day, giving way to another that doesn't fit. She tosses the tangelo into the crate for keeps. She wants to say his name again and stops herself, but the emotion it packs bubbles up from her chest all the same. She grips a branch in her fist and rests her forehead against her own shoulder. She catches her breath and begins again.

FIVE

Twenty-eight years ago Annie lifted a steak knife from the kitchen drawer and sneaked out through the screened-in porch. She waited for Calder near the tire swing at the front of the house with the knife hidden in the front pocket of her coverall shorts. It was summer, which meant they were on their way to pick peaches for Mr. Peterson. It meant four hours a day of slippery, risky ladder runs in the heat as they raced to see whose crate would fill first.

Annie never mentioned the knife during her shift. In fact, she nearly forgot about it until they were walking home down the dusty road and she heard, "Hey, retard!" coming up from behind. A breeze lifted the smell of hog farm, sweat, and oily teenage hair.

Annie and Calder weren't teenagers. They were twelve and eleven years old, and they picked up their pace.

"I'm talking to you, retard," one of the brothers said.

Annie turned to look at the boys. Their chests were bare and sunken, cherry colored from the sun. Both wore cutoffs with loose fringes fluttering at the knees. Josh had on red high-top tennis shoes without any socks. Gabe wore the same in black. Their rusty hair swung loose and curly, clownish around their ears. Calder had told her that mosquitoes bred in pet bowls and kiddie pools and could travel up to three miles in the muggy night air to thrive off the skin of sleeping kids. From the looks of all the red bumps covering their arms and legs, someone ought to have had enough sense to drain the standing water off their farm. Or else fix the holes in the screens.

Josh grinned. He flopped his hand in the air and gave a cutesy kind of wave.

Annie spit, quick and sharp. She turned her back.

"Mmn," somebody said.

All week long she'd tried to ignore them, keeping her sticky fists in her pockets where she jangled loose change from Mr. Peterson. She sang songs beneath her breath, church hymns, especially church hymns, ones she'd picked up the summer before when her mother decided that her children should learn about the Bible at Lakeview Baptist. They lasted three weeks, long enough for Annie to memorize a handful of hymns, and maybe too long for the congregation, including the smiley deacon who Annie could see had begun to count on their dollar in his basket. But a dollar a week wasn't worth Calder jumping up and down and grunting every time someone got dunked in the baptismal tank. The deacon finally hissed that the Holy Spirit didn't make people act like that at Lakeview Baptist.

This little light of mine. Annie hated that song. Hated the way it wouldn't leave her head, and that was the whole point. She could count on it to loop until she and Calder reached their driveway and the Pinckney boys lost their bluster and carried on down the road.

But as much as Annie had tried to distract herself from the Pinckneys, Calder had tried to win them over. "I saw your mama down at Lukeman's picking up some melons," he'd say, or something like it, while his legs did a jig on their own. "You know the thing about melons is..." Annie would grab him by the arm and spin him back around while he twisted his neck out and cleared his throat raw. The boys laughed until they choked.

"You stick your finger in a light socket, tard?" Gabe asked now. "Is that what makes you jump around like that?"

Annie thumbed the blade in her pocket.

The boys whooped and howled at the wonderful time they were having.

Her mother had planted a kiss on top of her head when Annie first told her about the Pinckneys. "Just walk away from those boys," she'd said, breezily, well aware of who they were, though never seeming to take them seriously. She was a popular middle school English teacher with flashing green eyes. Words came from her glamour-girl mouth as if they'd been scratched clean before they reached one's ears.

"Hey, stupid!" Josh yelled at Calder. "You jerking around like that cause you're a retard or what?"

Annie rolled her eyes far enough to the side to take in Calder's face. Her own muscles tensed as if willing his to do the same. But his eyebrows jumped and his mouth—rimmed in Tropical Punch—flicked sideways. He slapped the sweat from his forehead as if the sweat was the cause of all that was wrong with him.

A small, round ache formed in the bottom of Annie's throat.

The day after her mother had told her to walk away, her father pulled her aside where her mother couldn't hear and said, "Listen, songbird. A person needs to know what his own limitations are so when he gets pushed beyond them he can rest assured that no one, not even his own sense of right and wrong, can claim he's acted in any other way than self-defense. After that you can have 'em shakin like a dog shittin peach pits if you need to."

Annie let go of the knife, suddenly unable to figure taking on two boys with a single knife. She cut loose from Calder and darted along the shallow ditch, looking for a branch that was big enough. Fresh streams of sweat trailed down her sides.

Calder ran to catch up. He wasn't the least bit dumb like some people thought. In fact, he was smarter than anyone around, especially when it came to growing things in the hot Florida sun. He knew the difference between nimbus and stratus clouds for nothing besides his own pleasure, and his mind sometimes got so dreamy with tertiary roots and photosynthesis that he didn't see what was right in front of him.

Calder's eyelids fluttered. His hands rose to the sides of his hips, opening and closing like sticky traps.

"Here we go." Annie pulled up a branch that was twice as thick as a baseball bat and slightly shorter than a rake. She heaved it to her shoulder. The sweet smell of peaches under her fingernails mixed with bark and soil and compost. The Pinckneys' smart mouths were generally lined with spitballs. They made fun of girls with braces and shoved boys whose parents had a little money down onto the shiny hallway floors. In the wintertime with all the windows closed and the heat turned up, Annie had smelled them until she was sick to her stomach. She'd imagined this moment for years.

"Hey, boys. How's it going?" she said when the brothers caught up.

"Supposed to hit a hundred degrees today." Calder blinked so hard it was as if he were purposely putting on a show.

Gabe started throwing a fit like his skin was on fire. He slapped himself as if trying to put it out. It looked like it ought to hurt. "F-f-f-fine," Gabe said in answer to Annie's question, though he was looking at Calder as if accusing him of stuttering. He and Josh took a moment for laughing. "F-f-f-fine!" He swung his hips and jerked his arms in the air.

Calder sidestepped toward Annie. His shoulder shot at his ear and his eyes squeezed shut even as she knew he was now trying to keep still.

"You look fine," Annie said. "For an idiot. In fact I'd say you make a perfect example of an idiot, Gabe Pinckney."

Gabe put his hands on his hips, and it finally occurred to her which animal it was that the Pinckneys resembled. Dolphins. Eyes with too much lid, nose bottled out from the face.

"We're thinking of getting us a job," Josh said. "Picking peaches seems like an easy enough thing. What do you think, Gabe? Get us a little pocket money?"

"The thing is, you have to..." Calder sniffed the air once, twice, three times, "pay attention to the shade thrown over by the branches."

"Is that right. Well, there you go. Can't be that hard if a retard can do it," Gabe said.

Calder twisted his neck long and blinked. "Let's get on home," he finally said.

"Yeah, let's get on home," Gabe said in imitation. "So I can finger you with my quick action finger."

This seemed to be the funniest thing Josh had ever heard.

It took a moment for Annie's face to burn with awareness. The crude joke was directed at her.

Josh whooped and cried and doubled over. The thrill he was experiencing seemed to shed onto Gabe. They were both so busy having their hysterics that neither seemed to see the branch swinging left and right into their faces. Annie knocked them to their knees.

Josh held his hands out and shook his head in quick little spurts as if trying to keep the horizon from slipping upright. Blood dripped from his nose.

Calder ducked and scrambled backwards onto all fours and gouged his fingers into the ground and pulled up two fists full of gravel, which he flung at the boys. The rocks bounced like rubber balls off their chests.

It was like having the most satisfying fever dream of her life. The deep blue of the sky, the greens and browns of trees, the wet red blood on the boys' white faces sharpened into view as if all Annie's life color had been dulled and filtered out of focus, and only now could she see it in the way it was meant to be seen. Her mind sharpened, too, clicked tighter into place. A part of her was well aware that a person could kill someone with these kinds of blows to the head, but the thought of killing these two boys didn't equal to putting down the branch.

"The only retard around here is going to be the two of you with half a brain each," she said.

Gabe looked at her with an eerie grin. He seemed to be enjoying himself. "What a little bitch you are." He rose and stepped toward her. She swung with a force that began in her feet and worked its way into her hands. The wood made a crackling sound that startled her when it hit the side of his head, but the branch remained in one piece. Gabe yelled out and stumbled sideways. A ball of blood formed on the side of his head.

Her own head began to drift like a hollow, helium-filled skull above her neck.

Josh was still on his knees, rearing back from his brother's fall when he turned to Annie, arms hanging gorilla-like from his sides. He seemed unsure what to do without Gabe's direction.

Gabe raised his hand, then his head. Blood pooled in the dip of his sneer.

Josh leaned forward and offered him a hand. Gabe swiped it away.

Calder hopped quickly from one foot to the other.

Blood throbbed at the side of Annie's neck. The sharp swirl of undigested peach spun up from her stomach. She willed it back down and hit Gabe again, aiming carefully to the right of the bloody knot she'd already caused. He went down just like before, and his fall seemed to signal some direction for Josh, who growled and pursed his lips and lunged at Annie with fingers for claws.

Calder screamed so loud his voice broke midway through. He covered his head and stuck his long leg out and by some miracle tripped Josh and caused him to stumble toward Annie's knees. She brought the branch down with another *whomp*, and this time it busted in half on the back of Josh's head as he fell to the ground. A small trail of blood slid across the pale scalp beneath thin wisps of tangled hair. His smell sharpened as if more filth was let loose from his veins.

The piece of branch in her hands was hardly the size of a ruler. She threw it to the ground and pulled out the knife.

Calder seemed more shocked by the knife than anything else. "What the hell?" he yelled.

The bubble of elation suddenly burst. Annie tried not to cry as the dry fear of what was happening fully set in. The church hymns came back to her. But the reason wasn't the same.

Calder picked up the piece of branch lying near Josh's shoulder. He blinked at Annie and the two of them stood with legs apart, ready and waiting for whatever was to come.

Calder looked left and right down the road. "Put that thing away," he said as he crouched and shoved the boys' shoulders until they groaned. He stood and nodded to her and she took it to mean that she hadn't killed them after all.

"Put it away."

She slipped the knife into her pocket.

"Hey." Calder shoved each boy in the shoulder again. "Come on. Get up."

The boys stirred and gradually lifted themselves onto all fours. They cussed and balanced on their knees. Finally, they rose to their feet, brushing themselves off, swatting the flies already darting their wounds. And then they laughed.

Josh looked at Annie beneath a single thick lid. He smiled in a way that seemed shockingly tender. "You're something else, Annie Walsh," he said, his palms held up in surrender.

SIX

Annie's hands are stiff and raw with blisters. The tips of her fingers pruned from having stood too long in the shower, listening to tiny hailstones tick the bathroom window. It wasn't until the water turned cold on her back that she finally shut it down.

It's late. The sweet smell of burning maple and foggy windows give her living room the feel of a folksy country inn. Her hair hangs in wet ringlets around her face. She's chilled, shivering beneath a wooly, red comforter on the leather sofa.

"What if," she would like to say to Calder. He's the only person in the world who knows what it means.

After their father died they used to play a game they called "What If?" What would their lives be like in that very moment if their father had lived? It began the summer after he was gone, and they were eating bologna sandwiches in the kitchen when their mother stumbled in at noon after having just woken up. She hadn't showered in days. She'd stopped teaching. She'd stopped picking up around the house. She'd stopped everything except retreating from the outside world. "Why aren't the dishes done?" she asked, drunk on meanness and misery.

It was enough to blindside Annie with the grief. This happened from time to time when she least expected, like coming across her father's Swiss Army knife in the junk drawer when she was looking for a rubber band or accidentally knocking a small sample of his cologne from the top shelf of the medicine cabinet and breaking it in the sink until the whole bathroom, even halfway down the hall, smelled like her father for days.

Now her blood rose, bringing with it the words, "I wish you'd died instead of Daddy."

Her mother jerked her head up.

"He wouldn't have acted like such a coward."

Her mother slapped her face.

It didn't hurt nearly as much as one would think by the crack of it.

But then her mother grabbed a knife from the drawer as half-crying moans leaked from her throat.

"What are you doing!" Calder yelled, and Annie wasn't sure if he was talking to her or her mother the way his head swung back and forth.

Annie froze. Her hands leaden, useless. She'd crossed over into a hazy, unfamiliar place where she didn't care if any of them lived or died.

Her mother let loose a pathetic wail. She held the knife in the air like she intended to bring the blade down into her own chest. She screamed like a small child, her whole body trembling with frustration and pain. Calder leaped toward her and wrestled the knife away, but not before several teacups smashed to the floor and the two of them fell across the shards. Calder stood and tossed the knife into the sink while their mother wept into her bloody hands.

Annie did nothing. Calder blinked at the scrapes on his own hands and arms. He peeled their mother's fingers from her eyes. The cuts were only small abrasions. He wiped her face and hands with a wet dishcloth while she mumbled words no one understood. He lifted her from the floor. "Help me get her into the den," he said.

Annie glared at him.

"Come on," he said, and Annie flopped forward with exaggerated resentment.

Her mother smelled faintly of vinegar. Dirty strings of hair rimmed her eyes. They settled her into the recliner and covered her with the prickly orange afghan their mother's cousin had made, splashed with a pattern of poorly attempted blue stars and an uneven fringe. Their mother turned on her side and covered her whole face with it. Tiny drops of blood leaked like beads onto the watertight fabric.

Annie and Calder returned to their half-eaten sandwiches in the kitchen. But the shatter of broken glass and screams, the heat from her cheek, the way they'd skirted along the margins of death—and they had, she thought, all come eerily close—still echoed off the table and cupboards and floor. Annie got up and opened the window above the sink. She rested her hands on the pane while the grimy hem of the once white curtain stroked her arms in the breeze.

"What if Daddy had lived?" Calder asked from the table behind her.

Outside the air cracked with stiff palms coarsening against one another. Annie stared at the muscadine tendrils that had crawled all the way from the trellis just to suffocate the window box that her mother once filled with red geraniums.

"I'll tell you one thing," Calder said after the silence. "That ugly afghan would have never been allowed in this house."

Annie laughs, sadly, remembering. She tucks the comforter tighter around her cold feet. She thinks of a photograph that still hangs in the front hall of her childhood home. The first thing you see walking in is her mother in sandals on the red brick patio, holding a pitcher of iced tea, and she's smiling her gorgeous, glamour-girl smile. A man's blue sleeve lines the edge. Uncle Calder had stood beside her in the original, but someone had cut him away.

Hard to believe her mother was once curvy and lively, full of warm kisses and unreasonable optimism. She'd read most anything to them—newspaper columns, magazine articles, novels, essays, the latest research on the brain, heart, orca whales, glass blowing, space, anything she got her hands on— always hugging and kissing and reading, filling them up in all ways that mattered.

Annie feels the sting of tears when she thinks of the hole that separates the past from the present. She could fill a pool with all the poisonous things she has felt toward her mother, and now her brother, in between.

She wishes her mother had never come by and told her what she did. She wishes Calder had never come to see her on her birthday, wishes he'd never mentioned Magnus, wishes she'd never heard him say how mean the man was, wishes he hadn't sounded so much like their father when he said it. She might not have laughed and let him in so easily. She might not have learned about his love for Sidsel. *What if* he never showed up that day? Would he have done what they say he's done? What a foolish, hopeless game.

SEVEN

It disturbs Calder to think of how happy Sidsel makes him. He does it anyway, imagining Mateo's Mexican restaurant just as clearly as if he's sitting in one of its booths. He pulls in a long breath, and instead of the cold concrete walls and musty prison blankets, he smells the restaurant's lively mix of beans and spicy chicken, the linoleum floor and tables scrubbed clean with bleach. He sees the pale yellow walls, the sky-blue molding along the floor, ceiling, and windows where red and yellow striped curtains hang loose in the Florida sun. The air is chilled by a powerful air-conditioner, making the red Formica booths and vinyl seats especially cool to the touch. As a boy he used to come here with his father. He has come here his whole life.

It was nine months ago that Sidsel walked into Mateo's to have lunch with him. He thinks about that day as the turning point for everything. She entered the restaurant, and he stood from the booth and raised his hand to his heart as if he were saying the Pledge of Allegiance. Her gaze shot around the dining room as she walked toward him, but Calder couldn't turn away. Her husband Magnus could have been in the next booth for all he cared. It had been a full twenty-four hours since he'd last seen her white-blond hair glide across her bare shoulders. Twenty-four hours since he sang "Yankee Doodle Dandy"—a song she didn't know—softly into her ear while tickling her ribs, making her squirm backwards across his sheets and laugh with little bursts of screaming in between. Twenty-four hours since he smelled sugar and flour on her long neck. Twenty-four hours since he felt her breasts between his fingers and on the tip of his tongue, felt the inside of her like a drug that thrust him into some other place he had no name for and not a single word to describe.

Sidsel. She'd looked sideways once more as she slid into the booth across from him, and they situated themselves toward the center. Calder reached for her hand, and she looked across the room once more as she gave it to him. A flat, round freckle dotted the back of her hand, and he caressed it beneath his finger.

"Sid." He swallowed and looked at her closely. "We're going to work this thing out. I promise you."

Sidsel pulled away and tucked her hands beneath her armpits like a child on a cold day. "I like it here," she said, with what appeared to be a forced smile. "I like the colors of the walls."

He loved the soft trace of her accent. It was as if she were speaking with something hot in her mouth the way she sometimes pushed her lips toward a pout. When he first met her outside the red and white door of her Danish café, he'd had no idea how long she'd been standing there. He was planting a young magnolia in front of the law office next door when he heard a smooth voice say, "Hello?" His shovel had just chunked through the sandy soil, and he rested his hiking boot atop the turned edge of it and looked up. A freshly tanned face, big lime eyes, and all that white hair falling across a white, loosely fitted blouse. "Would you mind very much cutting this back?" She reached for a brittle branch of a small avocado tree in a planter on the sidewalk. She caressed its tip with her finger. "It's not been looked after."

"I wouldn't mind at all," he said, and she stepped forward and handed him a raspberry Kringle he hadn't noticed in her other hand. The need to touch her had been immediate.

"It reminds me of home," Sidsel said in Mateo's. The green of her shirt caused the green in her eyes to flash above her white teeth. "The colors, on the walls. They're like the houses back home."

She saw beauty in the cloudy skin of a blueberry, found pleasure in the weight of a spoon. Just being in the same room with her made him want to be a better man. She spoke French, English, German, and Danish, knew all about the constellations and other unlikely information, like the migrating patterns of Bean Geese and every joke the Marx brothers ever told. Her pastries left him satisfied and hungry all at once.

It couldn't have been more than sixty-five degrees in Mateo's, but sweat rolled down the sides of his temples like tears. He needed to get a hold of himself. He wanted nothing more than to have her every minute of the day, every day of the week, every year of his life. He imagined lying on top of her in the booth. Babies sprang before his eyes, then grandkids branching off into great-grandkids. He was seeing the future with her.

"You can file for a divorce," he said. What was he thinking? They'd barely discussed Magnus before now. His right eye twitched once and stopped.

Sidsel leaned back into her seat.

"I mean, is that something you'd want?" Calder asked.

She studied his face. "It's not so simple as that," she said.

"What can I get for you two here?" Mateo stood at the side of the table with a notepad and pen. His hair was as thick and white as his moustache. He looked more like a South American diplomat than a waiter.

Sidsel looked to Calder. "Anything is fine," she said.

"How are you, buddy?" Calder asked.

"I'm very fine, thank you." He bowed his head forward and smiled at Sidsel while rocking on the heels of his tennis shoes, pushing his protruding belly back and forth over the edge of the table.

Calder asked him to double the usual, and Mateo turned for the kitchen.

Calder leaned forward. "The way I hear it, more than half of everybody who's married has gotten divorced."

"That's not what I mean. You don't know Magnus," she said, whispering his name. "You have no idea how he can be."

"Hey, Calder!" A man's voice called from across the room.

Calder turned to see Gabe Pinckney, one of his landscapers, in dirty shorts and boots. He was wearing a purple Greenpeace T-shirt with a white whale on the front. It was Tuesday. Calder had completely forgotten that he'd be maintaining the Johnson house right around the corner.

Son of a bitch. Both Gabe and the situation here. Gabe grinned as big and manly as possible. Calder lifted a hand. "One of my landscapers," Calder whispered to Sidsel.

What was she saying? Magnus. He didn't know Magnus. No, he didn't, and the thought of Sidsel knowing Magnus the way she did made him feel a little sick. It was Magnus she was going home to. Maybe he waited for her in a chair that faced the door. Maybe he kissed her every time she walked in, the way Calder would, given the chance.

"Well. You're right about that," Calder said, leaning back in his own seat. "I don't know him and I don't care to know him but I sure as hell know that I'm not afraid of him and you shouldn't be either." He gave her a small smile and checked for a reaction. Her eyes seemed doubtful, maybe wistful, hard to gauge. "This is a free country. Somebody gets a notion to leave they just up and leave. That's the way we do it here."

"That's not what I mean," Sidsel said.

Calder opened his mouth but she cut him off. "Listen to me," she said. "Magnus has changed."

Calder let her go on.

"We hadn't been together long before we came here. I told you we only got married so I could come to the States with him when he took the job at Siemens."

"So what are you saying?"

"I don't love him. I never really loved him."

A rush of warm blood steamed from the pit of his stomach to the top of his head. Finally, she'd told him what he needed to hear.

"It was just a practical decision. The marriage and coming here. I could open my café in all this sunshine. It's so dark and rainy in Denmark. I know. It's stupid that I married him to live in the sunshine."

"My grandfather left everything and everyone he ever knew and loved, all for the sake of sunshine. It's not stupid. Hell, if it weren't for sunshine I wouldn't be sitting here with you right now." The idea that he might have never known her set off a flurry of urges beneath his skin.

"Your eye keeps jumping," she said. "Have you noticed that?"

"I have."

"And your shoulder."

"Just exactly how has he changed?" He rubbed the corner of his eyebrow with the tips of two fingers. When he tugged at his lid he saw Gabe shoveling pinto beans between his grin.

She leaned forward and whispered. "He tells me about seeing other women. He doesn't say who they are, he just says things like, 'I fucked another woman today,' and then he rolls over and goes to sleep."

"Good God."

"At first I thought he was joking. I asked him if he was serious because, I mean, he never said such a thing before, and then he held my arm up here like this and said, 'I'm capable of anything, don't you know that?'" Small green bruises poked from beneath her sleeve.

Calder started to come around and sit next to her, but she stopped him with her hand and the fear in her eyes that someone might see them together, and so he sat back down and bobbed his knee and felt his throat tighten along with his fist beneath the table.

"I don't know the word in English. *Ildevarslende.* It's like something threatening but not so clear. It's the way he stares at me. I'm afraid of him, Calder. You should be, too."

Calder examined his broken fingernails and small cuts from bristling palm trees. He looked up. "We're going to fix this," he said. "And don't you worry about me."

Sidsel dropped her gaze to the side and brushed her lap clean of something Calder couldn't see. She brought her head back up and sighed with closed eyes.

Then she stared at Calder for so long that Mateo had set two root beers on the table and walked away before either of them noticed. Her bottom lip quivered and she brought her fingers to rest there. "I'm sorry. I can't stop thinking about you." She covered her whole mouth with her hand. Tears spilled down her face.

A prickling heat stung Calder's feet. It shot up and tickled the roots of his lashes. He stretched his neck long to the side as if his collar were too tight, but it was no use. His eyelids fluttered until he finally squeezed them shut and opened them again, taking the edge off some of the urge. His fist opened and closed beneath the table. "I've got to tell you. I've never known anything like what's happening here," he said, and as quickly as he said it he realized that she might not know which thing he was referring to, their love or his tics or the threat of Magnus, but he didn't feel like explaining, and anyway she smiled and never asked.

The word she'd been looking for that day was *ominous*.

They had nine months of one another before Sidsel called with the news. She dialed the minute she heard from the police. That might have been the problem, calling her lover first thing. It was on record and it looked bad. He sees this now. So does she. But it was too late for all that. She went and called him again and again in fact, especially after having to identify the body. He didn't know what she was saying. She'd lost control of her English. It was all Danish in between the choking and sobbing and the single shrill scream she let out before he hung up and ran to her. Even now he has no idea what she said. By the time he got to her she couldn't speak at all so he held her and let her cry, and he didn't feel the least bit jealous about her weeping over her dead husband. He hated seeing her this way. He needed to do something for her, and he was trying, but at the same time his mind was flopping back and forth between worrying about her and jumping in a kind of floundering revelry over Magnus being dead. He had to help her. He would help her. He wiped her tears and held her and stroked her hair until she was quiet and thirsty for a glass of water.

After that she told him how the police had asked her all kinds of questions. She'd answered no to every one until they asked if she was seeing someone on the side. She told them the truth. Why shouldn't she? It had nothing to do with Magnus being dead.

* * *

Sidsel's face appears on Calder's screen in the Video Visitation Center and he forgets about the steel bolts and barbed wire. He forgets about the body odor, the smell of urine mixed with commercial-strength cleaners and cigarette smoke, the sickening taste of burned potatoes and watery coffee. All he sees is the splintered red of her swollen green eyes.

"Not my best color," he finally says of his orange jumpsuit.

She switches the phone to her other ear.

"Sid. I'm going to say this because God only knows what's going through your head. Listen to me. I had nothing to do with this. You know that, don't you?" His eyes squeeze shut several times. His right shoulder jumps at his ear.

Sidsel rubs her own eyes as if to make Calder's stop. Annie used to do the same thing.

"Of course," she says. But he can't take back what he said in Mateo's about how they were going to fix this.

"You have no idea what I'm going through," she says.

This takes Calder by surprise. It seems a selfish thing, considering.

In his moment of confusion he gazes at the row of inmates beside him. A red-haired guy with a red goatee and green tattooed fingers and thumb that spell I L-O-V-E wiggles his finger in his ear. A man with a clean haircut and gold wedding band on a tanned finger whispers into his phone, his words jumbled and whiney.

"It's a mess," Calder tells Sidsel. "Don't think I'm not sure as hell aware of that."

"I have reporters calling me all the way from France," Sidsel cuts in. "*The National Enquirer* is offering me money and the Danish Consulate won't return my calls. I've got to arrange for Magnus to be sent back to Denmark after the autopsy is complete." She stops and holds her hand over her eyes as if she's seeing Magnus dead in front of her. "His father's calling me all hours through the night. He thinks I killed him or had you kill him for me." Before he can say anything she's looking at the ceiling, switching gears. "Then there's the house. I never even liked the house. Magnus insisted on paying some Dutch architect to design it. He took out a big loan and now it's on me to pay it back." Calder opens his mouth. "And it's freezing outside!" she says. "Do you know how cold it is? The water has to be drained from the pool or it's going to freeze. I don't know how to drain water from a pool. How long do you think it would take to sell the house?"

She's manic. He's guessing sleep-deprived.

"And Siemens. You would think Human Resources would see that I need help, but all I get is that he wasn't there long enough to make him eligible for life insurance benefits."

"Do you need money?" Calder asks.

"No. No." His words have slowed her down. "I can take some extra from the café." She glances at her watch. "I have to get back to work. Every day I'm smiling at the tourists, hoping no one reads the local papers." She mocks her own smile. "I'm just a happy Danish girl selling her Kringles and pudding."

"Sid, please," he says, his knee hopping beneath the table.

"*Av mig God.* I can't do this by myself. I go home to this *warehouse,* and I think, what if this person comes after me, too? What if Magnus was involved in something bad? My family is begging me to come home. I'm sorry, Calder. I can't stand the thought of you in here. It's killing me in little pieces. I can't eat. I can't sleep. I can't remember the smallest things—my shoes, my watch, my purse. I don't even know when the last time was that I've eaten."

Calder grips his knee with his free hand. "Sweetheart." She's got everything bound up in his chest now. He needs to touch her. He does in his mind, and her scent seems to waft through the screen. His heart constricts. He coughs it free. "Have you got something to write with?"

She keeps her eyes on Calder as she feels around her pockets. She looks pale and sickly, as if she's lost and looking for change to call someone. She pulls a pen and address book from her purse.

"My bankcard is in the top drawer of my dresser with some other junk," he says.

"Calder—"

He tells her the pin. "Write it down. There's not a whole lot in the account but you can take it all if you need to. My accountant deposits money automatically every month. And the condo's paid for."

"It isn't necessary. No. I'll be fine."

"Sid," he says sharply. "Take what you need. Call a realtor and put your house up for sale. They'll take care of everything for you.

You can stay in my place." He thinks of her walking through his rooms, turning lights on and off the way his mother did after his father died. The thermostat up, then down. The windows open, then closed. Sheets off, then on, the rooms never feeling quite right.

"People live on the other side of the wall. Nice people. Friends. Write this number down, too. It's Annie's. She knows a lot of people. Just call her. She can help. You shouldn't be dealing with this alone."

"She must be dealing with it, too." She takes down the number. "In the papers. On the news. Everyone is paying extra attention because of who she is."

Of course. He hasn't even thought of how this will throw a light on Annie. Pressure percolates in his chest, his throat, his eyes. He needs to stay in control. He slaps his hand onto the video screen.

Sidsel presses her hand against her own screen, and the gesture makes his whole head ache.

Their visit is almost up. His knees bang one another.

"I've had a perfectly wonderful time," Sidsel says in an attempt at Groucho Marx.

Calder feels the burn in his knees. He smiles and says, "But this wasn't it."

Sidsel smiles, too—the softest, warmest, truest smile she's ever offered. "I'm sorry. I'm so sorry. I shouldn't have gotten so upset. I want to be strong. I promise I'll be strong next time. I just can't help wishing there was some way we could go back and change this. To make it so it never happened."

This is the thought that will stay with him through the night. But just how far back he'd have to go and what exactly he'd have to change is anybody's guess. It never does come to him in all the hours he's awake.

EIGHT

Annie is startled by the sound of branches snapping behind her. She nearly falls from the truck bed at the sight of a man in the grove. He's wearing a Channel 4 News jacket, his mouth in a twist as if caught while searching for the right thing to say.

"What the hell are you doing out here?" Annie says.

"I'm sorry," he says. "I just wanted to ask you a few questions." She doesn't like the sound of his voice. Genteel, almost ladylike. He's young and pudgy in the face. Annie throws a bruised tangelo at his head. It lands with a thud.

"Hey!" He holds his head.

"This is private property. You either leave on your own or I'm going to pull the shotgun out of this truck and point your way."

There is no shotgun, but there's also no way for him to know this.

"Can I quote you on that?"

He thinks he's funny. Annie slips off her gloves and throws them into the bed. Her hands have taken on a permanent grasp, claw-like. She tears her coat off as if readying for a fight.

"I read somewhere that you quit touring," the fat-faced boy says. "You haven't been back in the recording studio since

Gull on a Steeple. Of course, that can't have anything to do with what your brother's done."

She jumps from the truck and he takes off running. "It's none of my business what my brother does!" she screams, and runs after him. He's getting away. "You *better* run, you little son of a bitch." There's no time for this. The slight break in the rain has allowed her to make some headway on the tangelos.

She reaches the road with barely a breath to spare as the man jumps into his green sedan and locks the door.

Annie stands heaving on the side of the road. If she's not careful she's going to burst into tears. Swung out on either side of her driveway is an old iron gate that's hung open for years, its hinges rusted in place. She treks down the road to shove, and then pull the two sides together, wincing at the high-pitched grind of metal on metal. Then, just as she turns back for the grove, the man leans out his window and aims a telephoto lens at her. She's filthy and braless in an old long-sleeve T-shirt pulled from the back of her drawer. *ANARCHY!* is emblazoned across the front. Her hand shields her face as if from an oncoming fist.

She'll hire security guards the minute she gets inside. *Careful,* she says to her own tears, but they are starting to get the better of her.

She doesn't manage more than a few steps when another car appears on the road. Dark and masculine and sleek, clearly an unmarked cop car, pulling toward her gate. It stops and two men step out. They don't ask if she's Annie Walsh. She knows they already know. They only ask if they can speak to her. They show badges to be clear. Just a few questions if she doesn't mind.

"How many's a few?" she asks. "I don't have much time."

"Less than twenty," one says.

She accepts a ride up to her house. Her jacket is still in the back of the truck and she's cold now, shivering from adrenaline, too. Sitting in the backseat of the cop car makes her feel like a criminal. She can smell her own sweat.

Each man has dark hair, a square jawline, and white, healthy-looking teeth. They could be brothers, and she asks if this is how they came to be assigned to work as a team. They laugh a little. She washes her hands at the kitchen sink and they take a seat before she offers.

They're the first people to set foot inside her home in months. She imagines it through their eyes. A little too tidy. A little too quiet. Bleached. Pale, blond wood everywhere you turn.

She makes coffee. They don't say much until it's ready, until she brings three mugs to the table and slides theirs in front of them.

The guns on their belts catch her attention. The heavy brushed metal makes her want to tell the truth.

"He was here that morning but he never said anything to me about Magnus," she says when they ask. "Not that I remember. I would have remembered a name like that."

"Who wouldn't?" Detective Ron says.

"And so, I'm not sure what else I can help you with then."

"You'd be surprised at the kinds of things that help us," Detective Rick says.

Annie sips her coffee and looks at one then the other over the rim of her chunky mug.

"What was he like as a kid?" Detective Ron asks.

"Why do you ask?"

"Just curious."

"What were you like as a kid?" she asks.

"Hell on wheels," he says, and both men laugh.

Annie sets her coffee on the table. "He was sweet. Normal as any boy. He liked to fish. Liked nature and music. He liked watching things grow."

"We understand he had tics pretty bad back then."

So this is what they are after. Confirmation that her brother is a sideshow, a freak. Someone who was bullied and vowed revenge.

Annie shrugs a shoulder.

The detectives wait for her to say something else. She knows this technique. Lawyers use it, therapists, too. Wait long enough and they'll eventually fill the silence with their version of the truth.

"Was he ever angry?" Detective Rick asks.

"About what?"

"Life. Anything. It must have been tough growing up without a father."

"If what you're asking is whether or not he had some bone to pick, or some need to get back at the world, the answer is no. Never. Not even when he had a right to."

"He had a right to?"

"I think we're done here, boys."

"The last time you saw him, until recently I mean, was quite a while ago. Six months, something like that?"

Annie reaches into her purse on the counter. The detectives put their hands on their guns and jerk forward and then relax when she pulls out a card. "You get the urge to call someone and talk, here's my lawyer's number. She's a real chatterbox."

Detective Ron rises and slowly heads for the door. He stops and studies the photographs on the wall, lingering on one of

Detour as a puppy, licking Calder's chin. Detective Rick finishes his coffee at the table and then grins and asks for Annie's autograph. She signs his notebook, *Happy trails—Annie Walsh.* Detective Ron wanders into the living room.

"You live alone?" he asks.

"Not if you include him." Detour dozes in front of the fireplace.

"Smells like a lumberyard in here. Your boyfriend a carpenter?" he asks.

"Don't tell me you didn't notice my hands."

"Oh, I noticed," he replies, still looking around. "Abrasions on the right-hand fingers. Both hands severely chapped. The right one slightly bruised."

"I don't have a boyfriend," she says sharply.

"And no Christmas tree."

"It's not a crime, is it? Living alone? Not putting up a tree?"

Detective Rick joins him near the door. "No ma'am," he says, and both men smile and thank her and finally leave after what feels like hours but has only been twenty minutes and less than twenty questions.

She's furious. Not with them but with her brother. She picks up the phone and calls her old security team. The guys who used to work her local shows. They don't ask a lot of questions. They aren't impressed by fame. She always liked this about them. They agree to start immediately.

An hour and a half after she was first interrupted, she is finally back in the grove. Reaching, dipping, turning herself around. The colorful fruit piles in crates at her knees. It feels good to move her body. It feels good to work with her hands, to smell the tangy fruit, the cold air, and soil. She once heard of a famous singer who quit performing at the height of her career so she could move to Italy and learn the language. She never did return, not to music, not to America. There was another, an Oscar-winning actor, who'd stopped reading scripts to become a cobbler's apprentice. Of course, he did return, and won another Oscar if she's not mistaken. No matter. Annie could be a farmer, stay a farmer. She could adopt children. She could teach them to play music, and sing only to them.

This morning Allen, her manager, called first thing to tell her that Calder's story has become a twenty-second spot on the cable news networks. "Singer-songwriter's brother accused of murder," he said. He said it's true about any publicity being good publicity. *Gull on a Steeple* is flying up the charts.

"I'll be sure to thank my brother," she said.

"I'm serious. Yesterday the title song was the second most downloaded track on iTunes."

"What was the first?" she asked.

"That hip-hop guy's stuff. What's his name."

"DJ Whatshisname," she said, but Allen was on to the next thing. "How are the new songs coming?"

"Soon. They're coming soon," she said.

"Annie. The label is losing patience."

"We've been through this a hundred times. It hasn't been that long. They're just greedy."

"Maybe so but they pay the bills."

"You just said we're flying up charts."

"Promise me you'll come back."

"Allen."

"Promise."

"Where else would I go?"

Annie lunges above her head, slips on the ridges beneath her boots, and tumbles backwards smacking her tailbone against the uneven steel. "Goddammit!" Misty rain has already begun coating the trees, her hair, the crates full of tangelos. She could have filled another crate in the time it has taken to deal with all the nonsense.

She braces the side of the truck and hauls herself up. Pain snatches her breath when she lets go of the side of the truck. Enough rain has already gathered on the cab's window to spill a wriggling stream down the glass.

But she'll only come in from the grove after two large flashlights have sizzled down to meek yellow dots in the dark. Even after tumbling on her ass she still manages to fill another two crates and lug them into the barn with the others. The freezing rain, possibly snow, is set to arrive tomorrow.

Once inside, she starts a fire, lets Detour out, and then feels the pain flare in her back when she bends down to feed him. She removes her dirty clothes and slides directly into the silky, chocolate-colored robe Owen gave her two Christmases ago. She thinks of the last time he was here, the last time he would have seen her wear it.

He'd come down with a fever and she'd fallen asleep next to him with the robe on, waiting to see if his forehead would cool. She woke in the night with the damp silk plastered to her skin from his fevered body. His sweat smelled bitter. His mouth hung open, a mix of onions and sour milk. She thought maybe he'd eaten something bad at lunch that day. She leaned forward and touched her lips to his forehead. "I love you," he mumbled. He was burning up. She put an ice bucket beside the bed and wiped his face with the cold cloth she dipped in and out of it. She held a glass of ice water to his lips and made him drink. After a while the water in the bucket was nearly room temperature. She was drained by then. The idea of getting up and refilling the ice and then sitting over him and changing the cloth on his head filled her with a thick, clumsy fatigue. Her legs weighed into the mattress. Her brain felt heavy inside her skull. She sat with him until she thought she would cry the way a child cried from sleepiness. She wiped his hairline once more, and then she slipped out of bed and crawled naked between the cool sheets in the guest room. Detour joined her, and once he settled on the rug she fell into a sleep so deep and satisfying that the only thing that woke her was Owen in the late morning hour, tapping his razor against the porcelain sink down the hall.

I need to get to the store, she'd thought as she lay in bed. Chicken soup and grilled cheese.

The fire is dying now, and Annie doesn't have the energy to put another log on. She doesn't have the energy, even, to go to bed.

The memory of what happened next that day tugs at her. After the supermarket she would come home to an empty house. She knew the moment she pushed open the door. There were gaps in the shelves where his CDs and books had been. His guitar and stand were gone from their place by the window. But the reason she'd noticed these things in the first place was the air. She'd felt this air once before in her life. Like lights going out unexpectedly. Like being thrown into the dark unprepared.

She clutches a handful of silk at her leg. Embers pop, extinguish themselves. Cold air sifts through the flue.

He'd wanted children from the beginning. They'd gone in circles over this, and every time Annie was left feeling wronged in a way she had no words for, as if she herself had been cheated out of some essential piece that every other woman took for granted. *We should wait,* was all she could ever think to say. But then something shifted. Maybe it was the success of the CD or the fact that time was truly running out for her or maybe it was some kind of intuition that time was running out for *them.* All she knew was that after one of the last times they made love she heard herself say, "We need to get started on a family."

She can't remember the last time they made love. She might have done something different had she known, paid more attention, gone slower, breathed in the smell of his hair, traced the thin lines on the side of his neck. She might have told him she would never, could never love anyone else the way she loved him. But he knew that. Certainly he knew that. Even so, she might have had a chance to change what was about to come.

We need to get started on a family. "Roger that!" he'd said and kissed her on the mouth. *This* she remembers exactly. She remembers the feel of his hair between her fingers. Remembers the small kiss he gave the top of her head.

Not long after that he was gone, and she never got the chance to tell him that the family they'd planned on starting had already begun.

NINE

Nothing good can possibly come from this. Owen jumped into Tess's Miata this morning with the intention of going to work, and before he knew it he was on the freeway heading south with a knot the size of a walnut lodged in his throat.

Take me with you, babe. Take me, from here on out.

Gull on a Steeple has been playing for hours now. Annie's thick, sensual voice causes a whole pillow's worth of raw emotion to jam against his breastbone. His veins pulse with caffeine and tattered nerves, his cramped body feeling encapsulated inside the gunmetal Miata like a bullet about to discharge. The suck and pull of wind causes the canvas roof to thump somewhere behind his head, and he thinks of early fall when he and Tess kept the top down, her cords of blond hair swirling above her head, the seatbelt tucked beneath her small bump, their cheeks sun-kissed and freshly scrubbed as they made their way down the Emerald Coast Parkway, past the golf course and into town for dinner. It is an image that should make him turn around, her hand resting across her belly, the shy smile she gave when she noticed him looking. He doesn't turn around. Just eases off the gas.

In the beginning it wasn't clear what was wrong between him and Tess because they tore each other's clothes off every time they were alone. He now believes that's just the nature of affairs. To be filled with a kind of heightened desperation. It has its own appeal. Its own sense of purpose. But here's the thing. Deep down, the essence, and that *is* the word, the *essence* of what was quickly becoming *them* seemed to be missing a soul. Every time he tried to picture a future with Tess his mind cut to black and his chest filled with a range of buzzing, stinging, prodding discomforts. The only person he'd ever been able to see out there in the distance with him was Annie. Annie in the garden picking daylilies. Annie playing sweetly for a crowd. Annie planting kisses down the side of his neck. Annie making love to him in a hammock, flopping and swinging and laughing till she cried.

The thing with Tess had needed to end. He knew this. In fact, he'd asked Tess to meet him for lunch six months ago so he could explain himself in a public place and avoid a scene. A coward's way out, yes, but a way out of what felt like a miniature room with a hidden door. Not a lot of choices. Least none that he could see. But then the bell to the diner jangled and he glanced up as she breezed past the tables toward him with an expectant smile and he said, "What?" and she slipped into the booth next to him saying, "I have something to tell you, too," and he said, "Well go on," and she said, "You go first," and he said, "No, you," and all the while he was getting this feeling that his life had just turned into a second-rate script. A second-rate script, he thought again, only seconds before the grand finale. "I'm nearly three months pregnant," she said. "Now you go."

A mind can think a lot of things in the short amount of time it takes to open a mouth. His raced in circles, snagging along the reasons why this was a good thing, which, he later realized was a lot like self-hypnosis or the power of suggestion toward the things a man his age ought to want and have, and anyway, what came out of his mouth was laughter. The thing that made up who they were was now *literally* a soul. If he had done the wrong thing by having an affair, he was going to do the right thing now by..."Wow," he said. "Wow-wee." And if that sounded stupid, "I wanted to ask you to marry me," certainly took the prize. After that the train that seemed to be driving their lives barreled on down the track.

Almost. That night, his last night with Annie, he had planned to pack his things and leave, but he'd come down with a fever so unreasonable, so impervious to aspirin that he was sure the God he'd only half-believed in earlier in the day was not only certain but vengeful. He lay half-conscious, shivering beneath a stack of blankets Annie had drawn to his shoulders. He dreamed of being chased by a phoenix, his legs stuck no matter how he tried to run. He woke at intervals to Annie placing an icy cloth on his head. He woke to her watching over him while he shivered. "I love you," he told her more than once. Or at least he thought he had. "I'm sorry," he said, though he was even less sure of having said this.

He catches himself doing ninety and lets up on the gas.

The photo of Annie on the front of today's newspaper has dropped him into an icy crevasse from which he cannot seem to claw his way out. Her face had him holed up in the bathroom, sitting on the closed toilet seat beneath the halogen light, gripping the paper until it stained his fingers black. His eyes absorbed her in pieces. The hair he had stroked and lost his face into on so many nights. The curve of her neck and shoulders, her breasts in the ANARCHY! T-shirt he had bought for her as a joke when she refused to relinquish certain rights to her songs. There was the hand that had touched him everywhere for years. Her body so familiar, so much a part of who he was that he became confused, lost in time and space. He was sure he was going mad. He staggered out and slipped the paper in his desk drawer and then skulked around the cold kitchen, shivering, as a way of setting himself straight.

But it was no use.

There is still Calder to think of. He has always loved that man like a brother.

Prosecutors are seeking the death penalty. This is all Owen's fault. He didn't stop the two of them when he had the chance. He tried to tell Calder to stay away from Sidsel. She was married, he'd said. "You're as good as married yourself," Calder replied, and well, touché, buddy, what could Owen say to that? Calder had insisted that Sidsel was the only woman for him. Insisted with a fist to his chest. So Owen had gone into Sidsel's café with the intention of finding fault with her. He ordered a raspberry Kringle after watching a woman's eyes bug out when she bit into one. He ordered coffee because it smelled so fine and strong and at the price she was charging he expected it to be spectacular. It was. And he could see that, yes, Sidsel was indeed the kind of beauty that alarmed a man. A foreign kind, the kind you had to stare at to figure out how it was done.

But that didn't mean Calder had to be like every other idiot and fall in love with her. Owen studied her, checking off a list in his head. The way she moved: a graceful kind of dance. The way she talked: sexy, pouty lips, foreign accent. The way she dressed: all he really saw was her long, tan neck coming out of her white, open collared blouse like a calla lily. A calla lily? He swallowed the sweet, sticky pastry, thinking the sugar was going to his head. He had to look away before he fell in love with the woman himself. Not really, but part of him felt this way. The part of him that was his best friend Calder. More than anything it was the way she seemed to connect to people through her eyes. Calder did the very same thing. Staring a split-second too long, searching a face until he drew out whoever was behind it. Owen watched as Sidsel spoke to her customers with lightness and ease, the soft touch of her long fingers to an arm, offering her smile like a box of Kringles, something they could carry with them out the door and enjoy at a later time. Owen gulped his coffee down and pushed his way outside thinking, *Sonofabitch if Calder isn't screwed.*

Still. He should have insisted Calder wait to see if Sidsel would leave her husband. Who knew? Calder might have listened if he'd pressured him. A big brother kind of pressure. But instead, Owen sneaked around with Tess while Calder sneaked around with Sidsel, and on some level they became even closer than they'd been before. Partners in the same crime hidden from the other woman they both loved. Annie.

His sweaty hands feel tacky around the leather steering wheel. He feels worse than when he got into the car. He's been fighting off something, a cough that started small but now burns his chest as if the sticky phlegm is pulling loose from his lungs.

He passes a woman in a silver Mercedes convertible. Her big sunglasses and silky orange scarf seem more suited to the top being down. The whole picture of her seems more suited to a cliffy, Grace Kelly California highway. It's not until he passes her that he looks in his rearview mirror and sees that her license plate reads, LAST LAF. She can afford to look like Grace Kelly on any highway any day of the week. She's walked away from a divorce with everything.

His business. Everything's he's worked for. Everything he learned from Annie. Everything she helped him make.

He can't think about that now. Calder. There's just no way Calder could have killed Magnus. Owen saw Magnus once in Sidsel's café. He was twice as thick as Calder with fists the size of melons and an ornery look in his eye that said he'd made more enemies in his lifetime than friends. The evidence this prosecutor claims to have stacked up against Calder is purely circumstantial. So what if Magnus was beaten with a blunt object and Calder just happens to own a truck full of gardening tools? Owen hasn't come across any mention of a weapon or prints or even an eyewitness who could claim they saw Calder at Hal's that night. The only thing they have on him is motive. OK. It looks bad. Having an affair with a man's wife is number one on the list of motives. He'll give the prosecutor that.

But Calder is such an innocent. Owen can still see the look on his face when he first found out about Tess. Calder caught him and Tess parking like teenagers in the State Park off Route 41. What was Owen thinking? It was too close to the job Calder was doing for the Park Service down the road. He'd thought about this but decided to throw caution to the wind when it turned out to be the most convenient place for Tess to meet him before an interview she had. Calder recognized Owen's truck and walked up on them groping in the front seat. When he saw what was happening he stepped back and grabbed his shirt across his heart and ran back to his truck. Owen only managed to pound once on the tailgate before Calder sped away.

It was later that same day that Calder had demanded Owen either break it off with Tess or he was going to tell Annie. "You're a rotten bastard," he said. "You have any idea what this is going to do to my sister?" But then Calder must have realized the agony in Owen's face matched the agony in his own heart because that's when he backed off and confessed everything to Owen about Sidsel. The two men sat in silence after that. And then they called one another sonsabitches, and came this close to crying.

The air squeezes from his chest. He turns the stereo up. "Let's go back a year or two," Annie sings. "Back to knowing how it feels being right with you."

He and Tess made love last night. He needed so badly to feel some warmth. He needed so badly to feel some release. Afterwards he drifted in and out of sleep, his mind humming with thoughts of Annie. In the morning when he finally opened his eyes for good he rolled over, absorbed in his guilt, and placed his hand on Tess's hip, partly on the curve of her belly. When she placed her own hand on top of his it felt as if his heart was being prodded with a sharp, hot stick.

He isn't far now. Sixty miles at most.

In the days that followed him leaving Annie, in the months after that, even recently while watching Tess laugh with a circle of friends, he has burned to go back. The urge used to come on when he least expected until he realized it was seeing his wife happy that filled him with a nagging unease. He's not who she thinks he is. She has no idea that her happiness, which includes him, doesn't fully exist.

He should arrive in less than an hour. Tess will be calling any minute to see when he'll be home for dinner.

Early this morning he was listening to music while paying bills at his desk, and Tess walked in and asked, "Who's this on the stereo?"

One silly little phrase, *who's this,* crawled into his chest and gnawed away at the strings that bound him to his wife.

"The Kinks," he said without looking at her. He was ashamed of his feelings and wished they would go away. But how could she not recognize Ray Davies when she heard him? There was no one else who sounded anything like Ray Davies.

"Are you all right? You don't look like you feel well," Tess said.

"A chest cold. Something. My eyes feel tired. Maybe I need glasses."

"They say it happens in your early forties," she said.

Owen clicked his tongue. He tapped his pen on the desk. Tess stopped on her way out of the room. "What song is it?"

"'Misfits.'" A simple answer to a simple question, but he couldn't help but think that not only would Annie know the song and who wrote it, but she'd know when it was written and could play it for you.

He stood, rubbed his eyes, coughed, and left the house early.

TEN

Annie wakes with far less pain in her back than she expects. Coffee brews itself in the kitchen, and the rich smell draws her from the bed. She checks outside. Dark and gray, but dry.

Half an hour later she's heading out the door in what has become her harvest uniform of stiff jeans and boots, a dirty orange jacket and gloves, when the phone rings.

"Annie?" An old voice takes her by surprise. "I wonder if you wouldn't mind coming to see me."

"Uncle Calder."

"Just for a minute. I know you're probably busy."

"Well, in fact—"

"I wouldn't ask if it weren't important."

"I don't think I can. The weather is turning—"

"I know—"

"Can't we just talk over the phone?"

"I don't think that would have the same effect."

"I'm not sure I like the sound of that."

"Squirt. Please."

And with that she has no choice.

It's early. Maybe she can make her way out there and back within a couple of hours and still have time for the grove.

She changes into jeans and a black sweater, twists her mess of wavy hair into a barrette at the back of her head—careful not to pull too tight and walk out the door looking like her mother. This is the first time she's left home since Calder's arrest last week.

The air is charged, expectant, buzzing with some kind of energy when she opens the door. She's never seen this kind of light. Never seen such silvery white clouds. Driftwood in the sky. Her eyes water from the bitter wind, and now the lake, the whole pastoral scene is distorted, as if looking through a fisheye lens. She blinks away tears. The frosty air hums like an E flat. Maybe this is how it feels before a snowfall.

She yanks open the sticky door of the Land Cruiser. The feel of cold metal seeps through her gloves. Mrs. Lanie waves from her kitchen window now framed in multicolored lights, reminding Annie that Christmas is only days away. The curtain drops in a hurry, and Annie knows her front door is about to open.

"Annie?" Mrs. Lanie appears on her porch between bird-houses fashioned from gourds. The wreath on her door flops in the wind. She wraps her white cardigan across her chest. "I can't thank you enough. I was out in the barn this morning and brought in few. They're a beautiful crop. Even coming early like they did." The wind throws her voice behind her.

"I'll try to get back here shortly and bring in the rest."

"Are you headed out to see Calder?"

"No."

"Have you seen him yet?"

"No. I haven't. Not yet."

"It's not from having to pick the tangelos, is it?"

"Of course not."

"Well?"

"Go back inside. You'll catch pneumonia out here."

"I'm not scared."

Annie shakes her head.

"I can't believe he's still in there." Mrs. Lanie comes down several steps without holding the rail. "This is all nonsense," she says. "They must know that."

Ever since Owen left, Mrs. Lanie has dropped off canned jellies and baskets of corn and fresh berries and dense, home-baked bread on Annie's doorstep. These quiet, thoughtful gestures keep Annie from telling Mrs. Lanie how uneasy she feels about her brother.

"It'll all be over soon," Annie says.

Mrs. Lanie flattens the top of her hair back with her hand. She looks troubled by Annie's vague reply.

"I'm sorry. I'm in a hurry," Annie says. "I'm sorry about all them, too." She points at the press, now a constant gathering on the other side of the gate.

"Don't you worry about that," Mrs. Lanie commands, and tosses her kissed fingers toward Annie before heading inside and closing the door.

Annie starts the engine, turns the heat on high, and sits shivering in the blast of cold air. For the first time she imagines Calder in jail. The white cement-block buildings, giant chain-linked fences with looped barbed wire, dirty concrete floors, and armed guards in towers, all flash inside her mind like every cliché, every prison film she's ever seen. She remembers watching *One Flew Over the Cuckoo's Nest* with Calder when they were young. It wasn't a prison in the film. It was an institution for the criminally insane, but this is where she imagines Calder, wandering some hall, ticking himself crazy, being strapped down when he won't quit. Annie holds the steering wheel inside her fists for a stiff, breathless moment, remembering something else about the movie—Calder reaching for her hand, fumbling softly, and then squeezing tightly in the moments leading up to Chief suffocating McMurphy with a pillow. Then bam! Chief tosses a marble fountain through a barred window and escapes into hills of mist. He is free at last, the soundtrack rising with a haunting dulcimer and the thick beat of rawhide drums. The story ends, but it takes a little while before Calder lets go.

* * *

She drives through what feels like another country. Her pines and lakes and groves give way to golf courses, gated condos, and shopping centers humming with cars. Then come the oversized billboards advertising poker, line dancing, mechanical bulls, beachside pools with "real sandy shores" in the middle of Orlando. *Come experience the Caribbean at Sea World.* Traffic streams into sports bars, souvenir shops, and there is Rosie O'Grady's packing them in at two in the afternoon.

She feels dizzy and small, a turned-around insect making her way through all the buzz until the chaos trickles into lines of shoddy apartments, their white brick strung with fat, multicolored bulbs, roofs with plastic Santas in sleighs. Here and there a small clapboard house, tackle shop, and convenience store, and then acres of designer homes gathered around man-made lakes, long windows twinkling with the tiniest white lights.

The freeway finally spits her out going east into the small wooded town of Blue Springs. A white country church tucked between pines has the quiet, angelic look of Christmas without even trying.

Uncle Calder lives in the second-floor apartment of a Colonial Revival he's owned since before Annie was born. Her tires crunch over the short, pebbled driveway. She hasn't been here in nearly a year. She isn't proud of this. She thinks of all that happened when she was young. It shouldn't matter anymore, it doesn't matter anymore. It hasn't mattered in years.

The entrance to Uncle Calder's apartment is outdoors at the top of a set of long wooden stairs, and it is there that she sees him near the top in a blue baseball jacket and cap, lugging an elaborate red walker up the stairs. He fumbles once and catches his footing while his arm jets out to hook the stem of the walker, and in that moment it looks as if he might tumble to his death.

Annie jumps from the car and the air shocks her again. The wind pushes her forward, sucking her long coat against the backs of her legs. The silvery clouds hang low and thick, like blankets draped from a ceiling. Her uncle appears to be standing just beneath them. She nearly weeps at the sight. So many memories are archived inside him, a family library with pages fluttering open faster than she can turn away. She closes the car door and walks with a thickness in her step.

"Hey there!" she hollers.

He doesn't seem to hear. She follows him up the stairs calling his name until he finally turns, losing his grip on the walker, and then catching it again when he sees her.

"Whoa." He takes a moment to stare. "I'll be goddamned. I thought you was going to wait till I was laid out in a coffin before ever laying eyes on me again."

"Uncle Calder."

"What do you say, squirt?"

She grabs hold of one of the walker's back wheels. It's heavier than she thought, and the two of them continue up the stairs to the landing where they set the walker down with a thud.

"I'm just coming in from breakfast. You sure got here fast." The skin along his jaw has loosened. His eyes are the deep blue of her mother's woolen blanket. Darker than she remembers. The porch light catches moisture around the rims.

"What are you doing with this thing?" she asks.

His shoulders are still wide and straight. He lifts his cap with one hand while he smoothes his full head of gray hair with the other. The wind quickly slaps his hair forward again, and for a moment he wrestles it back and forth before cupping the cap on his head. "These people are paying me money to try it out. They call it a Rollator, the Prime 3 Deluxe Edition with a steel-reinforced frame. It's got lightweight baskets that pull out for groceries."

"It doesn't look to me like you even need the thing if you're carrying it up all these stairs."

"That's cause of the shoes."

She looks down at his white running shoes. "What do you mean?' she asks, but he is on to the next thing.

"You have any idea how old I am?" he says.

Despite the blotchy sunspots and papery paleness of his skin, he doesn't stand like an old man. He doesn't give off the bony, jittery gestures of the elderly. His voice is smooth and clear. "I know you don't act your age," she says.

He smiles and gently pats her cheek with his giant hand. He leans forward over the contraption and wraps her in his arms. "You're looking more like your mother," he says.

The mention of her mother, a trace of cigar, has shaken too many things loose, and she is teary-eyed by the time he lets go.

Inside the dark apartment, a small artificial tree is seized by an oversized string of blinking blue lights meant for a much larger tree. Annie recognizes the same ornaments her mother owns—elongated bulbs, tinsel, a tall, golden spire twinkling on top. The air is cooler than she expects. It smells like Uncle Calder. Like dust and stale cigars, and then a wonderfully greasy smell of something recently fried. She guesses the windows haven't been opened in a while.

Uncle Calder hits a wall switch, and a ceiling fan lights the room. The blades begin to spin. He walks over and pulls the fan's chain, twice. The blades slow to a stop, and Uncle Calder tells her he can never figure out how to turn one on without the other.

The living room is tidy, newspapers stacked into a neat square on the maple coffee table. Calder's mug shot is covered by a bowl of boiled peanuts. Two pairs of white tennis shoes make a line by the door. Uncle Calder's Purple Heart rests on top of its box beneath the lamp on the end table, and she imagines him sitting on the sofa, holding it in his hands, inviting memories to wash over him. When she'd first come across the satin box as a child her mother told her to put it back. "It's not a toy," she'd whispered. But it looked like one, like purple and gold jewelry for a girl. Her mother handled it like it was worth more than anything in their whole house. It wasn't until years later that Annie found a newspaper clipping among her father's things about Uncle Calder's ship in the Pacific. Of the thousands of sailors, only several hundred survived a torpedo attack by the Japanese. Uncle Calder had floated for days in freezing, shark-infested waters, waiting to be saved. The arms and legs of so many had been burned from the explosion, including Uncle Calder's. Their mouths had swelled with saltwater ulcers. At dusk the screams would come, first one and then another and another, and those who were left knew the sharks were taking men down in pieces. Uncle Calder never cracked. He didn't go insane like some of the others who were convinced they smelled fresh coffee and swam beneath the surface to find it. He stayed alert for four days, watching for fins, his sights jetting beneath the murky water and floating debris for the zigzagging shapes. Twice he lanced a shark's nose with the bones of his raw and swollen knuckles, twice saving another sailor along with himself. Annie remembers feeling confused by the picture of her gentle uncle, and even more so by the fact that in exchange for saving another man's life he was given a trinket, a heart-shaped gold charm on a pretty purple ribbon she had once thought of as belonging to a girl.

"Coffee OK?" Uncle Calder stops in the kitchen doorway. "I'm about frozen to the bone."

To the left of the doorway hangs a framed poster of Ronald Reagan in a cowboy hat. One hand is frozen out from his hip, the other sits on a pistol in its holster. Uncle Calder's head is now even with Ronald Reagan's, and she quickly sees a likeness. She slips off her scarf and gloves but leaves on her coat and slides her hands inside its roomy pockets.

"Coffee would be great." She sits down in a wooden rocker with blue cushions tied to the rungs. She faces the dead gray television set. "I must have asked you this before, but why do you live up here? Why don't you rent this one out and live downstairs?"

Uncle Calder fumbles around in the kitchen, and it isn't until he finally steps into the living room with two cups of instant black coffee that she realizes he's heard what she said. He hands her a cup, and when she takes it he squeezes his empty fist in and out as if it is cold or arthritic. Several bruises mark the back of his hand. "Stairs are a good form of exercise." He smiles and sits on the end of the sofa near her. "Besides, I like the view of the railroad from up here."

An old, metal-framed photograph is placed on the coffee table, and Annie has the feeling it was set there recently. It's a photo of her father and Calder on a dock with Parson's Lake shimmering in the background. Calder is no more than ten, grinning for the camera, showing off a bass on a line. Her father appears caught unaware, perhaps looking at her mother off to the side, his long arm dangling around Calder's shoulder.

"I found that the other day when I was going through some stuff," Uncle Calder says.

"He finally caught a bigger one than me," Annie says.

The coffee is watery, bland.

"Well? What do you say?" Uncle Calder lightly slaps his thigh and then holds his hand out several feet above the floor. "I don't think you've been here since you were this high."

"I'm still only that high."

He laughs. "I'm glad you came." A tuft of thick gray hair sticks out from the side of his cap above his ear, and Annie thinks this is exactly how Calder will look when he reaches old age.

Uncle Calder sees her looking and removes his cap, slicks his hair back once more.

"I'm sorry," she says. "It's been hard on me these past few months. I know Calder comes around to see you a lot. To be honest, I didn't want to run into him."

He eases his forearms onto his thighs and nods at the floor.

"You don't know the whole story." Annie thinks of the worst of it, and quickly pushes it from her mind.

"Which story is that?"

"What happened to me. I mean, between Calder and me."

"I heard some. Don't know if I heard it all. Probably not. I've got no way of checking the facts. I never heard your side of things."

She glances toward the window. A discolored plastic shade is pulled halfway down.

"Why did you ask me to come here?"

"I saw him yesterday," Uncle Calder says.

"How is he?"

"Why don't you go see for yourself?"

"I'm planning on it." She sets her coffee down on the pile of newspapers and sighs.

"He's holding up," Uncle Calder says. "Except for the tics. He's taken to jumping again."

"Mom told me." The mention of her mother hangs between them.

"How is she?" he asks.

"Seems to be holding up, I guess."

"Well."

"You can't expect too much," Annie says.

"No. She's been through plenty."

"Haven't we all."

"Coffee all right?"

"Mmn." Annie takes a sip.

"The thing is," Uncle Calder says, "the tics make him look half-crazy, which don't do a whole lot for his defense." He clears his throat and rubs his wrist across his mouth as if he is wiping it clean of sweat. His forearm is blotched with faint bruises.

"What happened to your arm?"

He looks at the back of it and shakes his head. "Eighty some odd years is what happened. You start bruising at the thought of moving." He glances at her hands. "What's your excuse? Looks like you caught your hands in a meat grinder."

"It's nothing, sanding, picking tangelos. Have you had blood work done? Just to make sure nothing's wrong?"

"You see that Rollator over there? Doctors are paying me to try it out."

"That's what you said."

"You have any idea how many people are willing to pay you to run a study on something you'd otherwise have to pay *them* for? The internist wants to study your cholesterol, the man on the radio wants to know if you're depressed, the billboard on the freeway offers to help your hair loss, the woman on TV wants to help with your high blood pressure."

"And the Rollator?"

"There's a whole other place that does nothing but gadgets. They're paying me to try out all kinds of things. In the meantime, all the other white coats are drawing blood and looking me over like the wife I never had. They want to know what kind of food I eat and how much exercise I get and how often I use the bathroom. All I have to do is try out these red and white blood pressure caplets and orange painkillers and fancy smelling shampoo for losing my hair."

"You're not losing your hair."

"Well."

"You're trying all this stuff out even if you don't need it?" She gestures to the Rollator. "Aren't they on to you?"

"You ever hear that song, 'The Great Pretender'?"

"I believe I'm hearing it now."

He laughs. "Who knows? Playing around with all this stuff might keep me from ever needing it."

"Not only does that not make sense, but you're likely to forget how to walk on your own if you keep pushing that thing around in front of you."

"You see these shoes?" He holds up his white, size-twelve sneakered foot. "Got battery powered insoles."

Annie raises her brow.

"That's the face your daddy used to make."

"I've been told."

"Anyway, what we're talking about here is balance control. Baby boomers are about to start falling and breaking their hips. It'll be a national crisis, just you wait and see. They're already coming out with a kind of air bag you attach to your hips."

She drops her head to the side. "I never know when you're joking with me."

"I swear."

"Uh huh."

"Speaking of which. Happy belated birthday. You're middle-aged, squirt. Where'd the time go?"

She honestly doesn't know.

"Listen," he says, lifting his foot again. "They put some kind of electrical current in these insoles. Runs from my feet to my brain. Supposed to steady out the balance that dulls with age. I thought I might take up dancing."

"Uncle Calder, you're going to mess up their research. You don't have trouble with balance, do you?"

"Not with these."

She shakes her head and lifts her coffee to her lips and drinks. It has cooled and tastes like plastic.

"Calder needs a better attorney." His words slice through the air. "That's why I asked you to come here."

She lowers her cup.

"You'd think in a case as clear-cut as this he'd be just fine with a court-appointed one. There's no evidence he was even at that bar. They act like cause he's got tics he's some kind of four-horned billy goat. I'm taking it upon myself to see that he gets someone else. One of those high-powered ones. Maybe you could help with that."

She's suddenly embarrassed by her hands. Cracked and blistered, taken up with other work, other concerns. She slips them back inside her pockets.

"Seems like you could use a little help yourself," he says.

"What? I'm fine."

"You don't look fine."

"Well, I am."

"You look like a short dog in tall grass is what you look like."

"What's that supposed to mean?"

"It means you look lost."

"Uncle Calder." She can't find the words to finish the sentence. *You look lost.* Such a simple thing to say. But it burrows through the hardest parts to the soft center of her core. She has the urge to spill everything, to tell him what she has told no one, what she has tried to hide even from herself about the morning Owen left her.

She felt queasy every time she pushed her cart down the aisle, every time the wobbly front wheel pulled in a different direction. She thought she must be getting sick, too, and realized as she ran through her symptoms that her breasts felt tender. Heavy. She was unsure of when her last period had been. Then she remembered several days in a row when she'd forgotten to take the pill. She was thinking about this when a teenage couple asked to have their picture taken with her. How many times had she forgotten to take a pill and nothing ever came of it? But then as she smiled and made a peace sign for their cell phone camera, she noticed the boy's boxers above his jeans and remembered the joke she'd made to Owen about him switching from briefs to boxers. A sure sign of his affair, she would later come to realize, but back then she'd laughed and said, "I've read that boxers make a man more fertile," and this was what was running through her mind after she was alone in the supermarket, her hand on her abdomen, eyes gazing at the laundry detergent she'd wandered toward, her eyes filling with circles of orange.

On the way home the ordinary ride down the graveled road had an airy freshness to it. She imagined a babbling toddler behind her in a car seat, asking, "What's that, and that, and that?" The thought, the possibility that this could happen, softened her, as if someone had poured a bubbly liquid into her veins. She recalled a song, just the essence of it, not the song itself, that a man wrote about his daughter back in the seventies. Annie couldn't think of what it was. "I've got a song lost in my head," she would say to Owen when she burst inside the house, and then tell him the one she was trying to think of and he would know exactly which one, and what a perfect way to deliver the news.

But Owen's truck wasn't in the driveway. And when she opened the front door her body registered the gaps in the room before her mind could catch up. It was June, and an icy cold settled in her bones. Things were missing from the shelves. Owen's guitar and stand were no longer by the window. But hers was, and worth far more than Owen's. Books were missing from the shelves. Thieves didn't steal books. The framed photographs of Owen as a child were gone. An old cigar box he kept receipts in was gone from the mantel. In its place was a note held in place by the tambourine. It was written on her own stationary as if she had written it to herself.

She stared at the note from across the room. How long did it take him to do all this? To pack his things and write the note? He must have been planning for days, weeks, months. She dropped the groceries to the floor and stood in place as it all tumbled from the paper bag. Detour crept forward and licked the damp cellophane around the meat.

She made her way toward the note. Floated? Materialized? Thinking back on it later she could never picture exactly how she had arrived, remembering only the jangle of the tambourine as it hit the floor.

My dear, dear, Annie,

This is the worst thing I've ever done in my life. Rest assured I'll be sorry for as long as I live, though I don't mean that as any kind of reparation. I know there's no atoning for something like this. I swear I never thought I'd do this sort of thing, I never pictured our lives ending up this way, but they have, and that's the part I can't claim to understand the way a man who's decided to go and do something like this ought to understand it. I've been involved with someone else. I've made a big mistake, and I'm afraid leaving seems to be the only way to put it right. "I'm sorry" probably has no meaning here. But Christ almighty, I am to the bone. And I know it doesn't make any sense, it doesn't help anybody to write that I'll always love you, but it only seems fair to state that truth in the face of so many lies.

Always,
Owen

This was all the explanation offered. Words plucked from his head in a state of hurry.

What she felt was dumb, numb shock. A blackout, really. And once that passed, the baby. What about the baby?

By the time she thought to take the test, she'd been crying for half an hour. She'd read the note and threw it away again and again, until she finally set fire to it in the sink.

Her mind remained cool and distant when the lines turned pink. She walked the rooms of the house and thought about raising a child by herself. She entered each room, picturing her baby in the tub, at the kitchen table, in the small bedroom that was perfect for a nursery. The baby, she imagined, had waves of chestnut hair just like Owen. In fact, the baby looked exactly like him, and this was where her thoughts began to twist, and the distance her mind had afforded her, closed in until it felt like a pillow on her face. Her days would begin and end with a child who reminded her of the day she was standing in right now. A child didn't deserve a burden like that. Children sense things. Like the way she had sensed there was something wrong with her father. The way she had sensed the truth about Uncle Calder.

Calder wasn't answering his cell. She got back in her car and looked everywhere for him and Owen. No one had seen or heard from either one. It was evening before she found Calder slung over the counter at Hal's. "I need to talk to you," she said, her hands and voice trembling. He focused hard on her face. He took her hand and she pulled away. "You don't want to know how young she is," he said, drunkenly, as if to himself.

Back home she stumbled through a fog, in and out of sleep for nearly twenty-four hours with very little to eat. When the phone rang she checked the caller ID but didn't pick up. It was never Owen. Or Calder. She kept thinking something would come to her. Some explanation, a solid plan she would know to follow. She picked up her guitar but found she couldn't sing. She couldn't stand the sound of minor chords. She grew weaker, and sicker.

Two days later, just hours before Calder showed up to get his Bobcat loader from her backyard, a violent sickness took over. A dull ache gripped her lower back. She felt dizzy and warm. Her forehead beaded with sweat. It wasn't until something wet slipped between her legs that she understood what was happening.

She walked her fingers along the hallway with the smiling photos of Owen. He mocked her unsteady steps toward the bathroom where the slightest trace of his aftershave still clung to the shower curtain, bath mat, something.

Stevie Wonder. It was Stevie Wonder's "Isn't She Lovely?" The song he'd written in the seventies for his daughter. "Isn't she lovely/ Isn't she wonderful/ Isn't she precious/ Less than one minute old."

She rushed to the toilet just in time. She closed her eyes and saw green and yellow. She opened them and saw the same thing. The pain in her back went from dull to hot, to knives piercing bone. She continued to throw up until there was nothing but bile, and then finally there was nothing left of that. Her arms and legs shook as the cramping bore down. The part of Owen inside her was cutting itself loose. She was relieved. She was mortified and heartbroken, though it no longer mattered what she was. She could no more stop the blood from slipping between her legs than she could make things with Owen go back to the way they were.

The pink and white mucousy blood in her underwear frightened her. She peeled them off and sat on the toilet and allowed herself to drain. She couldn't help but look down to see what was coming. Clots and mangled strings of dark blood. Bright, nearly clear red drops in between. Nothing that looked anything like the beginnings of a baby.

The bathroom smelled of vomit, and now the metallic smell of blood. She could no longer smell Owen's aftershave, and she wondered if these new smells would linger, too, the way his aftershave had, taunting her for days.

After a while the cramping began to lessen, and this is when she wept. Long, quiet, snot-filled cries. "I'm sorry," she whispered, though she wasn't sure what for or to whom this was directed.

She pulled a stream of toilet paper from the roll and blew her nose and wiped her face. After that came a burst of anger. It sparked and steamed and made her eyes ache. *You prick. You rotten sonofabitch.*

Another cramp took her by surprise. Her breath caught behind her ribs. "Son of a PRICK!"

She should call someone. Couldn't a woman bleed to death this way? She needed to call someone. But the only someone she wanted near her right now was Calder, and from what he'd said at Hal's the other night he'd known all along about Owen cheating on her. Did he know Owen was planning to leave her, too? Right then it didn't matter. When the next cramp seized her insides, her forearms and feet, every part of her body tingled with the release of sweat, and without thinking she screamed her brother's name. She screamed it again until it echoed off the bathroom walls and came back to her. It was Calder's hand she had wanted so badly to hold, his long arms she'd needed for comfort after the bleeding finally slowed and she'd stood for a time under a hot shower, and then walked back down the hallway with the photographs on either side like a procession of strangers smiling nervously over all that had gone on in the bathroom.

And all of this happening just hours before Calder had stood in her driveway on the day she'd told him to leave and never come back.

"Squirt?"

Annie glances at the door. The thought of going home brings tears.

"Aw, squirt."

"I'm sorry," she says, but allows herself to cry.

Uncle Calder puts his arm around her shoulder and draws her close. "Ever since you were this big you couldn't help but take it all in. And every little thing seemed to break your heart."

She cries harder, thinking how he himself once broke her heart. She becomes a child again in her uncle's big arms. She sobs uncontrollably against his scratchy sweater, unable to apologize for getting it wet.

"You see there?" He laughs a little as he squeezes her. "You're not fine, squirt. You're stubborn, that's for damn sure. And you *will* be fine again. But you're not fine right now."

It feels as if she's made of nothing but tears.

"It's all right there. It's going to be all right," he says, patting her back.

She finally pulls away and wipes her eyes. "What's going to happen to him?" she asks between breaths.

"Nothing. This thing isn't even going to make it to trial."

She wants to ask if he thinks Calder could have done such a thing. Of course she can't ask him that. Not that. So she says nothing, and by saying nothing he seems to feel the need to fill the silence.

"He didn't do this, squirt. I know what you're thinking." He stares at the tree and tosses a handful of peanuts in his mouth. He offers her the bowl and she shakes her head.

"I know why you think he might have," he says when he's finished chewing. "But he didn't. Look at me. You've got to trust me on this. There's plenty more I need to say here. I want you to think about putting to rights you and your brother."

She turns away.

"You want to hear what I have to say or don't you?"

She smiles, just a little. "Not particularly."

"I'll take that as a yes."

She barely gets out a sigh when he says, "I tried for months to talk him into going over there to see you in spite of you telling him to stay away, but he insisted on abiding by your wishes. He's been waiting all this time to get some kind of sign that you've forgiven him. It was me who told him to go over on your birthday and put things right."

"He told me he was in love with this man's wife, Uncle Calder. He said he couldn't imagine living without her. And then he said the only problem was that she had a husband named Magnus."

Uncle Calder stares at her, through her. "I know all that. He told me, too. I see where you're going with this."

"What am I supposed to think?"

She has only seen Uncle Calder angry one time in her life. The time her mother had refused to open her bedroom door and he'd hit it with his fist and then slid to the floor, yelling in a fusion of anger and, more than anything, misery.

He's angry now. Wiping his stiff mouth with the back of his hand and clearing his throat and taking in a breath so big it makes him cough a phlegmy cigar cough. "Listen here." His voice is steady, controlled. "Things aren't always what they seem."

"I know that." Boy, how she knows that.

"That Rollator in the corner. Seems a harmless thing, but like you said," he says, coughing again, and whether he forgets what it is he's going to say next or decides against saying it all together, Annie doesn't know. Either way, the coughing dies down, but Uncle Calder is finished talking. And so is she.

PART TWO

PART TWO

ELEVEN

Annie's mother had a way of clicking her tongue when she read the paper, adding sighs and chuckles at the end. Sometimes she read passages out loud to no one in particular, the way she was doing now.

"Oh, for Pete's sake," she said. "We're rolling back to the Middle Ages."

It was Sunday morning and the house smelled of cooked bacon and coffee and warm buttered biscuits. The family was gathered around the breakfast table, Annie's father to her left in a white T-shirt and red pajama bottoms. Her mother to her right, already dressed in blue shorts, her copper hair pulled into a ponytail that lay across her striped sleeveless blouse. She was the pretty center from which everything else seemed to flow. Food, plans for the day, the news of the world around them. Newspapers were splayed across both of their now empty plates.

Calder sat across from Annie reading the funnies. He hadn't looked at her the same since the Pinckneys the week before. He hadn't been acting the same, period.

"Those boys get into fights all the time," she'd said after the first day of the silent treatment. "Are you afraid we're going to get in trouble? Because we aren't. Everybody knows their daddy has a regular schedule of beating them. He won't be able to tell his own handiwork from someone else's. Besides, do you really think they're going to say a *girl* put those bloody knots on their heads?" This seemed to shut him out even more.

"Reinstating the *death* penalty!" her mother was saying. "My God. How can any sane nation...It says here..." She scanned the page, mouthing words as she searched.

Calder's eyebrows jumped up and down at the funnies. Annie swallowed her juice and chewed bits of pulp between her teeth.

A man's sad singing voice sifted from the radio's gold fabric speakers. The second pot of coffee gurgled through the percolator.

"That's Waylon Jennings, Annie," her father said from behind the paper. "Mark my words. He's going to be big."

Annie bit into a flaky, buttered biscuit coated in grape jelly. She listened to the smooth, baritone voice, and in that moment forgot about everything except the music and the biscuit, its crust lodged against the roof of her mouth. She freed it with her tongue, and her whole body relaxed into the sweet warmth.

Her mother clicked her tongue. "Here," she said. "This Justice Stewart! Quote, 'This function may be unappealing to many, but it is essential in an ordered society that asks its citizens to rely on legal process rather than self-help to vindicate their wrongs.' End quote. What does that even *mean*?" she asked. "That we'll all just go around killing people who break the law if the government won't kill them for us?" She groaned and took a sip of coffee. "How did they pull this crap over on us? We've been asleep at the wheel, Kearney." Her eyes never left the page, but her arms rose into the air. "It's 1976 and we're killing people to show killing is wrong. Am I the only one who sees the irony here?"

Annie felt Calder's eyes on her. She focused on her mother, feigned interest in what she was saying.

Her father drew the paper down as if he had something urgent to add. Her parents played off one another, each layering the conversation until they painted a single, agreed-upon picture. They were a set. Kearney and Miriam. Salt and pepper. Sun and moon. Shoes. One misplaced without the other. But now her father eyes glared across the room toward the sink and then up, with a tilt of his head, around the kitchen window and back down in little jerks as if he were following the trail of a skittish mouse. He didn't add anything to what her mother said.

He'd stared like this before, if not at the curtains in the breeze, then the doorframe, an African violet, a line of scuff marks on the floor. No one was exactly sure what to make of it. Last week her mother had found him on the patio, staring into the yard at the empty tree swing for who knew how long before she led him to the sofa and put a cold cloth to his head and told him to lie back and relax. He worked too hard she said, six days a week was too much. After a moment he'd jumped to his feet and said, "Goddamn, my head hurts," and he'd turned on the television with the wet cloth tumbling from his head to his lap to the floor.

Two evenings after he'd said that about his head, her mother whispered, "This is serious, Kearney," while they were reading beneath the lamplight on the living room sofa. Calder and Annie lay on the roped rug at their feet eating Pop-Tarts and watching *One Flew Over the Cuckoo's Nest* on Betamax.

"Look at me, Miriam," her father had whispered. "I'm fine. I probably work too much like you said. Why don't I take some time off and we'll all go someplace? We can drive over to Homosassa Springs for a few days. Get a look at some manatees."

"All right," her mother said, and by her soft tone it was clear she wanted to believe him. But then she added, "I still think it's more than that. Why don't you just go see someone?"

"Because I'm working so much," he said with a laugh, and Annie turned in time to see him kiss her mother on the cheek.

Her mother's hardcover book clapped shut when she tossed it onto the cushions. She stepped through Annie and Calder's legs on her way out of the room, and the tip of her cool toes skimmed Annie's calf.

Now, her mother released the paper. She set her palms flat and quiet on the table and watched Annie's father.

Annie swallowed at her plate. She didn't want to think about anything other than the fact that she loved Sundays—the way they all lingered at the table, her parents telling stories of customers and fellow teachers, the funny things people said and did. One woman needed a new hutch because her father had shot at her husband from across the dinner table and hit the hutch instead. Not only was the glass busted out but the frame on the door was split clean in half and the backside looked like it was hit with buckshot the way the hole sprayed open, according to this woman. "You couldn't fix it if you tried," the woman told Annie's father as she shopped for a new hutch in his store. "What about your husband?" he'd asked, and the woman shooed him like she was chasing away birds with her hands. "He's beyond fixing, too," she said, and Kearney was afraid to ask just exactly what that meant. Annie's mother's stories always unraveled from the same tangle of women. Fussy young teachers looking for husbands, and more often than not, finding the same kind of man who, in the end, didn't want any of them, which gave the women another day to bemoan having to teach *forever*. This seemed about the funniest thing Annie's mother had ever heard. *"Having* to teach, she said. *Forever*. Can you imagine? Then again, maybe Suzette *should* get her snaggletooth fixed so I wouldn't have to gag through her Charlie perfume and cigarettes in the teacher's lounge every morning." And on they went until everyone was hungry again, sandwiching bacon between leftover biscuits and drinking down the rest of the lukewarm juice for lunch.

"He's one ornery sonofabitch," her father suddenly said. "I'll say that much for him."

"Kearney!" Her mother jerked her head left and right at Calder and Annie. *"Who* are you talking about?"

"Well, Miriam. It's the truth."

The sun glowed orange in the white bowl of cantaloupe and peaches. Her father returned the paper to his face. Her mother stood without a word and cleared food and dishes from the table.

It fell quiet for too long, and Calder began mouthing the air like a fish.

Then her father dropped the paper into his lap again.

Her mother slowed with her cleanup.

"Y'all know I used to ski," he said.

Her mother frowned. "What are you talking about?"

"Water ski?" Calder asked.

"Snow ski."

Annie looked at her mother. Midway through she'd quit scraping cold gravy from one plate onto another. Annie turned to her father. "Really?"

"You know your fingers get so cold they burn when you heat them up again," he said.

Calder asked if that was true.

"I got to where I was kind of partial to it," her father said. "The frozen bones, and then the warm fire afterwards where everything thawed out and stung a little bit."

Her mother studied him closely.

"It's true. And the big steps it takes, like the abominable snowman, stepping through knee-high snow." He lifted his bare feet off the floor and let them drop one by one. "I loved the smell of snow."

"What's it smell like?" Calder asked.

"Well, that's the thing. I think it's different for different people. For me it was like brand-new upholstery."

Annie and Calder glanced at their mother and laughed, reluctantly.

"I'm serious." He winked and said, "It was during a trip up to New York with my mother and daddy when I was ten years old that I saw my first mountain and snow. Mother's cousin was dying up there of tetanus. A saw had sliced clear through his hand. Our intention for going was the funeral."

"What exactly *is* tetanus?" Calder asked, as if he'd been thinking about it all day long.

"It's a bacteria that poisons the body," their mother said in a slow, faraway voice. She watched their father. "Your jaw locks up and your throat closes." She brought her hand to her own throat. "Sometimes you can't breathe."

Calder asked if it could kill a person and she said that it could.

"The funeral was going to be up there in Utica where the cousin lived," her father said.

"My people are the ones who live in Utica, honey," her mother said.

Her father tilted his head to the side and stared at her with puckered lips.

"Kearney?" She placed the stack of dirty plates back onto the table. "*I* had a cousin with tetanus when I was young. That was *me*."

He turned to Calder and started again from the place he left off. "After two days of waiting on Henry to die and listening to my mother's people go on about his stiff jaw and the pain he was having swallowing a glass of water, my daddy finally said, 'I've had about enough of this,' and clapped his hands together and rose up off the sofa and he and Mother and me all piled into Daddy's Two Ten station wagon and drove up to Lake Placid.

"So we got there and Mother takes one look at the mountains and says, 'Lord, Daddy, I don't believe I will.' She stays in the base lodge reading *Life* magazine and drinking her hot cocoa. Daddy goes down the Silver Shoot bunny hill just once and decides he's cheated death well enough and there's no use in pushing one's luck. So he gets him a steady stool over to the oak bar and holds on like a hen shittin a goose egg."

Calder and Annie burst out laughing.

"Kearney!" Her mother picked up the stack of dirty dishes and carried them to the sink. "That sounds like a movie. Wasn't that from a movie or something?"

"Now *I*, however, took to the bunny hill like a jack rabbit. Then I took the, what do you call those things, the *gondola* to the top of some mountain, and imagine this, I zigzagged my way back down that sonofabitch like a ball bearing in a wooden shifter contraption."

Annie laughed until her stomach ached. Calder laughed, too. They stole looks at their mother between breaths, and even she had cracked a smile. Then she tied a yellow apron at her back in a hurry and Annie realized the smile had been for her children. When she brought her hands around they were shaking.

"I swear to God," he continued. "I went back up again for several more tries before I took to, what'd they call that, I don't remember what, but it was over four thousand feet tall, I'm telling you, this is the God's honest truth. I was a natural. Aside from landing on my ass a few times, I believed I'd found my life's purpose."

"Kearney," her mother said.

"Imagine coming from Florida and finding out you're a natural born skier," he said.

Goose bumps rose on Annie's arms. The smile dissolved from her face. She looked at her father, at the tiny black and gray flecks of stubble poking from the skin around his mouth. There was something, she didn't know what, but something to what he was getting at, even if none of it was true.

"I came back home after that trip and felt like I was trapped on an island where all the things I needed to keep me alive didn't exist," he said.

A breeze sucked the white curtains against the screen, and Annie's goose bumps lifted the tiny blond hairs on her arms. The idea he was getting at seemed vague and bigger than she knew what to do with, but somehow she understood. People got misplaced. She had always wanted to live in children's books where girls wore fat mittens and woke to snowy skies. She wanted to live where leaves painted streams of red and orange across hillsides. There was nothing she hated more than the heat, her shoulders always burned, peeling in raw patches, molting like a yellow rat snake. She hated swollen fingers in the summer. She hated mosquitoes sucking the life out of her when the grass was too high. Lizards in the bathtub when she pulled the shower curtain back. Somewhere in the world there was a place just for her, an exact place where she belonged. But what if she never found it? What if it turned out to be the coast of Lake Michigan? Or a place she would probably never go, like Iceland or New Zealand?

"Kearney," her mother said, as if to draw the truth, the real story from his mouth. Her hands slid down the front of her apron.

"I went back several more times as a teenager," he said. "But the snow was never quite the same. The winters seemed to get warmer every year."

"Kearney."

"The disappointment turned me sour," he said. "I'm still trying to put to rights my love-hate relationship with Northern skies."

"Kearney." Now barely a whisper.

The table was now empty of everything except biscuit crumbs, the fold of newspaper on the death penalty, and the remains of a biscuit in Annie's hand.

Her mother leaned her back into the sink, placed her arms in an X across her chest, and squeezed her shoulders.

"Did the man ever die?" Calder asked.

"What's that?" her father said.

"The cousin," Calder said, as much to their father as their mother. "Did he ever die of tetanus?" He gripped the edge of the table in a clear attempt to keep his legs from swinging underneath.

Her father's sights crept back along the frame of the kitchen window behind her mother, whose arms fell as she walked over and hugged Annie's father's neck. She rubbed the length of his arm as she kissed his hair above the temple, her lips frozen in that spot for the longest time.

"Was he really your cousin, Mom?" Calder's voice began to strain. He held on even tighter to the table as if he meant to anchor it to the floor.

Annie shoved the last piece of biscuit in her mouth. She focused on a dark knot in the pine and smeared a rigid finger back and forth across its cracks, wearing away the polished surface until it squeaked.

Her mother took hold of Annie's hand and squeezed. She smiled the saddest smile on earth, and it felt like a stream of heat rushed in to fill the empty space between them.

"Yes, Calder," she said. "Yes."

A woman's voice on the radio sang long and slow, like a cry, over having sweet dreams.

"Emmylou," her father said, as if Emmylou Harris were at the window. "Listen to that, Annie. That could be you someday."

TWELVE

Annie feels the weight of her lids from all the crying. Cold gusts of air bite her raw eyes. She closes herself inside her car in Uncle Calder's driveway, turns up the heat, and waits until she's sure her voice is steady again.

Icy rain ticks the hood. She opens her cell and dials Mrs. Lanie.

"The rest is done for, honey," Mrs. Lanie says. "I appreciate you trying. But the front steps are already solid ice, and they're up here next to the warm house. You can imagine the state of the grove out there."

Annie opens her mouth. A puff of white drifts from her lips.

Most of the tangelos go to a children's home in Altamonte Springs. She doesn't want to think of those kids going without, or receiving apples from up North as further proof that a person can't count on anything.

Anger snaps inside her. Hotter and deeper than is called for. This is her secret worry. That it's only a matter of time before everything is gone. Mrs. Lanie's daughter is a realtor whose business card reads *Abigail Lanie, Platinum-Diamond member of the Million-Dollar Club*. Annie knows because she's given her one. Twice. And every time she sees Annie in the driveway she asks if she's ready to sell and get rich, and every time Annie wants to tie her to a Longleaf pine and force her to take in a long view of open space until she appreciates the true meaning of rich. Mrs. Lanie's trees and corn and open field make up most of Annie's view from her porch.

"Those trees might be mature, but I don't think they're hardy enough to survive what they say is coming down the pike," Mrs. Lanie says.

Annie pictures the country club culture of shopping and golf bleeding across the open land, stopping only when it reaches the theme parks. She pictures giant parking lots and boxy home improvement stores. An invasion of dead-end sandstone culs de sac.

"Fuck it," she says. "Fuck it all to hell." She whacks the steering wheel.

"It's all right," Mrs. Lanie says, apparently unfazed. "Just a sign of things to come, I suppose."

The wind seems to have entered the phone, swirling and bending in place of their voices.

"You ought to go and see your brother now," Mrs. Lanie says. "You ought to. If you think you can manage the streets."

* * *

Annie treads carefully up the wooden steps outside Calder's condo. The cable railing feels like a rope of ice in her hand. She doesn't know if anyone is bringing in Calder's mail or looking after his plants or has thought to leave on a light, but has decided in the time it's taken to get here that if not, it isn't asking too much for her to do these things. She half expects to find yellow tape draped across the red door. But the door is undisturbed, and as she opens it with her spare key she's hit with the familiar scent of grassy shoes, bamboo and cork flooring, the rough sawn beams high above her head. She places her shoes by the closed door and sniffs her runny nose in the quiet.

The air is noticeably cool. Someone has turned down the heat. She makes her way toward the kitchen and considers flipping on the switch for the small gas fireplace in the living room. She decides against it. It's not as if she plans to stay.

Jade glass tiles glisten on the kitchen walls. Their transparency draws the light inside, then launches it back out. A red dishtowel is folded around the oven door handle. Everything looks tidy, orderly. The zinc counter reflects her hands. The stainless steel appliances are polished the way her brother likes to keep them, though a few of the walnut drawers have been left ajar, most likely from the police search. The garbage can beneath the sink is missing, as is the tin box from the side counter where Calder keeps bills, important reminders, keys.

It's only now that she sees the bundle of mail someone has left on the counter.

She massages her temples, surprised at how ropey they feel. She slips out onto the balcony in sudden need of air. It feels a lifetime since she was here. She rubs her arms in the cold and peers across the courtyard. Solar panels line the roofs, and down below the landscape is cut in staggered layers of green and red foliage, arranged in a way she doesn't exactly understand that will allow for the correct flow of rain, minimum erosion of the soil, things Calder explained to her even though he must have known she was only half listening.

She shivers in the cold. Winding jasmine pokes through the cable rails, and several tiny white blossoms flutter and strain to hold on. Potted palms veer in an arc above her head. A trumpet vine weaves above the glass doors. She decides to drag the palms into the kitchen, hoping the trumpet vine is close enough to the building to survive the drop in temperature.

The living room's big-leafed houseplants hang and stand, bend and twist toward the large windows whose wooden shades are closed. She pulls the heavy cords, and as the shades rise she can almost feel the plants sucking on the dim bands of light.

Everything looks the way it always has, simple lines and natural toned furniture and walls. Lots of green. His place has the feel of a Japanese forest in June, though the eye is always drawn to the exception, the red splash of an abstract painting above the fireplace.

The bedroom door is open and she's surprised to find the bed messily undone. The coffee-colored sheets and blankets are thrown from a corner of the bed. Calder seems to have jumped out of bed quickly, tossed the sheets off, and ran. Of course. The police at the door. He would have never left the bed like this if he weren't forced to. She thinks of him in his cell, blinking and grunting and jumping every time he remembers this unmade bed. She thinks of him holding a pillow like Chief, only it's not someone else's face he wants to press it into, it's his own.

A small photograph is wedged in the corner of the black-framed mirror above the dresser. Annie knows immediately that it's Sidsel. Blond, straight hair and a colorful scarf coiled around her neck. She's sitting in a garden bistro chair in what must be Denmark, her elbows propped onto the ironwork of the small table. She's smiling, her chin resting atop her hands. Behind her is a white half-timbered house with red and white floral-painted shutters. A thatched roof slopes downward like a neatly carved haystack with spotty layers of bright green moss along the edge. It makes her think of the Grimm Fairytales her mother gave her several years after Disney World opened.

Annie was ten years old. "These are the original tales," her mother said, and even though Annie had understood the intention was to show her all the whitewashing Disney had done to them, Annie was still surprised to find stories where children were locked up and punished, the big bad wolf's belly cut open, and not everyone lived happily ever after. Each story was made up of stark lessons for naughty children. Each one seeded in an undertone of darkness.

She places the photograph back in the mirror. She lifts the sheets and blanket off the floor and smells Calder in the puff of air. There's a faintly sweet smell. Sidsel's perfume or shampoo, then another that is stale and earthy, and she knows it is the two of them, together.

Annie pulls the sheets and blankets as tightly and evenly as she can.

She turns to leave and a wayward cricket chirps from behind a row of cacti in the windowsill. "Listen to that," Annie whispers. A memory has pulled the words from her mouth.

"Listen to that," Calder had said of an unusually forceful chirp of a cricket. It was June. They were sitting in lawn chairs in the middle of Annie's yard, far enough from the lights of the house to see the night sky poked full with thousands of stars. Her guitar lay across her lap. She was about to play Calder something she'd finished writing that morning. Owen was working late in the studio.

"Sounds like that cricket is chafing his wings for some cricket lady love."

"I didn't know that was why they did that." She strummed her guitar. "They're serenading the girls?"

"Yeah. But not the way you think. When one guy gets his song going, the others nearby stay quiet. It's like an invisible wall goes up and shuts them down. Only one act beneath the porch at a time."

"They have to wait till his wings get tired before they can give it go?"

Calder laughed. "That's the sweet part. Or the sick part, depending. The quiet ones actually sneak up and snatch the females while they're lost in lust for the singer. They're like teenage boys taking advantage of girls who've been staring at Tiger Beat all day."

"*Tiger Beat.* Jeez you're old."

"I swear. The females are so full of cricket lust they could care less. And that ain't the worst of it."

"Don't let Mom hear you say ain't."

"The sorry bastards that sing all the time are short-lived. They'll die off long before the silent types who steal their women."

"That is the saddest, sorriest thing I've ever heard," she said, laughing a little at the strangeness of it. "I don't want to know about the world working that way. Next time leave me in the dark, so to speak."

Calder cleared his throat. It looked and sounded more like a tic than a need to clear something away, and though she'd thought to ask if something was the matter, she was idly strumming her guitar and accidentally caught the rhythm of a melody she'd been trying to work out all day. "That's it," she said, and her whole body felt charged, her fingers plucking away while the moment of her asking him what was the matter passed into the song Calder had come to hear her sing.

The wind whips the stringy trumpet vine against the glass doors in the kitchen. Annie needs to get home to Detour. He doesn't like it when tree branches scrape the side of the house.

She doesn't think she's left any lights on at home. Detour'll be whining, hobbling from room to room if he can find the strength.

Without thinking, she flips open her cell and dials her mother.

"I'm going to get him an attorney," she says.

"Have you seen him yet?"

"No. But I'm going to."

"You said that last week."

"Do I have to make an appointment at the jail? Who do I call?"

Yes, she'll need an appointment. Her mother explains what she can and can't wear. What she can and can't bring. All of which seems obvious. Trench coats, firearms, knives, loaves of bread in which to hide the above. "You remember that scene in that movie," her mother says, "where he hid a giant file in that loaf of bread," but Annie is thinking of the steak knife hidden in her pocket when she was twelve.

"Who knows?" her mother says. "Maybe he'll be out of there before you even get a chance to visit."

"Mom. I just want you to think about this. Prepare yourself for what could happen. The man was killed at the same bar Calder was known to hang out in."

"What are you saying?"

"And then the man just happens to be married to Calder's girlfriend." Annie rubs her eyes in exhaustion. Her voice loses its intensity. "Please. Let's stop denying the obvious."

"There is nothing to deny."

"I saw Uncle Calder today," she says, not meaning it to be a slap in the face. But of course, that is exactly what it is.

Her mother hangs up.

Annie tosses her phone to the counter. The palm she's dragged in forms an arch above her head, and she thinks of the time she had her picture taken with Calder beneath a peach tree. Her yellow coverall shorts. His cutoffs and rainbow T-shirt. Calder had bought a camera with his own money and they were posing for Mr. Peterson with goofy grins, arms slung around one other as they leaned their heads together. They were inseparable then. Deeply happy in the way children feel happiness. Their father wasn't dead yet. Not for another two weeks. They had no way of knowing all they were capable of. They had no way of knowing what was to come.

A key jiggles in the lock and the front door swings open. A woman, who can only be Sidsel, fumbles in backwards with a bag of groceries and two bulging pieces of luggage. She mumbles to herself in what must be Danish. There is nowhere for Annie to escape.

THIRTEEN

A giant ball of fire lit up the cloudy back yard with a *whoosh*. Moments earlier Annie had seen her father in front of the grill clasping a bag of charcoal briquettes to his chest. He dumped half the bag into the grill and coated the charcoal with enough lighter fluid to fill a dog bowl.

And then he threw the match.

Annie lurched to the edge of the patio, but even there the heat reached her face and arms. She covered her hair.

Her mother ran from the kitchen, screaming her father's name. Calder jumped out the door behind her with balled fists and blinking eyes and kept on jumping even after he stood in place.

Her father felt around his head and laughed. "Did you get a load of that? Damn near lit up the sky."

"What did you do?" her mother yelled. Bits of bronze onionskin clung to her fingers. "You could have burned down the house!" She gaped at the flame on the grill and then up into the birch tree. Her eyes followed the line of branches over the roof.

Thunder rolled to the south as if God himself were calling for order. Damp air came in on the breeze and fused with the smell of lighter fluid. Lizards scrambled into the shrubs; mosquitoes buzzed along the patio lights strung from house to tree.

"Kearney."

He didn't turn around.

The flame was dying and he placed the wire rack over the coals, closed the lid, and rubbed his hands together.

He turned. "Look here," he said, and leaped forward and cupped a firefly in his hands. "An electrifly," he said, lifting a finger to show the glow coming from his hands. But the glow resembled fire and Annie stepped back. She knew enough to know that even grown men had fears, and her father's had always been fire.

Her mother was crying when she went inside the house.

Uncle Calder arrived ten minutes later.

Annie's mother buzzed around the picnic table with pitchers of lemonade and iced tea. Ringlets of damp hair stuck to the sides of her forehead. The patio lights reflected a piece of onionskin trapped in her hair. When she saw Uncle Calder she brushed her hair back with her arm and wiped her hands down the front of her apron. Her smile lit up like a fire all its own.

"There you are," she said. Uncle Calder lifted her in the air with his giant hug. She was nearly fifteen years younger than him, and the way he held her made her look younger still. He put her down and pulled the cinnamon toothpick from his mouth before kissing her cheek. She smiled and leaned into him and patted his big chest with her hand. Then she looked up, and for a split-second it seemed as if they might kiss on the lips. But then they looked in opposite directions as if some noise had suddenly drawn their attention, and Calder unexpectedly pulled his camera out and yelled, "Smile," and they smiled in time with the blinding flash.

"Smells good back here," Uncle Calder said.

"It was a bonfire," her mother said, apparently finishing what she didn't have a chance to say on the phone. She poured him a glass of iced tea. "He must have used a whole bottle of lighter fluid. He's grilling the food. It's like he forgot about the one thing he used to be afraid of."

Uncle Calder grabbed his toothpick, broke it between his fingers, and tossed it into the yard. "He still refusing to see a doctor?"

"I guess you could say that." She handed Calder and Annie paper cups of lemonade. "Why don't you two go practice your song before we eat?"

Neither made a move.

"Go on now."

Annie kept her ear turned as they crossed the patio.

"Hey!" Her father stepped out just as they reached the door. "Look who's here," he said, crossing the patio to Uncle Calder. The two men slapped backs, and her father quickly turned toward her mother and the grill and asked, "What on earth smells so good?"

She didn't move. "I can't take it anymore," she hissed to Uncle Calder. "You need to do something."

A sick, unsettled feeling billowed in and out of Annie's stomach. It'd been doing that for the past few weeks. Something bad was about to happen—and the thing that made it worse was the fact that everyone was pretending that it wasn't.

"Listen, Kearney," Uncle Calder started to say.

"The grill!" Annie yelled. She handed Calder her lemonade and ran toward her father. "The huge ball of fire!"

He rubbed his forehead and gave a small laugh.

"Annie please," her mother said. "Go to your room. Go play your guitar or something. I thought you and Calder were going to practice."

"I nearly lost all my hair wrestling around a campfire when I was a kid. She knows that story. You remember that, Calder?" he asked Uncle Calder. "You were the one who put it out."

"I remember," Uncle Calder said.

Her father clasped his hands on either side of his head as if a huge boulder were sitting there. "Goddamn if this sonofabitch isn't going to bust wide open."

Uncle Calder helped him to the picnic table.

"You ever have a headache that bad?" he asked Uncle Calder, his eyes squinting as if into a bright light.

"No. Can't say I have."

"Go, Annie," her mother said. "You too, Calder."

* * *

Annie sat next to Calder on the edge of his bed, the neck of her guitar braced between her knees. "What do you say?" Calder asked. When she didn't say anything, he lifted her hair into his hands and braided it the way she'd taught him years ago when they used to play house and hairdresser and afternoon theater and zoo. She closed her eyes and wished she could sit there all evening with his fingers roping the locks of hair from her scalp, filling her whole body with a soft tingling sensation. But she became aware of herself, aware of his hands as if she were watching from the doorway through someone else's eyes, and it didn't look right. It didn't feel right. They were no longer little kids. He ought not be playing with her hair. She scooted away and her hair unraveled at her back.

"What?" he asked. "Should we get our stuff and go out there?" Before she could answer he was up and digging through his closet.

An ache built inside her chest. She plucked the low E string on her guitar. She stared at the gloomy brown stagecoaches and horses on Calder's bedspread and traced the wagon wheels with her finger.

"What's wrong?" Calder asked as he emerged from the closet in his blue cowboy shirt with the pearly snaps and white looped stitching at the front of the shoulders. He looked silly. He looked like a boy pretending to be a man.

The idea of going outside and singing seemed foolish now. Childish. "You don't think it's stupid?" she asked him.

"What?" He turned back to the closet. "You seen my red cowboy hat anywhere?" He tossed the old white shawl toward her, and her fingers caught in the lace. "There it is!" He grabbed his hat from behind a jacket on a hook. "What are you talking about?"

She couldn't explain the way she felt. It was like walking into someone else's house for the first time. She was unsure of the layout. Unsure of what to do with herself in the open space. "I don't know. You don't think we're too old for this?"

"What are you talking about? Johnny Cash is older than you and me put together." He smiled a lopsided smile and plopped down next to her and patted her knee. "What d'ya say, squirt?" He sounded exactly like Uncle Calder. His legs were so much longer than hers, and the way he was sitting there crouched forward with his elbows resting near his knees made him look as if he'd just gone from an eleven-year-old boy to a man.

She wrapped the musty shawl around her shoulders and slipped on a pair of Calder's big cowboy boots. They walked out onto the patio, and everyone turned and clapped as if they were real musicians in a ticketed show.

Uncle Calder put his fingers to his mouth and pierced the air with a whistle. "Look how cute," he said of Annie. "Whose boots are those? Those your brother's boots? Lord God, would you look at this."

Her mother smiled but her eyes narrowed, concentrated like her mind was somewhere else. Her father gave a thumbs-up, his smile hard to see in the dim string of lights. Her mother leaned in and kissed his cheek, her lips plastered there longer than usual, as if she were stuck, waiting for him to react, to speak, to notice. He did none of these things.

Uncle Calder glanced at the two of them locked together and quickly turned away.

It was then that Annie felt something slip between her legs. Her mother had warned her, had had all those embarrassing talks with her, explained everything in anatomical detail, and still, that night, when the dull cramp bore down on her stomach she thought she was dying. A trickle of something warm slipped into her underwear. She knew it would be a drop of her own blood, and this only made matters worse.

A bead of rain hit her lashes. The storm was so close she could smell the soil on the wind. "You'll know it when it comes," her mother had told her. "They call it the change, the curse, the visit from Aunt Martha and all kinds of other nonsense, but it's your *menstruation*, honey, your *period* if you like, and it's normal. It just means you're going from being a girl to being a young woman. By the time you become a woman it'll turn into nothing more than a reminder that you're not pregnant with a baby."

Annie lowered her head and pressed her legs together. She squeezed Calder's hand as they stood against the white siding of the house.

"You nervous?" he whispered.

She squeezed so tightly that he yelped and released her grip. "What is it?"

She didn't answer. The night sounds—cicadas, frogs, wind—all disappeared. There was only quiet, a *heavy* quiet, like waiting for the sound of a giant firecracker to explode.

"Come on. Let's play. One, two, three," he whispered, his mouth a small twist of confusion.

Lightening blinked like a light shorting out behind the clouds. Calder took her hand back. His shoulder was jumping now. "We don't have to," he said. "Nobody's going to mind if we don't play."

Another trickle of blood, more warmth than wet.

"Tell me what it is," Calder said.

For the first time in her life she understood how things could be something other than what they seemed, the opposite even, of what a person believed in. Suddenly the whole world was exposed as a lie, the wizard's curtain pulled back to reveal the barbecue and the storm, the family get-together and the music she was about to play, all made up of layers and layers of something else. There was more to this story. Even her own body was splitting apart on the inside, going straight from a girl to a woman, while standing there looking to all the world like a child.

"I don't know if I can play," she whispered.

"Well, *I* know you can," Calder said. "Does that make a difference?" He looked at her the way he looked at the row of potted seedlings in his bedroom window every morning, his eyes filled with possibility.

She recalled a fight they once had over the TV set. It wasn't like them to take things so far, but this one turned vicious with the two of them coming to blows. A down pillow covered in needlework had split open, and feathers floated around the room like snow. The sight of it transported the two of them into stillness, as if it really were snow, something they'd never seen. Their mother marched into the room, and after screaming over what had once been her grandmother's pillow, she sat them both down and said, "Long after your father and I are dead and buried and all the people in your lives have come and gone, who do you think will be left? Who do you think will still care about you until your dying day?" She looked at each of them. She plucked a feather from Calder's hair, blew another that had taken flight again near her face. Nothing more needed to be said.

Annie strummed four measures' worth of D. She watched Calder's foot tap the flagstones and felt a prickle across her scalp. She switched to G, then looked up and saw a smile spread across his face. "You sing this one by yourself," she whispered. He nodded that he would, and a pleasant little hum lit her chest.

"I went down to the river to watch the fish swim by!" Calder sang, his body free of tics, his chin in the air, fingers snapping at his side. "But I got down to the river, so lonesome I wanted to die...Ohh Lord!"

Annie stepped to the side to give him room, and when she looked across the patio her father had disappeared into the shadow of the birch, cut away like an image from a photograph. It was then Annie realized how powerless he was making them all feel, especially her mother. Calder and Annie were just kids, rendered nearly helpless by size and inexperience, but their mother was a grown woman. And not just any woman. She was smart and successful, a teacher full of knowledge about the way the world worked. Why didn't she stand up to him? Why didn't she insist, for all their sake, that he see a doctor?

"And then I jumped in the river," Calder sang. "But the doggone river was dry."

Uncle Calder leaned forward in his lawn chair. He clapped and laughed and choked so hard he had to wipe his runny eyes dry.

They had just enough time to finish the song when the sky cracked open and rain crashed down like ground-up gravel on the patio, the grill, the pitchers of lemonade and iced tea. Everyone scrambled to grab what they could, her mother screaming about her hair and the burgers, Annie screaming about her guitar. Once inside Annie went to the bathroom and stuck the pad in a clean pair of underwear the way her mother had shown her, and before she knew it they were all sitting at the kitchen table with wild hair and blank faces, her father at one end and her mother and uncle at the other with Annie and Calder in between. Everyone chewed their crispy burgers in silence, their faces lit up now and again from the lightning, droplets of rain still glistening on their skin. In all the fuss no one had thought to shut off the string of patio lights. Her father said, "The lights are on out there," but no one got up to hit the switch. They went on eating in a kind of trance as if they were still listening to music, as if they were only watching the storm outside, but Annie knew it was the grill they were looking at. The dome knocked crooked from the rain, the ghostly steam rising up from the coals.

FOURTEEN

By the time Owen finally arrives at what used to be his home, he's trembling from what may be a fever. The day has lost nearly all its light. The gas tank is on empty.

Her gate is closed, locked he assumes, behind a line of cars, including a white van from Channel 4 News, its enormous antennae reaching the tops of trees.

Two men Owen takes for security guards step out of a black Suburban when he T-bones them in. He recognizes one as a guy who did security for some of Annie's shows.

Owen rises from his car, and the tips of his fingers instantly curl in the cold. He strains to peer down the long driveway. Moss dangles from the live oak, obstructing the view of where the Land Cruiser usually sits.

The men have small black guns clipped to their belts. They have flattop crew cuts and heavy black shoes.

Owen leans around the broad shoulders of the man he doesn't know but still can't tell if the Land Cruiser is there. Other than the porch light, it doesn't look as if any lights are on inside the house.

"Can we help you?" the one with big ears asks.

This is where the photo of Annie was taken for the paper. He feels his shoes dig into the cold gravel. He rubs his hands

together. His fingers have turned a whitish blue. "I'm Owen.
Pettybone. We've met before."

The man studies him. "I don't remember if we did."

"Sure you do. I was at all her shows. I produced *Gull on
a Steeple.*"

"Is that right."

Owen's jaw is now quivering. "Is she here? I don't see her
car."

"Maybe you should have called first," the other man says.
He's balding but young. They both lean down to look inside
his car.

Owen coughs into his hand. "I'm a friend of the family's."

"Maybe you should have called."

Suddenly a microphone and cameraman are lodged at
Owen's elbow.

"You're a friend of Ms. Walsh's?" the reporter with the
microphone and thick glasses asks.

Maybe this is the same guy who took Annie's picture and
put it in the paper. If it weren't for seeing her there he might
not be standing here now.

"Looks like no one's home," Owen says to the crew cuts.

Big ears looks him over, though Owen now sees that one
ear is slightly larger than the other. "It must be thirty-five
degrees out here," the man says. "And you're broke out in a
sweat."

"Can we get your name?" the reporter asks Owen.

Owen has left his jacket in the car. He wipes the sweat
from his forehead and shivers. "I've had a lot of caffeine," he
says. "I'm not feeling as good as I'd like."

They look in his car again.

The reporters lean in.

"Get the camera out of my face," Owen says. "Please."

He turns to the security guards. "Look, I'm a friend. I was. I actually used to live here," he says, and the last word catches in his throat making him sound even less convincing than the idea now seems.

They appear unfazed.

"Can we have just a moment of your time?" the reporter asks, the camera rolling in Owen's face.

"Not now," he tells them, and turns to the guards. "Come on. I know you know who I am."

"Why didn't you call? You've got her cell number, don't you?"

He thinks of all the miles he's burned to get here. He thinks of Tess having no idea she's been left behind. He doesn't want to say that if he'd called Annie she probably wouldn't have answered. And even if she did she would have told him to stay where he was. She would have said she didn't need him anymore and that he had no right to be there, which is true. He shivers again. His legs are weak. He hasn't eaten all day. "I'll just wait in the car," he says. "It's all right. I'll just wait like everyone else."

"Do you know Calder Walsh?" the reporter yells.

Owen shuts the door and starts the car. He looks down at the fuel gauge. The red warning light flashes. He turns the heat up as far as it will go and slips his jacket on. Then he digs out a packet of peanuts he'd tossed in the glove compartment months ago and pours them into his mouth. Soft and spongy. They don't even taste like peanuts.

He turns on his phone for the first time today and dials Annie's number inside the house. Detour will be looking in the direction of the phone. He has a habit of sitting up and scratching his ears at the ringing.

No answer. He tries her cell. The ringing is cut short. She seems to have answered and then immediately hung up. He leans his head into the headrest and searches the black canvas above him as if for stars.

The phone rings right back. He flicks it open with amazing speed. "Annie," he says, suddenly out of breath. "I'm right outside. It's freezing out here. Could you please let me in?"

A long pause.

"Annie?"

"I guess I don't need to ask where you've been all day. Or the reason your phone has been turned off."

"Tess!"

"Could you please *let me in?*"

"Wait—"

"What's the matter? Don't you still have the key?"

"No. It's not. There's a gate. Never mind. Listen—"

"Don't tell me."

"Hold on."

"I can't believe you would do this to me."

"I haven't *done* anything."

"And to Caroline."

"I just want to talk to her, Tess. And see Calder. It's got nothing to do with you or our baby."

Her silence suspends his soul into a kind of purgatory. He's finally going to account for his sins. A news crew is ready to broadcast what will be left of him when he rises from this car.

"Tess?" he says. She doesn't answer. Maybe she's trying to believe him. Maybe she's taking stock of what she wants in the divorce. He will give her the goddamn house, no doubt about it.

"I was right," she says. "It was Magnus I interviewed last year."

"What?"

"He's the one who hired the Dutch architect and built the house I wrote about. I found the article in my files. Did you know Calder was sleeping with his wife?"

"Not then. Maybe. I don't know. About the timing—"

"The *timing*? Why didn't you ever mention Calder was having an affair? As many times as you've talked about him I can't believe you'd leave something like that out. It might have made me feel a little less guilty about cheating with someone in a relationship, seeing how your best friend was doing the very same thing. Or is that why you didn't mention it? So you could keep me feeling guilty?"

"Why would I want you to feel guilty?"

"How many more things haven't you told me?"

"Come on, Tess."

"I can think of at least one. The article in your desk drawer. The one with Annie's picture."

"What were you doing in my desk?"

"Oh, I'm sorry. Is it off limits to your wife?"

"No. I mean. Don't put words in my mouth. Were you looking for something in there?"

"What difference does it make?"

He has no idea.

"What did you expect me to do?" she says. "At first I thought you were acting so weird because the due date is so close. *First Time Father* mentions that men can get a little panicky right before the baby comes. But it seemed like more than that. I've had this awful feeling you were lying to me. I mean, you lied to Annie, why not me?"

"That's cheap."

"*You're* cheap! You're a cheap piece of shit."

"Whoa! OK. I'm going to chalk that one off to hormones. We read about it. We knew it was coming, and now here it is. I'm not cheating on you, for Christ's sake. I just need to talk to Annie and Calder. I need to see if there's something I can do. I can't sleep."

"You can't sleep because you're thinking about Annie."

"This can't be good for the baby."

"You should have thought about that before you decided to run off."

"I didn't *run* off. Christ. I'll be home as soon as I have a chance to talk to them."

"What do you mean? You've been gone all day."

"I'm waiting outside Annie's gate. She isn't home."

"Stalkers wait outside gates."

Owen looks at the guards still standing in the cold. They cross their arms.

"You're taking this too far."

"What about Calder?" Tess asks. "You know exactly where he is. Why didn't you go there first?"

"You need an appointment. I didn't know. You have to give at least twenty-four hours' notice."

"Whatever," Tess says as if she is fourteen years old.

"Look. I didn't tell you about Calder cheating with this guy's wife because I didn't want you to get the wrong impression. I didn't want you to think that me and all my friends were assholes."

"Well, guess what? You and all your friends are assholes."

"Tess, please. I didn't plan this. I wasn't thinking. It was just a spur-of-the-moment decision. I'm sorry. I didn't think this through. And once I was on the road, I didn't want to hurt you by telling you where I was going. I was afraid you'd get the wrong idea, and I was right. I thought I could just explain myself after the fact, but now Annie isn't home and it looks like I'm going to have to spend the night."

"Are you fucking *kidding* me?"

Owen rubs his eyes. His cold fingers feel good against the lids. "Honey. I love you," he says, though the sound of it rings hollow. "You know that. I left everything I knew for you. Please. It's not like it looks."

"You're not coming back, are you?"

"Of course I'm coming back."

"I was so stupid. How could I have been so stupid? People warned me and I wouldn't listen."

"People *warned* you? What people?"

"They said, 'Once a cheater always a cheater,' and I said they had no idea what they were talking about."

"Who said that? Your mother?"

"I'm tired of hearing how you married me as some kind of proof that you're where you want to be. I don't think you have a clue where it is you belong."

He doesn't dare open his mouth. He doesn't dare take the chance that his voice will give anything away.

It sounds as if she's muffling a cry with her hand.

"I promise I'll be home tomorrow," he says, and in his mind he somehow sees himself doing just that. "I promise you the only reason I'm here is to see if there's anything I can do. I'll come home to you the minute I'm through."

"It wasn't my mother," she says, and hangs up.

FIFTEEN

"I don't give a goddamn who said it." Calder's face is hot, his eyes blinking so hard he can barely get a look at his court-appointed lawyer standing on the other side of the table. Ms. Thompson, a thick-armed woman in her thirties with short brown hair, leans forward and sets her briefcase on the table. The veneer beneath it is worn away by the countless briefcases that have come before.

"Let's go over all this one more time," she says. "And keep in mind, if you're not honest with me, I can't give you fair representation."

Her bottom row of teeth are crooked, small discolored pegs crammed one against the other, and the appearance, coupled with the way she's stacking and restacking her papers, leaves him with the feeling that she is new at this, that she tried and failed at some other career, and now she's taking a shot at law.

"I *am* being honest with you. I never once said I wanted Magnus dead. I might have thought it. Sure I thought it. Hell yes, there you go, I thought how nice it would be if he would just disappear, but I never said it out loud to anybody."

"You've got Tourette Syndrome, Mr. Walsh. Don't you blurt things out without meaning to?"

137

Even though the meeting room is opposite the cafeteria, the smell of burned potatoes saturates the concrete walls and penetrates Calder's nose. "Now you're a doctor?"

"Don't you?"

"No. For your information I don't blurt things out. I don't have those kinds of tics."

"I see."

"Whose side are you on?"

Ms. Thompson sits across from him and folds her hands together on the table as if she's praying. "We need to look at this from all angles. The prosecution thinks your inability to control your tics helps build their case. They think you got it inside your head to kill Magnus and just like one of your tics you had to get it out. They're saying you told a landscaper who works for you..." She pauses and leafs through her notes. "This Gabe Pinckney. How many years has he worked for you?"

"Three. And he's slobbered after every single woman I ever dated."

"You're aware he was one of the men in Hal's that night."

"I've been told."

"He says he never saw you there." She looks through her notes. "But he also says he wasn't paying a whole lot of attention to who *was*."

"Well, there you go."

"He also said that you once told him Magnus was, and I'm quoting here, 'a mean, giant son of a bitch that someone was going to put out of his misery.'"

"The dumb bastard is not only a lousy landscaper, he's a liar, too." Calder leans back in his chair and shakes his head. "That's not what I said. He's twisting my words around. What I said was that Sidsel had told me what a big guy Magnus was and had warned me about his temper. She was worried about what was going to happen if he found out about us. She was afraid to leave him. I think that's more or less what I told Gabe."

"Was it more or was it less? What exactly did you say?"

"That was it. I don't remember word for word. All I know is that I never threatened to do anything to Magnus."

"I see."

"No, you don't see at all. You don't understand. My family's got a long history with the Pinckneys. We've known each other our whole lives."

"Which means?"

"I hired Gabe a few years ago when he came to see me about a job. I had the impression he'd changed after his brother ended up going to college. His brother turned out to be a great guy."

"What brother?"

"Joshua. Listen, we're getting off track here. What I'm saying is I hired him knowing he used to be mean as hell when we were kids. But that was a long time ago. He's got a family to support. He talks all the time about wanting to be a better father to his kids than his own father was to him. I guess I felt a little sorry for him."

Ms. Thompson writes something down.

"But it turned out that once I hired Gabe he started making comments about every woman I ever dated, like he was jealous. I only kept him on all these years because of his wife and kids."

"You think he said these things because he's jealous of you?"

"Who knows? The only thing I have to go on is the look on his face when he saw me with Sidsel."

"He saw you with Sidsel?"

Calder chews the inside of his cheek and blinks.

"The two of you were open about your affair?"

"Well, no. I wouldn't say that. Once or twice we met at Hal's if she was free in the evening, just to get out and be like other people. We knew we were taking a chance. But as far as I know he never saw us there. We had lunch sometimes at Mateo's on the edge of town. That's where he saw us. That's why I told him what I did about Magnus, because he started asking all kinds of questions and I knew he wouldn't let up until I told him something. Anyway, just so you know, Sidsel and I mostly met at my place. I don't think anyone ever saw us there."

Ms. Thompson pushes the sleeves of her suit above her wrists. She is wearing a band on her ring finger that looks like a braided friendship bracelet in gold. "This Gabe Pinckney claimed you assaulted him once. Can you tell me about that?"

"Oh, Jesus Christ."

"I need to know what happened."

"Nothing happened. We got in a fight. He was insulting my sister. He tried to kiss her one night at a bar and she didn't want anything to do with him. She walked out and Gabe was pissed at me cause I wouldn't talk her into coming back and giving him a chance, and then he made some comment about me wanting to keep her for myself. So I hit him."

Ms. Thompson lets out a sigh. "Are you prone to that sort of thing?"

"What? No. Of course not."

"Did he require medical attention?"

"God, no. He hit me back, like I said. It was a fight. We got over it and went back to work the next day."

"Why would you keep a man on like that? Why didn't you fire him?"

"First of all, I grew up in the country. Men fight. It's not the end of the world. They move on in the light of day. It's as simple as that. And second, it's like I told you. He's got a wife and kids. His wife calls up at least once a month and asks shyly if he got paid that week, and I tell her of course he did. He gets paid every week, but she still calls and asks the same question and I know it's because he's not regular about bringing money home and those kids are going hungry sometimes because she's told me as much. What am I supposed to do? He'd be hard pressed to find somebody else to hire him on short notice, and that family of his would be out on the street."

"Mr. Walsh."

"Calder."

"Calder. Can you please relax?"

Calder realizes he's been banging his knees and stops. "This whole thing is getting the tics out of control."

"Try not to use the term *out of control*," she says.

Calder holds her in a steady gaze.

"When did the tics start getting worse again?"

He thinks for a moment. "Months ago. When I first fell in love with Sidsel. Or when she first fell in love with me. After that they kicked up another notch when she told me Magnus had hurt her."

"He hurt her? How did he hurt her?"

"She had bruises on her arm. Ask her about it. She'll probably tell you more than she told me. And just so you know, he probably had more enemies than you can count. Sidsel said he told her all the time about sleeping with other women. Flat out told her he had just come from some other woman's bed. The man was crazy. He could have had any number of husbands looking to kill him."

"Good. This is good to know." She writes something down.

"When she told me he was murdered the tics got worse. And then after they accused me of killing him, well, let's just say I've been going off like popcorn in hot oil ever since."

"I'm going to ask you something and I want you to give me a straight answer."

"They've all been straight."

"Could she have killed him herself?"

Calder laughs. "You're not serious."

"You said yourself that he told her all the time about sleeping with other women. It sounds to me like he was taunting her."

"That's just…No. How can you say such a thing? It's not even practical. You know how badly he was beaten. Have you seen the size of Sidsel's arms?"

"No. It isn't practical. But the smallest of people can put a fist through a solid block of wood. I've seen my nephew do it. Ten years old. A purple belt in karate."

Calder raises an eyebrow. "Yeah, well, Sidsel doesn't know karate."

"How do you know?"

"I just do."

"How well do you really know her?"

"What is this?"

"Just so you know, they're investigating her, too."

"No."

"Yes. This is a major investigation. The press is digging in deep on this. It's taken the prosecutor all the way back to Denmark." She lets out an enormous sigh and places her hands flat on the table and leans in. "I think you may have been framed, Mr. Walsh. And under the circumstances you better hope that's the case because the prosecutor loves nothing more than an execution. Whether it's you or your friend Sidsel. It'll make no difference to her. In fact, if she can get two for one she'll get a better night's sleep."

Calder winces.

"I'm just telling you like it is. She's a bloodthirsty woman. The women in the DA's office joke that she keeps a python just so she can throw bunnies at it."

Calder looks around the room trying to keep still. "I need some medication for the tics. You need to get me some Haldol."

She writes on her legal pad.

"Listen. Sidsel's no black belt in karate. She couldn't protect herself against Magnus," he says, though he pictures her graceful hand barreling through a block of wood and it seems possible that she could do or be anything she wished.

His eyes burn to blink. His shoulder itches to jump. He refuses to let go but cannot control the steady bang of knees.

"It's all true what I just said. I only added the python to see for myself what happens to you under stress. We can't let this get to court."

"I didn't do it and neither did she," Calder says.

"I'll get you the Haldol by five."

SIXTEEN

Streams of sunlight bent through the leaves, reflecting the amber glow of ripe peaches. Annie clung to a ladder high inside the tree and grabbed hold of peach. Her fingers sank into the overripe flesh, and there were other moist patches of brownish orange where the insects had gotten there first.

Two rows over Calder was singing "Don't Go Breaking My Heart" by Elton John and Kiki Dee.

"I couldn't if I tried," Annie sang back, and Calder laughed at the way she exaggerated the drawl.

She was about to toss the peach into the "rotten" bucket when a bee landed between her finger and thumb. She was aware of more buzzing in the trees. Mr. Peterson always warned them not to swat. "They'll come back after you," he'd say. "You'll get turned around and they'll come back after you from behind just as sure as I'm standing here."

Annie had never been stung. Not once in all this country full of lush growing things and the equally rotting dead, had she ever been stung.

She shook the bee gently to the side, but it clung like it was glued. She watched as its head dipped into the moist insides of the peach without leaving her skin. She thought to lean her hand and release it like a ladybug against a branch. She thought it would simply walk off. But when she reached her hand out toward the branch she jerked back and nearly fell off the ladder at the sight of Josh Pinckney's wispy hair on the other side of her tree.

"Don't go breaking my heart," Calder sang out.

A sharp sting between her fingers drew her head down. She slapped at the bee and dropped the peach. The stinger poked like a splinter from her yellow-stained skin. Pain seared through her hand. "Hey, Kiki!" Calder yelled. "What's going on over there?" Pain spread to her wrist. She couldn't think of what to do next. She didn't remember climbing down the ladder but she must have because the next thing she knew she was surrounded by the inescapable smell of peaches spoiling in the heat.

She sat on the ground and rocked the ache deep inside her arm. Flies buzzed her head. The grass beyond the grove confused her. Everything seemed out of place. She didn't know how long she was sitting there. All she knew was the sun was hot on her scalp when she quit moving. Her eyes itched and puffed as if her face were filling with water.

"Hey!" She finally thought to holler for somebody, anybody. Her voice sounded like it came from somewhere else.

The bee sting was the cause of all the pain. She knew this. But she kept seeing Josh Pinckney's face above the tree, his hand waving, his hair flopping in the wind as if he was the one who had done this to her.

Her throat felt lined with cotton. She coughed and dug at the stinger stuck in her skin. Her hand was so swollen it no longer looked like her own.

"Cal-der!" she yelled, though it didn't sound like much. She could feel someone near, sense him coming toward her. She couldn't see clearly. Her skin turned cold and her bare legs shook. "I got stung between my fingers," she said. Her hand lifted like a balloon.

She lay back onto the ground, her face to the sun, her hair in withered, rotten peaches. The air seemed too thin to make a difference to her lungs. It became even thinner when the silhouette of Josh Pinckney took shape above her head.

* * *

Rain ticked the hospital glass and the smell of wet soil seeped beneath the windowpane. Annie opened one eye and saw Calder glancing at the large round clock on the wall. The three o'clock rain was coming down hard enough to bypass gutters and soak every living thing to the root. Annie was thirsty. She closed her eye and imagined the rain saturating the earth. She felt Calder on the end of the bed, heard the pages of a small book flipping, flipping, flipping.

Then she smelled minty soap and cigar and knew Uncle Calder was there, too. She sensed him leaning toward her and sighing from his chair. He touched her arm lightly before he sat back. A moment later he did it again.

She slowly opened both eyes and tried to sit up but couldn't.

Uncle Calder stood and patted her leg. "I thought I told you to stay out of trouble." His big fingers brushed the hair from her eyes.

"You're a war hero," Annie said, as if he had just rescued her. She closed her eyes again. There was laughter in the room, and she realized she must have been dreaming of the stories. She often did back then. Uncle Calder punching sharks in the face. Uncle Calder lifted onto a lifeboat, handed a drink of fresh water, a pretty purple medal on a stage.

Her eyes opened wide. Her uncle and brother were like big and small versions of the same person.

Calder slid up next to Annie. "You're awake."

She blinked.

"You all right, squirt?" Uncle Calder asked.

"I feel sick," she whispered.

Calder placed the book on the bed. A field guide to insects. He drew his hands behind his back, but she could see that his forearms were blotched purple and red with cuts and bruises. "They've been giving you all kinds of stuff in that tube," he said.

She peered at the bottle hanging from the pole. She examined her arm and hand, connected to a tube and wrapped in gauze the size of a boxing glove. She gave a slight motion of her head in the direction of Calder's arms. "What happened to you?"

He looked down at himself. "I fell out of the tree," he said, but his tone didn't ring the way it should. She must have raised her eyebrow like her father. "What?" Calder said. "I fell out of the tree."

Annie turned to Uncle Calder. "Where's Mom and Daddy?"

Calder started bouncing on the bed.

"Get off," she said, and swallowed to calm her stomach.

He got up and stood at her side and held his hands behind his back.

"Your daddy's not feeling so good," Uncle Calder said. "But don't you worry about him right now. He'll be fine."

The truth escaped through his eyes.

Calder blinked several times and then blurted the news. "He was in here but you were sleeping. Then I don't know what happened. He started talking crazy. Saying stuff about catching rats in steel traps, using peppermint candies as bait. The doctor took him out. Mom told me to stay here. Then Uncle Calder showed up."

"How long have I been asleep?" she asked.

"A couple hours."

She looked around the room trying to take it all in. Walls the color of frosted glass. Everything white. The small table, curtains, and bed. Silver and white. Only Uncle Calder's chair was black patent leather with wooden arms and legs as if it'd been brought in from another room to accommodate him.

"Listen. You've got enough to deal with, squirt," he said. "Don't worry about your daddy. He's in good hands."

She slowly shifted her head on the pillow. She ran her fingers through the back of her hair. It was matted with small clumps of peaches she imagined must look like a head wound. On a wave of nausea she thought of the Pinckneys. She smacked her dry lips and burped.

Calder shrugged his shoulders at least five times. "Mom poked her head in here a minute ago and said they want to run some tests on him." He rose up and down on the balls of his feet. "At least she finally got him to the doctor. That's what she said."

Annie glimpsed the wet window. A quick bolt of light flashed through the room. A second later thunder rolled. Calder rubbed his hand along the surface of his bruises.

"I can't believe you've never been stung," Uncle Calder said. "You're allergic. That's what's happened here."

She looked at her swollen hand. She looked at Calder.

"You're a lucky girl," Uncle Calder said.

"*Rat bait?*" she asked.

Calder shrugged in quick succession. "I'm wondering if he's going nutty like old Mrs. Peterson did when she came knocking on our door that time, saying she had ants under her skin." It wasn't a joke. His bottom lip quivered. He grabbed it between his teeth.

"Come on, now," Uncle Calder said, pulling the toothpick from his mouth. "It's not like that. Your daddy's sharp as sawgrass."

Annie struggled, and then managed, with the help of Uncle Calder, to sit upright. She untangled the IV and reached for Calder. He came and sat on the bed next to her, laying his head against her shoulder. She wrapped her arms around his back and felt his spine beneath her open fingers.

Then his back started shaking and it took her a moment to realize he was crying. Her stomach felt sicker. It was all she could do to keep from throwing up. She stroked his bony shoulder blades and gently shushed him the way she'd done so many times when he was little and constantly scraping his knees on the gravel driveway.

"He's going to be—" Uncle Calder never finished. He patted Calder's shoulder and cleared his throat and left the room.

Annie held Calder to her chest until the rhythmic jerks of his shoulders gave way to the random jerks of his tics. She squeezed him once more before letting go.

She wiped his face with the corner of her stiff sheet. She looked at his arms and a scratch on his temple. She touched it lightly with her finger. He was lying and she didn't know why. "What'd you do?" she asked. "Fall through the whole tree?"

"Yeah." He sounded just like their father when he said, "Like a ball bearing in a wooden shifter contraption."

* * *

The Pinckney house was less than a mile through the woods from Annie and Calder's backyard. The first thing she and Calder spotted was the rusty rooster weather vane atop the barn, spinning in a squeaky circle. The air fanned the sour smell of pigs. The same smell that came off Josh and Gabe. There was no one outside when Annie and Calder came snooping along the far end of the split-rail fence.

The great door of the barn stood open to both sides. Annie was still a little weak from the bee sting two days before. She rested her hands on her knees and looked in.

"What do you think they do with that thing hanging over the beam in there?" Calder asked.

"The cable pulley?"

"Uh huh."

"I don't know. Something bad or something stupid," she said.

Calder blinked several times. "You want to go look in there?"

"Inside the barn?"

"Yeah."

"What for?"

"Maybe we can figure out what they do with that pulley."

"What are you up to?" she asked.

"What?"

"I'm asking you what."

"What do you mean?"

"Calder Walsh. Who do you think you're talking to? You've never once in your life gone looking for trouble."

"I ain't looking for trouble."

"Don't let Mom hear you say ain't."

"I ain't."

Annie gave him a sidelong glance. "Then why'd you want to come snooping around out here so bad? This was your idea."

"Don't act like I twisted your arm," Calder said.

The weight of her body sank her heels in the sand. She thought of her mother at home wringing her hands, her red eyes staring at the phone, all the sighing and distraction, fussing in the kitchen while she waited for the doctor to call about her father in the hospital. It was hard for Annie to know what to do with herself at home. She couldn't get a clear breath in any of the rooms. It was summer when they were normally free to do as they pleased once they finished picking peaches, and a part of her resented feeling so much restraint.

The pigs in the sty to the right of the barn squealed and rolled in mud. "Look over at the house," Annie whispered.

Josh Pinckney was framed inside the kitchen window, no more than fifty feet away from where they stood. He was leaning over the sink, washing dishes in the sun. His mother's big apron hung loosely around his neck.

"Just seeing that is worth any bit of trouble," Annie said. They ducked behind the side of the barn and couldn't keep from laughing.

"You think he's wearing her house slippers, too? The ones she wears into town?" Calder asked.

The mention of Josh's mother's shoes brought back a sliver of memory. In the peach grove Josh's face had leaned over hers, and now, for the first time, she remembered the feel of his fingers lifting her hand. She remembered his smell. She remembered his shoe near her face.

"What was he doing when you came up on me in the grove?"

"Who?"

She nodded toward the kitchen window.

"What makes you think he was there?"

"Wasn't he?"

"I didn't say he wasn't. I just thought you were out of it."

"I was. But I saw him there before I passed out." The memory came to her in pieces like a dream. "He leaned over me. He was doing something with my hand."

Calder shrugged once, and then his shoulder kept jerking at his ear. "I didn't see anything. I just called for old man Peterson."

"What was he doing, Calder?"

"What do you mean? I told you."

"You're the worst liar in all of Seminole County."

"I ain't lying!"

She grabbed him by the arm.

The door to the house slammed shut. She let go of Calder and motioned him into the back of the barn where they could no longer see the house. The door slammed shut again, and Annie figured that someone had either come out and gone back in, or two people had come out and stayed. She glanced up into the rafters. Plywood was gathered across the crossbars and nailed, creating a platform like the early makings of a fort. This must have been what they used the pulley for. She looked around for a ladder. There was none. She couldn't figure how they got up there and didn't have time to consider it before she heard what sounded like Gabe and his daddy.

Annie and Calder crouched in the corner, halfway behind a stack of wooden chicken crates.

"I didn't see it," Gabe said.

"It was right where I told you it was," his daddy said. "Why do you bother to go to school anyhow? What the hell they teaching? How to make your daddy do all the work around here?" Annie could hear what sounded like the man's hand striking Gabe. Gabe yelled for him to stop.

The breeze took a turn and swooped through the center of the barn and lifted the smell of something dead. Annie plugged her nose and looked up to the side. A row of skinned rabbits hung from a beam, each by their ears, and she thought it was as bad as stringing up a row of babies, the way it sickened her. Their taut muscles glistened with dark blood. Bits of fur clung to their ears, but their feet were sawed clean off. Annie lowered her gaze and caught sight of the skins laid out across the railing of an empty stall. Next to that a row of rabbit feet were lined up like seashells on a windowsill.

"Jesus." Calder gazed upward with a plugged nose. "What do they want with those?"

"I don't know." She recalled the sound of an animal being skinned. Uncle Calder once dressed a deer in his garage. It was like duct tape tearing off the roll, getting stuck, then tearing again. Uncle Calder didn't seem to mind it. Annie had covered her ears and shook at the thought of losing her own skin. She thought of how only hours before, that buck had been running through the forest with other deer, eating grass, breathing fresh air, completely unaware of what was about to happen.

She felt a little sorry for the Pinckney boys just then. It was like they were forced to hear the skin peeling off an animal every day of their lives. A person was bound to get ornery and mean if they had to work in a pigsty and get slapped in the head for no good reason and live in a house with holes in the screens and dead rabbits hanging in the barn. She thought of how she'd added to their misery by beating them in the head with the branch. This was their *life*. They had no choice but to get up and live it every day.

Annie felt a sharp ache for her mother. Her jasmine perfume, the touch of her fingers in Annie's hair, the way she sent Annie off to class by squeezing her and telling her to go teach those people something.

The door to the house slammed again and they waited. When nothing came they crouched low to the ground and hid first behind the tractor in the dirt yard, second behind the old pickup with flat tires and a wooden tailgate, and third behind the row of scrub palmettos along the woods that led to home.

* * *

Sobs could be heard all the way into the kitchen. Then a wail so thick it lingered in Annie's head for days afterward.

Her father hadn't been home for days, but it was only then, as Annie and Calder came in from the Pinckneys' farm, that Annie felt the fullness of his absence. It was everywhere, and it was final.

They found their mother sitting on the edge of her bed, facing the wall with her head down. She held a wadded tissue in her fist. She turned to the sound of Calder bouncing on the balls of his feet.

Annie filled with an ache so deep and powerful her arms and legs began to tremble.

"His voice," her mother said as if she were midway through a conversation. Her face was wet and swollen, altered in a way Annie had never seen. "I was always so taken by that voice of his."

Annie's hands sweated. The pale pink walls made her legs sway. She lowered herself onto the bed with her mother.

"I could never stand all that slang he used, but the soft lilt of it, you know, the way he said *Flahrida* so gently, like it was rolling off his tongue." She gestured with a wave of her hand, and then she stopped and looked at Annie as if seeing her there for the first time. "The way you and Calder say it."

The ache bore deep and hot in Annie's stomach.

"At least I've got that."

"What's wrong with Daddy?" Calder asked from the doorway.

Annie straightened her back.

Her mother seemed not to hear.

"What happened?" Calder asked.

Her red eyes were wet again. "He didn't get to finish the table."

They sat in silence. The only sound was sniffling.

Annie was afraid to touch her own mother. It was as if they'd never met.

"Finish what table?" Annie finally asked.

"Hmn?"

"What table are you talking about?"

"It was going to be a surprise." She shook her head at the ceiling like she was faced with something ridiculous. "He was making a new table for our kitchen."

Her father had pored over projects in his workshop, surrounded by scraps of wood and saws and glass jars full of nails and a whole collection of chisels and mallets. A range of wood stains lined a single shelf as the final step in making rocking chairs, chests, and bevel-framed mirrors. The air was thick with turpentine and sawdust and sweat. Annie had helped him build cedar birdhouses for swallows with slotted holes to keep the sparrows out. Every day her hands and hair, her whole body smelled like resin. The birdhouses were sold from a stand they built on the road, and some of the money was used to buy her first guitar, which, her father had said, was nothing more than a funny looking birdhouse with a hole big enough for cowbirds to lay eggs in.

She'd been in his workshop nearly every weekend this summer and never once saw the makings of a table.

"What does it look like?" she asked.

"What?"

"The table."

Her mother took a moment to wipe her nose and eyes. "He called it a farmhouse table. He had this dream of making a whole line of tables out of Tiger Maple. He wanted to spend his days listening to the radio in his workshop and building these custom tables for families to sit around."

"On Sundays?" Annie asked.

A gasp escaped her mother's throat. She shook her head at the floor.

After a time Annie said, "Where is it?"

"The table?"

Annie nodded.

"In Uncle Calder's garage. I imagine it's still in pieces."

She dropped the wadded tissue into her lap and wiped her face with her hands. She wept quietly into her hands and they waited for her to stop. She did, finally, abruptly, like she was forcing the tears down her throat, and then forcing words up past her tears. "He had cancer. A tumor. It was in his brain and there wasn't a thing they could do for him."

In the silence a fly ticked the window, trying to get in.

"I want to see him," Calder finally said.

"There's nothing to see," their mother said.

"Take me to see him!" Calder yelled.

"There's nothing—" Her face turned rigid, her jaw muscles stiffened, determined to stay shut.

Annie swallowed dryly. Her father was dead. She knew this was the part her mother hadn't come out and said. He was dead. She knew this. At least a part of her did, but this other part seemed to be watching from the outside, aware that her mother had somehow forgotten they were only kids, *her* kids, and her husband had been their father, and now he was dead, and there was no one here to tell them what to do, to help them understand, to get them through the next minute, the next day and year.

Calder ran down the hall and slammed the door to his room. Annie turned to her mother but she was no longer there. She'd been replaced by a woman who gritted her teeth and stared at the ceiling with hateful, untamed eyes. Annie thought again to touch her, but didn't dare.

Where was Uncle Calder? Annie couldn't bring herself to ask.

SEVENTEEN

She blows in through the door as if propelled by wind. A bag of groceries in one arm, dragging her luggage with the other. She has no idea Annie is standing in Calder's living room, and Annie can't think of what to say to let her know. And then there's no need because her cell phone suddenly rings on the counter.

Sidsel turns and screams, *really* screams, as if someone is about to kill her.

"It's all right," Annie says, but she can see by Sidsel's round eyes and the way she's still backing away that she doesn't believe her. "I'm Annie. Calder's sister."

Annie opens and shuts her phone to stop the ringing.

"*Av mig God!*" Sidsel says, or something like this and sets the groceries on her luggage. She grips her knees beneath her red trench coat and catches her breath like a runner who's just finished a final mile. "Why are you here?" A statement more than a question. Her intonation is flat, and Annie isn't sure whether this is because her head is lowered or she simply talks this way. There's the accent, too, the trouble she seems to have with her R's. Before Annie can answer her question she says, "You really frightened me." She's still leaning into her knees in the doorway, her long blond hair obscuring her face. The cold air, damp and woodsy, rushes through the open door.

They're so quiet it's as if they've stopped to listen to the wind rustling the plant leaves.

"I came to water the plants," Annie says. "And bring in the mail, but I see someone has already done that."

"Thank you," she says, as if Annie is doing her a favor. She straightens herself and shakes her hair behind her shoulders and peers around the room as if she's lost.

Annie rubs the sides of her arms. Sidsel finally turns and shuts the door. What little heat there is in the room slowly wells around them.

"I'm Sidsel. Jørgenson," she adds, from the back of her mouth and Annie realizes this is the way it's pronounced in Danish. She takes off her jacket and folds it in half across her luggage next to the groceries. She sighs and pulls her white blouse out of her jeans like a man loosening his tie after work. Annie's discomfort grows. Sidsel doesn't live here. Neither does Annie.

Sidsel pulls her luggage and groceries away from the closed door as if someone needs to get by. Fresh herbs hang from the top of the bag. A small box of what looks and smells like cookies sits next to them, probably from her café. Annie looks around her brother's home, and though she's been here for more than twenty minutes, it feels strange now without him in it. With Sidsel here instead.

"It's so great to finally meet you," Sidsel says, no longer sounding flat. "Calder asked me to call you and here you are." She comes toward her. "Sorry I was so frightened. My nerves," she says, and throws her arms around Annie. She is tall and thin like Calder but she smells like Mrs. Lanie's kitchen. Sugar and butter and flour. It is faintly what Annie smelled on her brother's sheets.

Annie starts to let go but Sidsel holds on to her. Annie waits like a child seized into the breasts of an aunt, though she can't help notice Sidsel's breasts are smallish and firm along her cheek.

Annie pats her, feeling the lean muscle of her back. She finally lets go.

"You're a beautiful singer." Sidsel has no choice but to look down at her when she speaks. "Your voice is like a scratchy whisper. So delicate, but big. It reminds me of Iceland."

Annie feels herself blush, embarrassed, and finally confused. She doesn't know a thing about Iceland. She doesn't know a thing about Sidsel. "Iceland?"

"They believe in fairies."

"I see." But she doesn't.

"There's a quality to your voice. Something. I don't know. It reminds me of their language."

They look around the room and sigh at the same time. This makes them smile. The tension seems to ease.

Sidsel is stunning. Annie doesn't think she's ever seen more beautiful skin. It's like the flawless, velvety finish on a fine piece of oak.

Sidsel folds her hands together in front of her. They are surprisingly rough and aged. Dishpan hands, completely out of place with the rest of her. They look like Annie's.

She scratches the back of one when she says, "Calder suggested I stay here. I've been a little scared at home by myself. I feel like I'm being watched by whoever did this to Magnus."

The air shifts at the mention of Magnus. "I'm sorry," Annie says. "About your loss." Her words sound inappropriate, obligatory.

Sidsel nods at the floor and rubs her eyes. "Magnus wasn't a very nice man," she says. Annie waits for her to say something more. Something that will make what she has already said seem less crude, less comical. But she isn't saying a word, and now Annie can't stop the awkward smile breaking on her face. It's tight and fixed and fake and she cannot seem to change it.

"I'm sorry." Sidsel finally shakes her head at herself and rolls her eyes. "I seem to be mixing things up. My English is normally very good, but now my thoughts have switched back to Danish and things are getting lost in translation."

Annie can't imagine what she might have meant to say. "Don't worry about it," Annie tells her. "We all do that. Even in our own language."

"I don't think I did it back home, though. I never had people look at me the way they look at me here, with such blank faces." Annie thinks to tell her, "They're just stunned by your ridiculous beauty, not by your words," when Sidsel says, "But then I never had a dead husband back home."

Annie slowly points her finger. "Right there. That's—I don't think you mean it like that."

Sidsel growls. "I give up." She rubs her arms as if to warm herself. "I just came from meeting with a realtor," she says.

A childlike quality, an innocence flashes in the way her thoughts seem to bounce. Annie imagines Calder charmed by all the non sequiturs and the accent coming through those pouty lips. Sidsel crosses the room and flips the switch to the fireplace. A flame of blue and then a fire swooshes behind her legs as she turns to speak.

"Calder said I should meet with a realtor to try and sell my house. I don't ever want to go back there. I never liked it to begin with."

"I can't imagine," Annie says. What else is there to say?

"She was really helpful. The realtor. It turns out a while ago some woman wrote an article in *Architectural Digest* about the Dutch architect who designed the house. People still drive by to have a look at it. I never knew. I haven't lived there very long."

"Hmn."

"The realtor is attaching the article by this woman to the fliers and the Web site, hoping it will distract from the fact that Magnus lived there, you know, if they see his name somewhere and put it together it might be hard to sell."

"Have you seen my brother?" Annie asks.

Sidsel moves to a chair and sits. She scoots back, crosses her long legs, and runs her hands down the upholstery. "Yes," she says, swinging her foot nervously. "Nearly every day."

"How is he?" The room may have gone dark if not for the fire. Annie turns on the floor lamp and sits on the sofa across from Sidsel. She sinks, easily, into the down cushions. Outside the wind has picked up, causing a whistle in the kitchen window. She needs to get home to Detour.

"He keeps saying he didn't do it. As if I'd ever think he did." Sidsel glances down the hall toward the bedroom. The lamplight catches her face. Tiny puffs rim her eyes. "It's not like I don't know how much he loves me. I think he'd do anything for me, but I don't think he'd do that."

A jealousy she can't explain pinches Annie's chest. "Why'd he ask you to call me?"

"He said you could help."

"How?"

"I don't know anyone here, aside from a few young girls who work for me. I have no family here. My parents are old and not in good health."

"Do you have brothers or sisters?"

She shakes her head no. "Calder was hoping you would befriend me. Be friends with me. However you say it. So I won't go back to Denmark."

Annie imagines their friendship but can't seem to develop a clear picture. And now she sees that she's hurt Sidsel's feelings by not speaking quickly enough. By not immediately inviting her into her life.

"It's silly anyway," Sidsel says. "He doesn't need to worry about that. I won't go back to Denmark. I won't leave him. No matter what."

If they were friends Annie would tell her, "Oh, but you could. People do things, say things, end up with lives they never imagined."

"His tics are getting worse," Sidsel says.

"I know. My Uncle Calder told me."

"I love your Uncle Calder." Sidsel smiles with what appears to be memories of him.

This is the second time today his name has been used like a slap across the face. "You *love* my Uncle Calder?" He never even mentioned meeting her.

"He's a funny man. And pretty charming, don't you think?"

"Yes. I do," Annie says. "A lot like my brother," she adds, trying to take some control. She can't know Annie's own family better than she does. "Have you met my mother, too?"

Sidsel's smile dissolves. "Not yet. I have a feeling she doesn't like me. I'm sure she thinks this is all my fault."

A thread of warmth pulls Annie toward her. "Don't worry. She doesn't like me much either."

Sidsel smiles a full open laugh of a smile. Her teeth are large and white and straight. Perfect. Annie doesn't understand why she isn't on a runway somewhere making millions of dollars instead of sitting in Calder's living room.

"I grew up in a small house on a cobbled street," she says, and Annie thinks of Calder trying to keep up with the way her mind works. Then she realizes the mention of Annie's family has reminded Sidsel of her own.

"We had two black cats named Trudel and Lille. My parents were teachers."

"My mother was a teacher, too."

"I know," she says.

Of course.

"I used to spend my summers swimming naked and eating strawberries on this island called Aeroskobing."

Annie nods and smiles and sits back for the ride. It's easy to imagine Calder pulled in by the intrigue, the beauty, the crush and curiosity of her.

"The stone houses stand all in a row there." Sidsel clasps her palms together. "Red and yellow and blue. People throw the shutters open at the same time every day so the breeze from the North Sea can come in. The pillows on the furniture feel damp. Everything smells like salt."

So she's a storyteller. This is how they'll connect. An unexpected knot rises in Annie's throat.

"I haven't thought of this since I was little. Nearly every window on the island has a pair of porcelain spaniels on the sill." Sidsel laughs inwardly as if some insight has just been revealed to her.

"There's this legend about the fisherman," she says. "When they traveled to London they visited prostitutes whose business was supposed to be selling these porcelain spaniels. The fishermen brought them home as gifts for their wives. But the wives weren't stupid. They knew exactly where they came from." She shakes her head. "The wives were so clever that they placed the spaniels in their front windows as a sign for their *own* lovers. Facing out meant the husband was away at sea. But if the back and curly tail was turned to the street, then the husband had returned and the lovers knew to stay away."

It's as old and common as dirt, this game of lying and pretending, this whole business of cheating. Funny how Sidsel speaks with such ease, considering what cheating has made of her life, not to mention Annie's. She must know about Owen. She must know what happened between Annie and Calder. Assuming Sidsel knows all this, her ease appears callous.

Then again, maybe it's only her nerves. Maybe it's lost in translation.

Sidsel drops her head back and sighs at the ceiling, and they are both quiet and Annie doesn't feel the need to say anything. She stares into the fire, its predictable shape never changing.

She thinks of the time Owen came home with a peculiar smell on his clothes. It wasn't perfume or lotion or makeup. It was the smell of cooked meat and broth and smoke, and she knew he had spent hours in a restaurant somewhere. A nice restaurant. He was supposed to be working, and she told herself that maybe he and the guys had hit a wall, it was like that sometimes, when no one can agree on the tiniest melody and you need to leave the studio and come back with fresh eyes and ears; and so she'd rolled away from him in bed, and though it tugged at her for a while, it wasn't so powerful that she couldn't sleep.

The next morning she looked at his shirt on the back of the chair but didn't pick it up. She didn't examine it. She simply allowed a finger to brush along the sleeve as she left the room. Then she did something she rarely ever did. She made him eggs Benedict, his favorite. She sat across from him and watched him eat. He didn't say a word about hitting a wall the night before, and Annie never asked. She sees now that she was already steeped in something meant to protect her from what was happening even as a part of her seemed unaware that it was happening at all. He took long, slow bites, and every now and then he smiled at her above his coffee cup; and then he said something about a red-tailed bird at the window but when she looked it had already flown away. It makes her heart physically ache just thinking about all that went unsaid that morning. What would have happened if he'd come right out and told her? What if she'd slammed her fist on the table and demanded to know where he'd been? Could they have worked things out? She has no way of knowing. She has no way of knowing if he even felt guilty as he sat there eating his breakfast. For all she knows he was thinking how unfortunate it was that of all mornings she could have made eggs Benedict, she picked the one when so much rich food was still sitting in his stomach from the night before.

"Men can be so confusing," Sidsel finally says, but it's the wind slapping the trumpet vine against the glass door in the kitchen that fully brings Annie back into the room. It's grown even darker in the room, though maybe this is only because she's been staring into the fire and now she's looking at Sidsel and it just now sinks in what she's said. Annie feels the need to stand up and go. But she doesn't. "I'm sure they think the same of us," she says.

"Sometimes I wish we didn't need them at all," Sidsel says. "And then sometimes I wish we needed them more than we really do."

Annie tilts her head to the side and nods to let her know she may be onto on something.

"Calder told me about his problem with drinking," she says.

"Yes. Well." She's caught Annie off guard.

Sidsel sighs and crosses her other leg and swings her foot. "Why are you bringing it up?"

"I worry when he gets out that he may start again," Sidsel says.

"I was under the impression that he had it under control. And he's certainly not drinking in jail."

"No. But...It's something else. Something that happened before he went in."

"What?"

"He started drinking."

"When?"

"Magnus found out about our affair the day before he was killed."

Annie waits for her to continue. She takes too long. "What does this have to do with my brother's drinking?"

"I don't even know how Magnus found out about us. I knew the day would come sooner or later. But I always imagined when it did that I would be the one who would be killed for it. Really. The whole time Calder and I were together I thought it was only a matter of time before Magnus found out and came after me, and yet I couldn't stop seeing Calder." She presses herself forward as if a small ache has formed in her stomach. "I love your brother," she says. "More than anything."

"I have no reason to doubt that," Annie says, unsure if this is true. "But what does this have to do with his drinking?"

"Magnus met me at the door when I came home from work that evening and said, 'I know all about you two.' He was very calm. Not at all the way I thought he'd be. He told me he was going to have a little talk with Calder and he left the house and that was the last time I saw him alive."

The papers have said nothing of this. Annie wonders if Sidsel has told this to Detectives Rick and Ron. "What did you do?"

"I called Calder and he told me not to worry. He said he could handle whatever was going to happen. He said he was glad that we wouldn't have to sneak around anymore."

"Then what happened?"

"A couple of hours went by and Magnus didn't come back and I tried calling Calder again but he didn't pick up. I left several messages, and then I finally drove by his house and his truck wasn't there. Then something strange happened. I can't explain it but I just knew Calder was safe somewhere. I trusted he had a good reason for not answering his phone. Of course, Magnus never came home, and early the next morning when I talked to Calder he sounded different on the phone. I asked if he'd seen Magnus. He said no, but his voice was, I don't know, heavy, and tired, like he was sick. I asked what was wrong and he said he did something really stupid."

Annie's insides twist. Here it comes.

"He was drinking."

"Oh," Annie says, and can tell by the quickness of Sidsel's eyes that she sees the relief in Annie's face.

"He said he just wanted one drink to help him relax and think of what to do next but he opened a bottle and ended up drinking until he passed out."

"So his alibi is that he was passed out drunk the night Magnus was killed?"

"Yes."

"Well, obviously the police don't think that's what happened."

"They know he bought the whiskey, they just think he drove out to Hal's after that and waited for Magnus in the parking lot."

"How would he know Magnus was at Hal's?"

"Of course that's the part that doesn't make sense. He had no idea where Magnus was. Maybe they think I told him. Maybe they think Magnus told me where he was going and I told Calder. I don't know. No one even saw Calder at Hal's that night. But there's something strange about it. The police said someone called Calder's house from the pay phone inside Hal's that night."

"Who?"

"Nobody knows. Calder wasn't home so he didn't answer. The police think it was some kind of signal."

"For what?"

"To tell him Magnus was there, I guess."

"So if Calder wasn't at Hal's and he wasn't home when you drove by, then where was he?"

"Out buying the whiskey. I'd just missed him."

Annie rubs her hands down her thighs and pulls in a deep breath.

"I know how it looks but he didn't kill Magnus," Sidsel says. "I already said that. I'm just worried that he isn't strong enough to withstand all this when it's finally over."

"You have no idea what my brother can withstand," Annie says. "I've known him since the day he came into the world." For the first time tonight she has something over on Sidsel, though the satisfaction she ought to feel isn't there.

"You're probably right," Sidsel says, and Annie can see in her face, hear in her voice that she believes this.

169

"No wonder the prosecutor is going after the death penalty," Annie says. "Who's going to believe an alibi like that?"

Sidsel suddenly bursts into tears.

"I'm sorry," Annie says. "I didn't mean that the way it sounded. See? We all mess up what we mean to say, even in our own language."

Sidsel covers her face and lowers her head and her shoulders shake with tears.

"Listen." A soreness fills Annie's throat. "I'm going to help him get a better lawyer."

Sidsel bolts upright in her chair. "I can't talk about this anymore," she says, wiping her tears. "Please. It's late and I haven't even offered you anything. Can I cook something for us? Can you stay?"

Annie hasn't eaten since breakfast and realizes at the mention of food just how hungry she is. "That would be nice."

"Thank you." Sidsel rises from the chair with a dancer's long grace. Annie recognizes the sadness that weighs in her arms as she lifts the groceries and steps into the kitchen. She washes her hands and takes a plate from the cupboard, places it on the counter, and then remembers to grab another. She must have lived alone for many years. Annie does the opposite in her own kitchen, choosing two plates before remembering that she only needs one.

When she stands to join Sidsel in the kitchen she finds she's light-headed from hunger. Sidsel greets her with a saucer. At the center is a home-baked Christmas cookie in the shape of a star. Annie lifts it to her tongue, and there is nothing she knows of in this world to compare it to.

From her grocery bag Sidsel grabs a small plastic box of red Christmas lights. "I thought I would string these on the Bird of Paradise. For when he comes home."

Annie thinks of her brother's words on her porch that day. *I've never known in all my life what it is to love like this.*

Sidsel has her back to Annie when she says, "I think you and I are going to be great friends."

But Annie is still thinking of Calder. Of his happy face whistling a tune on her porch that day. She wants to warn him to stay away. "This love is like sharks," she wants to tell him. "Taking us all down in pieces."

EIGHTEEN

It was the hottest Thanksgiving on record and her mother refused to turn on the air-conditioner.

"It'll be fine," she said. "It costs a fortune to run that thing."

The ceiling fan spun the smell of roasting turkey and sage to all corners of the house. The scent was so familiar, so comforting, that the possibility of having a normal holiday bubbled through Annie's veins for the better part of the morning. She made her bed and swept the sand off the porch and trimmed her own bangs. Calder watered the begonias along the house and spent the next two hours reading quietly in the blue, oversized living room chair. Her mother hadn't left the kitchen for hours. She'd cooked more in a few hours than she'd cooked in months. They were turning a corner. Annie could feel it. They were repairing, at least beginning to, the damage that'd been done.

But by the time her mother plopped the turkey on the table Annie felt weak beneath the boiler room heat. Sweat beaded across her forehead and streamed down her ribs. Her mother was now making herself another drink while the mashed potatoes dried out on the counter and the rolls burned and the green beans shriveled in the pan.

Calder sat across the table from Annie holding an Avenger comic like a fort in front of his face. His upper lip glistened with sweat. "I bet he can figure out a way to come back if he wants to," he whispered, referring to their father.

How could she have thought for a minute that today could be a normal holiday?

Their father had a glossy black tombstone with flat gray lettering. *Our Beloved, Kearney Riley Walsh, 1938–1976.* He had been dead for nearly four months. How long was Calder going to talk like this?

He flipped the pages and the back cover caught the sunlight. Annie strained to read the ad. *Miracle Plant, Instantly Brought Back to Life.* It had *before* and *after* photos. One brown and wilted, the other upright and shiny green. She knew what they were selling. She'd grown up with these plants, the dense furry coat of what looked like dead plants lining the bark and forks of live oak trees. They were no better than weeds. Swarms of brown and green spikes curled on the ends like fiddle heads. Those plants weren't dead. They were Resurrection Ferns, capable of "coming back to life" within minutes of a falling rain. Somebody was charging five dollars plus shipping and handling for those things.

"Why are you starting this again?" Annie whispered. For someone whose mind had always been bent on facts Calder now seemed willing to believe anything.

"Cause it's true."

"It's not true."

"You don't know."

"Of course I know. People don't rise back up, Calder, unless you happen to be Jesus Christ."

"That doesn't mean it can't happen." His knees banged beneath the table.

"It sure as hell *does* mean it can't happen," Annie hissed.

"Happy Thanksgiving," her mother said with a tone of irony as she came back in with the rubbery green beans and sat in her chair, suddenly motionless, staring at her father's empty seat.

Two days earlier, Annie had lost track of her in a department store. Annie was outgrowing all her clothes, which struck her as odd, that she should go on growing while her father was dead. It didn't seem right that anything should go on as it had before without him. But it had, and she felt guilty and distracted, looking for a new dress to wear on Thanksgiving. She played along and held up dress after dress to see what her mother thought of each, and she guessed her mother was feeling the same way because the dresses all seemed wrong to her, too. But then Annie came across one that she really did like. It was sleeveless and blue, the same blue as her eyes, the same blue as her father's and Calder's, and the dress had tiny white stitching along the hem and neckline and when she held it up she knew it was the one. She said (maybe a little too loud), "This is the one!" But when she turned there was no one and nothing but Muzak streaming through the ceiling. Her mother was gone. At some point Annie put down the dress. This was how it felt to have no parents. It was a long and seemingly endless black hall where there was nothing and no one to help her make sense of the world. She'd had no idea a person could feel so alone.

She searched the aisles. Makeup, jewelry, accessories. Her mother always liked scarves but there was no one there, and for a moment Annie stopped to gather her scattered thoughts, calm her panic between the swatches of silk. It was in the men's shoes that she finally found her. A sales lady was patting her mother's back and trying to get her to drink water from a Dixie cup, but her mother just kept sobbing with a man's black dress shoe hanging limply in her hand.

Now Annie sat at the table in the old yellow dress that pulled across her back and beneath her arms. She had begun to grow breasts since the last time she wore it, and it was only a matter of time before the seams tore apart. So she held still, watching Calder bang his knees and read his comic. His arms on the table trembled slightly from the movement of his legs, and the whole table shook just enough to get on a person's nerves.

Her mother jumped up to fetch something else from the kitchen. She wobbled and caught herself in the doorway. "Whoop," she said, apparently having started drinking since before she started cooking. Annie was afraid to cut into the turkey and find it raw, or worse, stuffed with a man's shoe.

"I want him to come back as bad as anybody ever wanted anything," Annie whispered to Calder. "But it's not going to happen. It's just not. He had a tumor in his brain, Calder. He had cancer. "

"Mrs. Brinkman had cancer and she's still walking around the halls of Lakewood Elementary, yelling at everybody," he said from behind his comic.

"That's not the same."

"What's not the same?"

"The same cancer. She didn't have a brain tumor. Hers was different. They caught it in time and got rid of it. It's gone. That's why she's still here, yelling at everybody."

"Daddy never yelled at anybody."

"No. He wasn't much for yelling."

"Then why'd he have to go and Mrs. Brinkman got to stay?"

"I don't know."

"Then how do you know he's not coming back?"

"Cause he's not!" Annie shoved her chair out and felt the seam give along the zipper between her shoulders. She walked to the doorway leading into the hall. Stepping all the way through it seemed mean and final, so she turned around as the ceiling fan blew warm air into her opened seam. Calder had slapped his comic onto the table and her mother froze opposite Annie in the kitchen doorway on the other side of the room. Another drink sloshed in her hand.

"He's not coming back!" Annie screamed at both of them. "Ever. Not ever. Not even for a minute. So stop saying it, stop acting like a little kid, Calder. Stop asking like asking itself is going to make it come true!" She smelled the whiskey in her mother's glass and on her sweaty skin as she stomped past through the kitchen and out into the screened-in porch. She threw herself down on the chaise lounge with the moth holes. Her stomach growled loud enough for anyone to hear.

Calder cleared his throat when he opened the door to the porch. He walked over with blinking eyes and slid next to her. She sat up.

A dining room chair scraped and crashed inside. A glass broke and she had no doubt it was her mother's drink against a wall. Calder and Annie didn't even look at each other, they just looked outside at the patio and the grill and the big grassy field beyond. It could have been the middle of summer for the heat.

Calder cleared his throat again. "Should we call Uncle Calder?"

"I shouldn't have said what I said." Annie glanced toward the kitchen. "I'm sorry." But even as she said this she was still reeling from how good it felt to get it all out and she wasn't the least bit sorry at all. As for Uncle Calder, she'd tired of calling him long ago. Every time he knocked at the door their mother glared as if she were ashamed of them, of her life, of the fact that her husband had died, and they were putting that shame on display for the whole world to see. "Don't answer that door," she'd say. "Don't you dare answer that door." After the last time when he came straight through the back door without knocking and stuffed her in the shower with her clothes on, even as she threw punches in the air around his head, she'd forbidden Annie and Calder, with a loosely pointed finger, to ever call him again.

"Let her go," Annie said. "Let her do what she's got to do around here. It's not like we have to sit here and listen to it."

Annie stepped outside where the air was even thicker than she expected. The sun beat down and reflected off the backyard like a toaster cooking everything from both sides. Calder let the screen slam behind him when he came out, and the sound of it must have caught their mother's attention.

By the time they reached the tire swing, their mother was wedged between the screen door and frame like she was caught in a trap. "I made this dinner for you!" she hollered. "I'm not even hungry." She started to go inside and then turned. "Don't go swatting at bees." There was an edge to her voice. "That Pinckney boy is nowhere in sight." She glanced from side to side as if she were searching for him.

Sweat trickled down the center of Annie's chest. A dragonfly buzzed past her ear, the sun burned through the hole in the back of her dress. Ever since her father died the world had turned into one giant riddle. She could no longer wake up and move around inside it without thinking, without needing to figure something out. She couldn't just do the things she liked to do. Every day was a maze she had to work her way out of. "What are you talking about?" she asked her mother from across the yard, and then she turned to Calder. "What's she talking about?"

"Nothing," he said. "Forget it."

"Didn't anyone tell you?" her mother asked. A sudden look of confusion, of concern came over her face. "I thought I told you in the hospital that day." She stumbled into the yard and reached for Calder. "I guess I had other things on my mind—"

Calder backed off and she stumbled forward in the sandy grass and caught herself with flailing arms.

"You've got five seconds to tell me or else," Annie said to Calder, not knowing what she meant by *or else*, but guessing that the image of her beating the Pinckneys was now fresh in his mind.

"She's nothing but a drunk," he said, and the shock of those words stopped everything—birds, dragonflies, wind, everything.

Her mother looked at Annie and her mouth fell open as if Annie were the one who'd said it. As if Annie were the one who should apologize. Then she laced her fingers across her face and her back shook and Annie didn't know if she was laughing or crying. Either way was bad. Her words were muffled when she said, "You know what I'm talking about, Calder. You nearly got both of you killed by that Pinckney boy."

Now they were getting somewhere.

Her mother threw her arms out at her sides. "I could have lost every single one of you that day." She wiped her face and stumbled in a circle, seeming to consider this. "Hey!" she suddenly barked, like the drunks downtown near the train station. "Hey. I'm *lucky*," she said. "We're *all* lucky. We're the *lucky* ones here."

"What happened, Calder?" Annie asked.

He scrunched his eyes and bobbed up and down on his heels.

"Stand still and tell me!" She took a step toward him.

"Tell her." Her mother tottered away and flung an arm into the air behind her as if to ward off a bird. "About the day your father went into the hospital and never came out. *That* day." She pointed at her head with her finger, pecking her skull the way people do when they've got a bright idea. Only it wasn't a bright idea she was referring to. It was the tumor in her father's head.

Annie jammed her fists onto her hips and glared at Calder. Her dress pulled and the threads gave one last time until it finally fit comfortably across her chest.

He cleared his throat and blinked.

"Stop it!" she screamed.

His mouth jerked sideways. "I thought he was trying to hurt you. He had a hold of your hand and was spitting. I didn't know what he was doing. You were laying there like you were dead and I heard him spitting and I ran as fast as I could."

"What do you mean?"

"I jumped on his back to get him to stop."

"He was spitting on me?"

"No. I thought he was hurting you."

She looked to her mother for an answer.

"He was saving your life, sweetheart." She rubbed her eyes like she was only tired now. Tired from making such a big meal on Thanksgiving. "He scraped the stinger out and spit in the dirt to make mud. He was trying to pack it on the sting to draw the venom out. His mother's allergic just like you."

"I didn't know!" Calder said. "You were on the ground and he had a hold of your hand."

Annie couldn't speak.

Calder held still.

"That's where your bruises came from?" she finally said. "You never fell through the tree like you said?"

"No."

"He was trying to *save* me?"

Calder blinked and cleared his throat.

Her mother drew in a long breath and sighed. "That Pinckney boy laid him out flat." Her face twisted to the side and her eyes were wet in the sunlight and Annie knew she didn't want to think about that day for another second. But she went on. "It's a good thing," she said and Annie looked at her, really looked at her for the first time in months. The ends of her hair were dull and frayed. Her dress hung off her shoulder and a bony knot popped out where her round shoulder used to be. Her collarbone scooped beneath her skinny throat.

Fresh sweat rolled down Annie's sides. She glanced at Calder but couldn't stand to see the humiliation in his face. It took a lot to humiliate Calder. But even as a part of her wanted to hold him, to mess up his already messy hair and give his shoulder a shove and forget any of this ever happened, another part of her had already walked away and left him standing there alone. All this time he'd lied. She understood he'd tried to do the right thing, but he'd *lied* to her and if that wasn't bad enough he'd nearly gotten her killed.

She closed her eyes and imagined what it would have been like had she vanished from the world with her father that day.

It felt like spring, blossoms and seventy degrees, like funny stories around a Sunday table, like birdhouses and cuss words and her father's aftershave and wearing a blue dress with white stitching. She could have stayed there, easily, tucked inside that small opening forever. But she opened her eyes and pushed back into the heat, back to her mother and brother in the yard when she realized that no matter how long she lived, every day of her life would be a day for which she had Josh Pinckney to thank.

NINETEEN

The Miata ran out of gas and shut off sometime in the night, and Owen has never felt the kind of cold he feels when early morning seeps in and he peels himself away from the steering wheel he's been sleeping against. Fingers, knees ache deep inside the bones. His dry lips pull apart when he coughs, and his breath comes out in great white puffs. His watch says five minutes to six. A varnish of condensation coats the windows. Beyond them, a blinding white light.

Owen moves to open the door, and he's stiff from his head to the base of his back. He coughs as he rises from the car and shivers profoundly when the air touches his neck.

He stops. Something creaks beneath his shoe. Flakes the size of down feathers, trees covered in crystalline white, branches of glass along the field. Snow. It's snowing. Must be an inch on the ground. "Christ Almighty," he says and coughs until he catches his breath.

The air smells faintly of burning gas and chimney smoke. Owen scoops the snow into his hands. Enough to pack a snowball, and his fingers burn with cold as he presses it into shape. Annie's green Land Cruiser pops through all the white. It's parked beside the house. She must have driven past him in the night while he slept. He tosses the snowball back to the ground and it falls apart.

The black Suburban with the two guards from last night has been replaced by a white Suburban with silver pin striping. A young man sits behind the wheel snapping photos of the snow with his cell phone.

Owen pulls his own phone from his pocket. The battery has gone dead. He steps through the snow and knocks on the window of the Suburban. His socks are already wet at the ankles.

"My phone is dead," he says as the window comes down.

"What's that?" The man is blond and pimply and can't be more than eighteen years old.

"I need to use your phone. Mine's dead. And I ran out of gas."

The young man shakes his head at the snow. "Can you believe this?"

The wind sends an icy chill up the back of Owen's jacket and he coughs again, deeper than the last.

Maybe the man is taken by the snow, or just naive when it comes to matters of security. He hands his phone over without a word.

Owen pecks in Annie's cell number with a stiff finger. It rings and rings and he wonders if she's watching through her father's old binoculars, laughing, letting it ring some more.

"Yes?" she answers like a blow to the head. His knees bow beneath him.

"Babe," he says before remembering he shouldn't call her that. "Tell him to open the gate. Please." His hand shakes when he hands the open phone back.

"Ms. Walsh?" the young man says. "OK…No, he doesn't."

No, he doesn't what?

The man climbs out of the Suburban and unlocks the gate.

The driveway looks as if it just got longer. The man doesn't offer a ride. Owen wouldn't take it if he did. He needs to work his legs. He needs to think.

He buttons his jacket and begins the trek toward her. A crow flies overhead like a tiny black cutout in a giant poster of white. Flakes fall onto his face and burn like pieces of white ash. He feels faint and nauseous, coughing with every few breaths. His head has the funny, faraway feel of fever.

He pictures himself inside the warm house with its soft chairs and plush rugs, the round angles of tables and instruments, the smooth round angles of Annie. He feels warmer now, even as the snow flips and melts inside his shoes. He thinks of the August when the air-conditioning broke in the middle of the night and he and Annie barely slept from the heat. They were sticky and bad-tempered when they finally quit trying at dawn. It was already pushing eighty degrees, and Annie had the idea of driving out to Cypress Springs before the park opened. The thought of a cold spring made them giddy and silly, and they rushed from the house laughing, each with a towel in hand. When they reached the spring an orange and pink sunrise was ringing the tops of the Cypress trees and reflecting off the icy blue water. It reflected the lush palmettos and oaks, and they could see the swarms of mosquitoes in the surrounding woods where it was warmer. Nothing seemed real, everything burst with color, and the golden glow of the morning sun illuminated the air as if it, too, were rising up from the ground like the spring. Detour jumped out of the car, scrambled under the gate, and barreled into the water. He swam back and forth as if practicing for a race. Owen and Annie ran around the locked gate and left their clothes on a picnic table and jumped naked into the spring that was so clear and blue they could have been jumping into the sky. They screamed at the cold and laughed and splashed like children, and when they looked down they could see yards past their feet all the way to the limestone.

Cold burns the moisture running from Owen's nose. He swipes it with the back of his sleeve. Even now in the snow and freezing temperature he can still see Annie's tanned face, the white lines across her shoulders where her bathing suit would have been, her round breasts, the whole of her naked body beneath the clear water. She was happy, and so much of that happiness had been due to him. He'd pulled her against him in the water and she closed her legs around his waist and gave out a small, sweet-sounding sigh and they kissed on the mouth and the sides of each other's necks and she told him that she loved him in a playful voice and he was about to tell her the same, except right then his love felt a lot more serious than hers. He'd wanted her to know that, to understand just how deep it ran, how heavy it sometimes felt to love her, but he never got the chance because Detour barked and leapt onto the shore toward the park ranger's truck pulling in.

They'd scrambled from the water and back into their clothes while the ranger waited, shaking his head behind the wheel. Once they were dressed the ranger got out with his hands on his hips and came toward them in his stiff brown uniform, still shaking his head. "I won't write the two of you a fine if you promise this is the last I'll see of your bare asses in my spring."

Owen apologized for both of them, and the ranger saluted as they hurried for the car and drove away. They laughed the better part of the way home. But Owen had always felt that something had been lost that day. Something he never quite got back.

He walks in the snow and thinks of the aquifers below him, so pure and cold beneath the whole of Florida. They spring so easily to the surface, no effort at all, just knowing where to go and when. He imagines the blue water bubbling up and out onto the white snow like a blue Sno-Cone. He knows this is not how it would be, but he imagines it this way, blue instead of white as if the sky has switched with the ground. He's warm now, hot even, sweating beneath his coat, pores like aquifers releasing all that's inside him, and he thinks that what he feels is happiness, seeing himself closed up inside the house, hearing his own voice whisper into Annie's ear. *It has never run so deep.*

* * *

When Annie got home from dinner with Sidsel it was past eleven and the only cars at her gate were the guard's white Suburban and a bluish Miata she didn't recognize. The news van had finally gone home and the other stragglers, amateur reporters in small sedans, had apparently given up and gone, too. She stopped for the guard to let her in and he came to the window and told her there was only the one guy left. He pointed to the Miata whose windows were full of moisture. "He must be about frozen to death in there," he said. "The car stopped running a while ago but he refused to leave."

Annie could see the shape of a figure in a tan jacket sleeping against the steering wheel. "Knock on the window again," she said. "Remind him of his wife and kids. It's Christmas, for heaven's sake."

She hadn't planned to be gone so long, and when she opened the front door it was so dark she could barely see in front of her. She hadn't left any lights on for Detour. It was quiet. Too quiet. Not even a bark at the creak of the door.

She called out. The furnace was running and she could hear the brass vent with the loose screws rattling in the bedroom. "Here, buddy," she said, feeling the dread crawling up her neck.

Her boots squeaked in the dark as she moved through the living room, kitchen, and bathroom, flipping on lights the way her mother had done when she'd wake from a dream of Annie's father, sure he was only hiding, playing a trick, a harmless, great big joke. "Detour?" Annie shouted. "Detour, come!"

From the bedroom doorway she saw the outline of his body on the braided rug near the bed. The room smelled sharply of urine. It smelled of sickness. She turned on the bedside lamp.

He blinked at the light in his eyes. A dark wet circle soaked the rug beneath him. He'd lost control of his bladder, and from the looks of it, his eyes seemed to be the only part of him he could move.

Annie dropped to the floor and lifted his head into her lap. His rib cage barely rose with each breath. She stroked his long ear, and his eyes rolled up to look at her with that same guilty look he'd had as a puppy when he chewed her leather sandal, when he scratched a hole in the upholstery of the bedroom chair, trying to reach his ball between the cushions. He felt bad about wetting the rug. She was sure he was feeling bad about what was coming, too.

It didn't seem like eleven years could have passed since Calder had brought him to her. But the gum maple Calder had planted in front of the guide-dog school was now huge, throwing shade across the yellow-spotted lawn. He'd gone in after seeing a sign about puppies who'd failed their training, and the next thing Annie knew he was in her driveway holding a gangly golden creature with a knot of bone on his head. Her first thought was that the puppy didn't look right. "What's wrong with him?" she asked. His ears were long for a Retriever's, his jawline slightly large. Maybe there was hound in the line, or maybe he was simply malformed. He'd walked over as if he were already old and laid his big head down across her foot and fell asleep. "They named him Detour at the school," Calder had said. "How were they supposed to know that this was where he was headed?"

"You're a good boy," Annie told him on the rug, stroking his ear.

He didn't wag his tail. He'd never failed to wag his tail when she spoke these words.

A sudden convulsion of tears took her breath. His eyes were fixed on hers and she had to turn away. She recalled how frightened he'd been when the hail came crashing down on her birthday. She squeezed his neck and buried her face behind his ear. His breathing came in uneven puffs and she wanted to comfort him with words, but tears got the best of her voice and she wailed in a way she'd only done a few times in her life when she couldn't catch a breath, and the bellowing she made seemed to come from an animal in the woods. It took a while before she could make herself stop. She pulled in long breaths of air, and when the anguish slowly turned to calm she leaned over and whispered in his ear. "Let's hope there's a guy named Kearney who'll throw sticks in the water for you."

If Calder were there he'd tell her how corny she was, but it wouldn't be what he meant and they'd both know it. She could practically hear his voice, and it threw her into another round of tears she had to work her way out of.

She stroked Detour's head and his eyes closed and it didn't take more than a moment for him to slip through an opening and go wherever he was going because all of a sudden his fur felt like nothing more than an empty coat in her hands.

* * *

She wakes to find herself on the floor in her heavy jacket and boots, Detour's body lying next to her. The phone rings in her pocket. She sits up in the strange white light of the room. It's morning but she can't tell what time it is. Early, she's sure of that. She brings the phone to her ear, more out of habit, less out of understanding what is happening. Detour has gone completely stiff against her, his tongue pressed into his teeth. The sight jerks her fully awake.

"Yes?" she says, though this is never how she answers the phone.

"Babe," a voice says. Annie looks around the room for someone or something help her understand. Owen's voice is in her ear. Owen is asking her to open the gate.

And then suddenly the security guard is on the line. "Ms. Walsh?"

"How are you?" she asks, as if on autopilot. There is something carnival-like in the way her head is going round and round.

"OK," he says.

"Does he have anyone with him?" A strange question, perhaps from the back of her mind? Is she wondering if he's brought his wife?

"No. He doesn't."

* * *

Owen expects to find her waiting at the door but instead the door is ajar and snow has lined the open space on the floor. He quickly shuts the door behind him and pounds his feet into the floor mat. "Annie?" The house smells like raw wood. He removes his shoes and looks around the living room. The furniture has been stripped. The mantel, too. The heat and smell of resin throw him into a coughing fit. He braces himself on the arm of the leather sofa and remembers the day he and Annie toted it in from the back of his truck. She'd cut her hand on a loose tack underneath and he fetched her a Band-Aid and kissed her temple and told her to be careful. "Careful, careful," he now mouths the words.

It's possible his fever is quite high. He left this house with a fever, and he's returned with one, but that's the least of what makes him feel like no time at all has passed since he called this place his home.

"Annie?" He finds her in the bedroom. It smells like urine and the cold that blew through the open front door. She's on the floor in her coat, her back against the bed, her scarf in a pile next to her. She's looking down at Detour's head in her lap. His eyes are closed and his front legs jut straight out as if he's stretching. It's clear he's not.

* * *

She has no idea why he has come or what he wants or how long he plans to stay. She knows she's not thinking as clearly as she normally would first thing in the morning. But last week, in a fleeting attempt at normalcy, she'd pulled a box of ornaments from the garage, only to find that Owen had left behind the flat, wooden ornaments he'd painted as a child. Gingerbread men, sleighs, thorny wreaths, a skinny Santa, all forgotten in a box filled with her mother's red and golden balls and a white snow angel her father gave her the last Christmas he was alive. She dropped everything back into the box and closed the door and never made it to get a tree because all she could think about was Owen's innocent boy hands painting so carefully within the lines, his tongue pressed out the corner of his mouth in concentration, and how that blameless little boy with nothing but the best intentions in his heart would grow into the man who'd hurt her in a way no one else ever could.

It seems a reasonable thing to ask, "Are you here for the ornaments?"

"What?"

She doesn't look up. "It's almost Christmas."

"I know. I don't need the ornaments," he says.

"You can take them though, when you leave."

"I just got here."

She feels him eyeing Detour. She feels him eyeing her.

"Oh, babe," he says. "I am so, so sorry."

He coughs long and hard and gets down on his knees and touches Detour's head. He touches Annie's face.

His skin is hot. She leans her face into his hand and smells his smell and immediately feels a rhythm that is her, the person she once was, vibrate just beneath her skin. Her chest aches and her throat feels thick and she puts her hand to her cheek and feels the cold band of gold on his finger.

She lifts her face to meet his eyes. From the tan color of his jacket she realizes he was the man sleeping in the car. He looks like a man who's been losing sleep long before he spent the night in his car. His mouth is gaunt and rimmed in stubble, the same color of his hair in sunlight. Circles ring his eyes, and his cheeks are flushed against his otherwise sallow skin. "What's happened to you?" she asks. But it doesn't matter. It's Owen. He's here, and it is all she can do not to reach up and brush away the wavy hair that has fallen near his eye. "What's all over your hair?"

He shakes his hair out and sweeps his shoulders off and dries his hands on the thighs of his jeans. "Snow."

She waits to hear he's joking.

"Everything is covered in white."

This strikes her as funny. Absurd. More ridiculous than anything she's ever heard. Laughter rises in her throat. It brings tears, so many of them, enough to distort the room. She shakes her head at the floor and rubs her eyes. "You look like hell," she says.

His eyes are glassy and red. He gives her a weak smile, just enough to show a corner of his sexy-crooked teeth. He scratches his stubble, the only sound in the room, like sandpaper on wood. "Yeah. Well. So do you," he says, and coughs through his laughter.

She brushes her hair from her face and turns to the window, unable to see the snow from where she sits, only the glare of white light through the condensation. All her life she's had to imagine what snow looks like and now she's imagining it still, even as it lies outside her door.

"Yeah. Well. Someday I'll be the one who does the leaving around here. Then we'll see who looks like what."

* * *

Owen raises Annie's worn yellow quilt to his cheek. "I think we should use this. It smells like you." He begins wrapping Detour inside it. Annie leaves the room.

Outside, the porch has been transported into another time and place. Snow is meant to fall on rolling hills and trees whose spindly branches have no leaves. But here it is, blanketing the flat swamplands like clouds, like heaven resting on earth. Annie's throat aches at the beauty. Even more at the grace.

Owen comes out with the bundle in his arms. Annie turns away. Together they walk to the side of the house and stand beneath the willow tree with the shade Detour always chose above the others. Annie keeps her head down. They don't have to say anything. They know this is the place.

It needs to be done and Owen insists on digging, even as his coughs echo across the frozen field. His hands shake as he breaks through the hardened surface to the moist and warmer soil underneath. The lump of quilt lies nearby in the snow. A well-worn paw pokes from the folds, and Annie finds the strength to bend down and tuck it back in. It feels cold and foreign in her hand, nothing more than a rabbit's foot on a chain. She recalls the footless rabbits in the Pinckney barn. She stands, rubs her eyes, and pushes the image away.

The wind sweeps snowflakes through the branches. Annie blinks them free from her lashes. She brushes off what gathers on the yellow quilt before she realizes there's no point.

Owen places Detour in the ground and covers him with clumps of soil.

A high-pitched ringing fills Annie's ears the way it does when she's trying not to cry. Owen cries freely, wiping his nose on his sleeve. When he's finished he drops the shovel to the side and reaches for her. She steps forward and he pulls her against him and rocks her gently inside a tight embrace. She lets go a torrent of tears. They remain latched, one onto the other against the cold. She wants to say something, but there are no words she can think of that come close to the way she feels.

* * *

They lie on her bed in their coats and talk to the ceiling. "You're really sick," Annie says. "When was the last time you ate something?" This conversation is surreal. The flakes floating past the window do nothing to ground her.

He shivers. "The house smells like sawdust."

"I used your toothbrush on the fireplace."

He seems to be falling asleep.

"I think in some ways I loved Detour more than I loved you," she says.

His laugh is muffled and side-mouthed. He coughs. "I don't blame you."

"He never made me worry."

"No."

"He never left my side. Well. He couldn't help this time."

"No."

"As far as I know he never lied to me."

"I'm sure that's true."

Owen slides his hot hand over, and she doesn't pull away when he hooks his small finger through hers.

"How is Calder?" he asks. "Is he all right?"

Annie thinks of Sidsel breaking down on the sofa and then of the dinner they shared, which was as good a dinner as any she's ever eaten, and all the talk about her music and Sidsel's café as if they'd been friends for some time, and the way they purposely said nothing more about Calder and Magnus because it was a natural fact, as her father used to say, that what they needed was a break.

"I don't know how to answer that," Annie says.

"I'm sorry," Owen says. Annie doesn't ask what exactly for. She's close enough to hear a rattle when he coughs.

She squeezes his finger. "You need to see Doctor Collins."

"It's the day before Christmas Eve," he croaks.

"You need to."

"Christmas Eve, Eve," he says, and thinks this is funny.

She can feel the heat through his coat. She rises up onto her elbow. It's obvious how sick he is, but she can't help but be reminded of the countless times they made love in this exact spot. He's lying on the same side of the bed he slept on. "Does your wife know you're here? Does she know you're sick?"

"How did you know I was married?"

"Calder found out. Besides, you're wearing a wedding band, stupid."

"What else did he tell you?"

"What else is there to tell?"

He doesn't say anything.

"Does she know you're here and that you're sick like this?"

He coughs and closes his eyes. "Yes," he says. "And no." He's groggy, on the verge of saying something else but nothing comes.

"I should call her."

"No." He rolls his head side-to-side in a weak protest.

"Give me your phone."

He seems to be drifting off. After a minute his face is soft and vulnerable, taken over by sleep. She knocks his shoulder, hard. His eyes pop open.

"What are you doing here?" she asks.

He looks around as if he's not sure where he is. Then he closes his eyes again and sighs and pats her hand. "I just need a minute." He falls back asleep.

She reaches in his coat pocket and takes out his cell phone. He doesn't move.

She slips on her rubber boots, grabs a magnifying glass from her desk drawer, and goes outside. The thing she quickly learns about snow is the thing she has known instinctively all along. It has a ruminating, meditative quality that stills her insides. It's made for daydreaming. For turning things over in one's mind. She follows a single flake to the ground, then another as they disappear into a blanket of white. Some flow one way while others go another, all in the absence of wind. She could stand here all day, figuring out the mystery of this.

She steps down and moves through the snow with a graceful awareness, savoring the creak beneath her boots. Her father once said snow smelled like new upholstery. He was right, even if he made the whole thing up. She walks all the way out to the edge of the lake and presses her boot tip into the thin layer of ice, which splits and floats apart and reattaches itself in the cold.

Years ago Annie saw a scene in an old film where a circle of children took turns gazing at snowflakes through a magnifying glass. They were thrilled at what they saw, overacting with rounded mouths and bugging eyes, but the idea had stuck with her. Someday she would look at snow through a magnifying glass to see for herself if she really felt like yelling, "Golly, it's just too much!"

She catches flakes on her sleeve. Magnified, they become sculpted crystals in the shape of Christmas ornaments.

Elaborate, six-sided stars. Scandinavian art. Each looks different from the other, and golly, it really is too much. She can't
believe this is how they actually look. She suddenly feels the
loss of her brother, the loss of a moment that will never exist
of him looking through the magnifying glass with her, the
sheer joy spreading across his face.

She drops the magnifying glass into her pocket and takes
out Owen's phone. He needs a doctor. This is what she'll tell
his wife. He's lying in her bed. No, she won't say that. He's
inside, asleep. He's very ill, she'll say. But then maybe she'll
want to come get him.

The screen on the phone is black. The battery has died.
Annie pictures a young wife, shocked and confused, waiting
for a call, for an explanation to arrive that will make sense of
her world again.

Annie drops the phone into her pocket and it clinks against
the magnifying glass. She treks back to the house, and when
she reaches the porch she turns and eyes the tracks in her wake.
The flakes are even heavier than before. The footprints leading
out are already disappearing.

PART THREE

PART THREE

TWENTY

The next time Annie saw Josh Pinckney was three years after he saved her life. He'd run away the summer of her bee sting. It wasn't the first time he'd taken off, but it was the time he'd made it the farthest. He was picked up in Jacksonville and shipped off to an aunt in Tampa where Annie had heard he'd been living ever since. She was fifteen years old by this time, spending most of her summer days alone and writing songs that hadn't yet measured up to the way she heard them inside her head. Josh was at least a year older than her. She didn't even recognize him. It was he who recognized her.

Someone called her name in Lukeman's Grocery, and she turned to see an attractive teenage boy with short, strawberry-blond hair. His bright green eyes were rimmed with pale lashes. He was freckled and slightly sunburned and could have been a relative of her mother's, so familiar, yet distant was his face. He held a gallon jug of milk in his arm. She studied his short sleeve shirt and clean jeans and blue boat sneakers, and it slowly dawned on her how he knew her name.

"Joshua," he said. "I go by Joshua now."

She dropped the lettuce back onto the pile and instinctively felt for her hand, the one he'd spit on to save her.

"Pinckney?" she said.

"That's the one." He shifted the milk jug to his left hand and held out his right for her to shake. It was cold from the milk and the full size of a man's. He smelled like fabric softener.

"I live in Tampa now. I'm just over visiting my folks for the day with my aunt." He motioned down the aisle to a woman with a grocery cart and a tiny black handbag on her shoulder. She was as freshly groomed as Joshua, her straight dark hair combed neatly off her face. Her eyebrows were finely drawn, smart looking and smooth. She reminded Annie of the clever, lesser attractive, though still attractive Charlie's Angel. She must have been listening because she turned when he mentioned her and waved at them both and then kept on with her shopping.

"I have to visit my parents," he said, as if apologizing. "They've got visitation rights and want me to come every other weekend."

She'd hopped on her bike at the last minute to buy lettuce and ketchup for the burgers Calder was about to grill. She was taking too long. The charcoal would be ready in few minutes and he'd be waiting, flipping the burgers from side to side to keep them from burning.

She hadn't paid attention to what she looked like when she left the house, having jumped out of bed early that morning and thrown on her clothes from the day before so she could hurry and write down a melody running through her head.

She glanced down to see charcoal smears across her yellow tank top whose hem had come undone at the hip of her cutoffs. She smelled like dust from the road. She wasn't wearing a bra, and though her breasts were small, they were obvious, given the air-conditioning. Her feet were filthy inside her flip-flops, dusty as a coat of pollen. She realized she looked like this all the time.

"You've changed," she said, putting the focus on him. The bottlenose dolphin look was gone. So were the eyes with too much lid. Maybe his floppy, unkempt hair had caused him to look that way or maybe he'd grown into his features or maybe she'd just hated him so much that she imagined he looked that way. He didn't look that way now.

"So have you," he said, and she wondered if they were both thinking, *Him for the better, her for the worse*: then she saw him glance at her breasts.

The last time she saw him he was wearing his mother's apron, doing the dishes in the window, and she was laughing at him. She remembered thinking there was something sad about him, something out of place, even as she'd laughed. It seemed impossible now for her to picture him anywhere near that house and those people and the manure and skinned rabbits in the barn. The white trim around his blue boat shoes would get ruined out there, and she imagined his aunt so practical as to bring an old pair he could change into before stepping out of the car.

The white seam of a scar near the corner of his eyebrow crinkled when he smiled, and she was sure she was the one who'd put it there. She wondered to her own embarrassment if he thought of her every time he looked in the mirror. This was the boy who'd made the crude gestures, said the cruel things, the boy who'd deserved a branch upside his head; but all she saw in front of her now was the boy who'd saved her with his spit.

"You staying away from those bees?" he asked, and she felt as if she might faint into the lettuce. She took a breath to prevent the blood from pooling in her face.

"I carry a kit now," she said, though the truth was most days she forgot it at home; in fact she didn't have it with her then, only her wallet in her hand and she thought, *Wouldn't it be funny if one of those bees in the supermarket melons decided to sting me right now and Joshua here jumped into action and saved me all over again?*

"That's a good thing," he said.

"You ready, Joshua?" his aunt called down the aisle. She winked and her sharp eyebrow dipped and there was something in the way she called him Joshua that made Annie think of when she was little and her mother sometimes called her Annie Oakley for fun. She never called her that anymore. It was two in the afternoon and her mother hadn't gotten up yet, which in its own way was fine because when she was awake a deadening mood stifled the air and Calder ticked himself into a frenzy and her father was still dead and Annie's life seemed so unbearably *ugly* now in the face of freshly scrubbed *Joshua* and his Charlie's Angel.

She smiled nervously, imagining the two of them agreeing to pick up a gallon of milk on the way to the Pinckneys' and once they got to the farm the Angel would refuse to take any money and all through the visit she would wink from across the room and smile in secret every time Mr. Pinckney said something mean or stupid and Joshua would feel at ease knowing she wouldn't let anything bad happen to him, because maybe she really was a graduate of the police academy, and the two of them together, this team of capable people, were clearly nothing like the other Pinckneys. At the end of the day they would laugh all the way home to their tidy house on Tampa Bay, feeling closer and stronger and more accomplished for having proved there was nothing they couldn't handle together.

"I guess I've got to go," he said.

Annie couldn't think of what to say, and he didn't make any motion to leave.

So many things were supposed to be one way but instead were another, and she tried not to think about this and as she tried she felt herself start to get angry. "You take care, Joshua," she said, and touched the side of his arm like they were friends.

"Will do, Annie Walsh," he said, like a sweet country boy with a sweet country boy smile. "Will do," and then he reached out and shook her hand again and this time it was warm and they shook firmly and longer than most people shake hands, like they were sealing some deal that was long in the making. It wasn't until she returned home and was eating her crispy burger in silence with the secret of Joshua and that handshake, and still that melody from the morning running through her head, that she realized for the first time what was really meant when people said, "Let bygones be bygones." She rose from the table and closed herself up in her room and wrote her first good song, one that matched pitch perfect with the melody inside her head, and the whole experience made her softer around Calder and even her mother for the rest of the day.

TWENTY-ONE

O wen snores softly in Annie's bed. She's turned up the heat, and the moisture on the windows begins to drip. Streams of clear glass reveal slivers of snow, a collage of winter plastered around the room. Annie pulls a duvet from the pine armoire, and the smell of sawdust lifts into the air when she opens it across Owen's body. He doesn't stir, not even when the magnifying glass clangs against his phone in her pocket. The bedroom door closes with a small click behind her.

It can't be as simple as this. She blows dust off the neck of her guitar in the living room. It can't be as simple as him walking through the door. She plucks the low E-string, the sound so foreign, so familiar that even the furniture seems to take note.

She needs new strings.

But first things first. Dr. Collins lives nearby on several acres that Calder maintains. He's been the Walshes' family doctor for as long as Annie can remember, and she thinks nothing of asking him to check on Owen. "I can be there in an hour," he tells her on the phone. He even sounds a little eager. He's always had a crush on Annie's mother and maybe he thinks she's there. "No less than two," he says.

Within seconds she's out the door and in the car, driving cautiously to get a feel for the grip of the tires beneath her.

But by the time she passes the security guard it's clear that the Land Cruiser is more than capable of trekking through snow.

Fifteen minutes later she's standing in front of the shellacked pine counter in Willy's Guitar Shop and Willy's asking bronze or coated, light gauge or medium. Her nearly colorless reflection appears in the long mirror behind him. Her eyes feel bulbous and dry, her teeth unclean. She's wearing yesterday's clothes.

"Coated. Medium," she says, and takes a mint from the bowl on the counter, rolls it around her tongue, and crunches loudly, echoing the lively pulse beneath her skin.

"Good to see you," Willie says, and they both know what it is they're not saying and that's just fine. Willy is an old-fashioned Southern gentleman. He won't be asking questions. He won't be handing out advice.

Back home she peers through the crack in her bedroom door. Owen is right where she left him—snoring, arms thrown to his sides.

Light floods the large window in the living room, so still and tempered by the porch, silver and blue from the snow. Annie lifts her guitar by the neck and with a snap of her wrist spins the first peg to loosen the string. She clips it near the top with wire cutters, and the string launches wildly into the air from the release of so much pressure.

She remembers how the threading of metal on metal, like nails on a chalkboard, always made Owen's teeth ache. She zips the string through the eye without care, winds it around the twisting peg, and moves on to the next.

When she's finished tuning the new strings she lifts the curvy underside of the guitar into her lap. There's no question that she's missed its rich palette of sound, the color and full-ness, the emotion that lasts long after words have inevitably failed. But she's also missed the weight of it, the smell of wood and sweat and metal on her fingers. So much like a lover, she's missed the feel of it in her arms.

A knock at the door jolts her back into the room. She places the guitar on the stand.

Dr. Collins enters in a flurry of cheer. He immediately wraps her against his overcoat. "Where's the patient, Annie Lou?" Her middle name is Louise, and he's called her Annie Lou for as long as she can remember. The familiar rasp of his voice, the smell of his aftershave reminds her of childhood fevers, of tonsillitis, the bee sting in the grove.

She shows him to the bedroom and sits opposite on the bed as he opens Owen's jacket and shirt. He places a stethoscope to his chest. Owen wakes with a groggy hello. He even smiles and pats Annie's hand before drifting away again. They roll him onto his side facing Annie so Dr. Collins can listen to his back. Owen's shirt falls all the way open and Annie is shocked at just how thin he's become.

"He's likely got walking pneumonia," Dr. Collins says, listening to points on his back. "Can you take a deep breath for me, Owen?"

Owen opens his eyes and draws in a breath that makes him cough.

"Again."

Another cough and more listening to points on his back, and Dr. Collins finally draws the stethoscope from his ears. "It's not as bad as it sounds, but he ought to get an x-ray if he doesn't start improving with antibiotics." Owen helps to button his own shirt and there's a quick moment of recognition of his wedding band. The doctor's eyes lock onto Annie's. She glances down and rubs her empty finger before catching herself.

He digs through his bag on the floor and then hands her a bottle of pills. "I figured he might need these. Make sure he takes every last one. It doesn't look like he's been taking care of himself."

Dr. Collins gathers his things and they meet at the front door. "I think the man's exhausted more than anything," he says.

He's lost sleep over what he's done, Annie thinks. Lost his appetite, maybe even a little of his mind. This whole time she's imagined him healthy and happy. Tanned and carefree. And all this time he's been nothing more than a rope fraying through his young wife's hands.

"Can I get you something? Some coffee? Tea?"

"No, thank you. I've got some last-minute shopping to do."

"Thank you so much for doing this."

"It's the least I could do." He buttons his jacket. "Well. Let's not ignore the elephant in the room here, Annie Lou. How the hell did Calder get mixed up with that murder?"

She can still see Calder as a seven-year-old boy, sitting on the table in Dr. Collins's office. Along his jaw, a giant knot with a one-inch gash. A batter lost his grip on the bat while Calder was playing catcher. Doctor Collins leaned in to take a closer look. "How the hell did you get mixed up in something like this?" he asked.

"Well," Calder said in all seriousness, "people don't always have good sense."

Annie explains as best she can that it's true what the papers are saying. Calder was in fact seeing the man's wife. "So in answer to your question—apparently *love* is how he got mixed up in this."

"That boy could no more harm a flea on a pig than kill a man."

"And they'll see that. It'll all be over soon," she says, and maybe it's the fact that he's a doctor, a man who shows up to fix them when they're broken, or the fact that Owen is right there on the other side of the wall and he's going to be fine, or the simple fact that her guitar has new strings. Whatever the reason, she feels a wave of reassurance for the first time since Calder's arrest.

"How about your mother?" he asks. "How's she holding up?"

"You sure I can't get you some tea?"

"No, thank you ma'am. I've got to get going." He rests his hand on the doorknob.

"She's fine, I guess. She's stronger than she used to be."

He nods several times, pulls in a deep breath, and Annie can practically see the sticky details of her family's past spinning through his head. He glances around the room. "Where's Detour?"

No sooner does she tell him than his arms are wrapped around her again. She gives him one final squeeze and their conversation comes to an end with hopes of a Merry Christmas anyway. "At least we have the snow," she says before remembering the acres of orange and lemon trees Calder planted on his land.

She watches the falling snow as he drives away, and then she closes the door and stands listening to the silence. Even after Owen left her there'd still been the jangle of Detour's tags when he scratched his ears, his claws clicking across the wood floors, the old moans of his dreams.

TWENTY-TWO

Six months after Annie saw Joshua in Lukeman's he appeared on her front porch. In place of the gallon of milk was a poinsettia. It was two days before Christmas. Annie had just turned sixteen.

"Merry Christmas," he said.

He wore a jean jacket and his hair was slightly longer than the time before. His freckles were pale without the summer sun. He was taller and smelled even better than fabric softener. She imagined his aunt giving him the early gift of aftershave to cancel out the odor of the other Pinckneys in the room.

He thrust the poinsettia into her arms. She didn't know what to say. She couldn't think. The red cellophane embarrassed her when it filled the silence with a crunch.

His aunt waited in the car in the driveway. She wore a red scarf and looked even more like Sabrina Duncan. Charlie's Angel. Ready at the wheel. She waved against the windshield. Annie waved back. The Beatles played loudly on the stereo inside the car.

"*Sergeant Pepper's Lonely Hearts Club Band*," Annie said.

"She loves the Beatles."

"Not a bad thing."

"No." He smiled. "You listen to a lot of music?"

"All the time."

"You play anything?"

"Guitar."

He looked surprised. Maybe he was expecting her to say the flute. "Electric?" he asked.

She laughed. "Acoustic. I don't think I could even write a song for an electric guitar."

"You write songs, too?"

"A little." Though the truth was she hardly did much else.

Calder suddenly towered at her shoulder. This time of year the postman knocked on the door and handed them gifts from their mother's relatives up north. Nail kits and bubble baths for Annie, money clips and pocket flashlights for Calder. He'd been expecting another Christmas box of things they'd never use, and here was a teenage boy, and Annie, holding a poinsettia.

Joshua took a step back and nodded a small greeting toward Calder. "Merry Christmas," he said.

Annie looked down at the velvety red leaves. Heat swelled beneath her skin. "You remember Josh Pinckney?" she said, breaking into a sweat. Her tongue stuck to the roof of her mouth. "He goes by Joshua now." The recognition slowly spread across Calder's face, and she could tell he was trying to keep still.

Calder was taller than Joshua but nearly the same size across the chest, which didn't say a whole lot for either one of them.

"Oh," Calder said. "Nice." He looked at Joshua's aunt in the car, and then he turned for the kitchen and Annie knew it was so he could blink his eyes in private.

Joshua glanced at the yard while his aunt busied herself digging in her purse on the dash. Annie didn't know what was expected of her. She didn't understand why he was there.

She studied her own yard, overgrown and littered with tree debris. She gazed at the woods beyond and cleared her throat. Joshua did the same. The sky felt high and empty. Cold and clear and blue.

"So. How's it going?" she finally asked.

"Good. I was just, we stopped on the way and picked up a few of these." He motioned to the poinsettia. "I thought I'd just drop one by." He nodded continuously and she nodded with him.

He glanced at his aunt, and she gave him an apologetic smile and tapped her watch.

"I can't stay." He leaned into her ear. For a second she thought he was going to kiss her. She had never been kissed. She froze with fear. "There's a number tucked inside the cellophane," he whispered, and put his hand across hers on the poinsettia. He left it there long enough for her to consider when the last time was that someone had touched her. It must have been years but it seemed like never since she'd felt something so tender. He drew his hand away, and cold air swept against the shape where it'd been. He straightened up and said, "I'll be a senior in the fall."

"Nice. You're almost done then."

"I got into a private school upstate. That's where I'll be going," he said, and it suddenly felt as if she'd been waiting all this time for him to show up here, although she hadn't really thought of him much at all; but just then it seemed as if she'd been thinking on him every day, and now that he was finally here he'd only come to tell her he was going away. "Anyway. I thought maybe we could talk sometime on the phone. If you want." She squeezed the poinsettia against her chest and thought of how ugly he'd once been. She thought of how it would really be something if they could all transform themselves the way he had.

"Thank you," she said.

"So you'll call?"

"OK."

She waited for the car to disappear before she shut the door and set the plant on the kitchen table. Then she reached inside the cellophane and found the small fold of paper.

"What the hell was he doing here?" Calder asked as he walked into the room.

She squeezed the paper inside her fist. "I don't know."

"How'd you even know it was him? He looks completely different. He looks normal."

"I saw him last summer at Lukeman's. His folks have visitation rights and want to see him every other weekend." Those were Joshua's words from six months ago, and she felt a small thrill at having them inside her mouth.

"How come you never said anything?"

"I didn't think it was important."

"You didn't want me to know."

"Don't be silly. Why wouldn't I want you to know?"

"I saw the way you two were looking at each other, Annie. For God's sake, he's still Josh Pinckney no matter what he looks like or what he calls himself or who he's living with. Did you forget all the hell he put us through?"

For all the kindness Calder had once shown the Pinckneys in the face of their cruelty, he now showed an equal amount of disdain toward kindness.

But no one could have been more shocked than Annie at what was happening. A warm excitement still thrashed inside her body at his presence on the porch, at having had him so close to the place she ate and slept and played music. "Did you forget that he saved my life?"

Calder tightened his jaw. "Did you forget that you tried to kill him?"

She snatched up the poinsettia and took it to her room and set it on her dresser where she could see it from her bed. She wanted so badly in that moment to have her mother back. To tell her how Joshua had changed. How he'd touched her hand and ever since her stomach wouldn't stop twisting. The heat in her face seemed as if it'd never cool.

She pushed back against her pillows and took a deep breath and opened the piece of paper to find the moisture in the cellophane had smeared the ink and the last two numbers had disappeared.

TWENTY-THREE

Annie doesn't sleep with him. It doesn't seem right. He's hardly been awake in all the hours he's been here, and she feels it would be taking advantage just to crawl in next to him, if only to watch him sleep. Instead she lies awake most of the night in the guest room listening to him snore and cough in her bed down the hall. She gets up several times to help him drink water and broth and take another pill, and then she parts the curtains in the guest room and watches the snow fall in the dark. Each time she looks for Detour on the floor, and each time she remembers why he's not there, and that Owen is here instead, and it's through this revolving door that she swings until the sun rises behind another front of snow clouds.

It's Christmas Eve. She leaves the house before Owen wakes, to buy a small balsam fir, no taller than herself, from John Smiley, whose lot is next to his house with a year-round sign that reads, *Smiley's Tree Lot, Come Get It*. The streets are mostly deserted. It snowed all night and there must be four inches on the ground. She doesn't know for sure. She doesn't want to listen to all the talk on the radio about the damage and loss of the crops.

She lugs the tree inside and wrestles it into the stand in the corner near the window where she hides its lopsided gap against the wall. She lights a fire, pulls her hair into a ponytail, and brings in the decorations from the garage. She is nearly done decorating the tree when she hears him stirring in the bedroom.

"How are you feeling?" she asks from the bedroom doorway. He's a stranger, and yet more familiar than anyone she knows.

The room smells stale from his coughs, his clothes. He sits on the side of the bed rubbing his bloodshot eyes, and then he looks at her with a seriousness that causes the huge smile on her face to shrink.

"Better. I think. What time is it?"

"Almost noon."

"Shit. I need to make a call." He doesn't need to say to whom.

"Well. You know where the phone is," she says, feeling unsteady, feeling the need to run into the living room and pick up her guitar and hold it against her like a child caught in a custody fight. "There's coffee in the kitchen," she says.

In the living room she snatches up the last few ornaments, places them on the tree without care, and drags the empty box to the front porch. The sight of snow loosens her shoulders and she steps back inside to the smell of pine and burning maple logs and fresh coffee. She plugs in the white tree lights, and they reflect the silvery cast of the needles and it *feels* like Christmas. She pours herself another coffee and sits on the floor in front of the fire. She brushes her hand back and forth through Detour's loose fur in the rug.

Then she hears Owen yelling on the phone. She can't make out what he says, only coughing and a muffled *yes* and *so do I, yes, yes, yes.*

He hangs up and goes into the bathroom and she hears the shower run and his bare feet skid against the tub when he turns around in there; and after a while the water shuts off and the medicine cabinet opens and he must have found the packet of new toothbrushes because there's the familiar sound of him brushing his teeth. He taps it on the side of the porcelain when he's finished and she hears it land in the holder on the sink. The medicine cabinet opens again, and next she hears him gargle and cough and spit and the water running and then it's off again.

She's collected a mouse-size clump of Detour's fur from the rug by the time he comes into the kitchen across from her in his rumpled clothes. He pours himself coffee. It can't possibly taste good after brushing and gargling, she thinks, but those thoughts are as thin as the skin of a peach. *What did she say? What does she want? What are you doing here?*

He holds his mug and squints into the living room at the tree and then the fire. He doesn't look at her.

"I just went out and got the tree from Smiley. Not bad for five bucks. It'll probably be the only sale of the day, too. Look outside."

He cleans the sleep from the corners of his eyes and peers through the oval glass in the door. "Jesus. Tess wasn't kidding about the snow."

Tess. Annie squeezes the fur inside her hand.

He drinks his coffee and smacks his lips and walks into the living room. "How does the Land Cruiser handle in it?"

"Fine," she says, passing him on her way into the kitchen with her cup and a fist full of fur, which she throws into the trash beneath the sink. She sets her cup down and turns around and leans into the counter with crossed arms. "What are you doing here?"

He sits on the sofa and stares at the tree. The lights reflect in his face and mug, and then his back gets taller when he glimpses her guitar on the stand. "How are the new songs coming?" He coughs but it doesn't sound half as bad as yesterday. He still doesn't look at her.

She lifts her cup and sets it back down without drinking. "I asked you a question."

He stares into the fire. "There's a million reasons and none at all for me being here, Annie."

"Let's start with the first."

"Calder," he says without hesitation, and she feels the coffee in her stomach slide to a place she didn't know was there.

"Calder," she repeats.

"Yes." He glances back at the hallway as if thinking of the phone and *Tess*, still fresh in his ear, his head, his heart.

"Look at me." She walks toward him.

The muscles in his jaw tighten. He doesn't turn from the fire.

She kneels on the floor in front of his knees and places her hand on his arm. The fire and tree lights reflect in the red of his eyes.

"Look at me and tell me why you're here."

"I never wanted to leave."

"I didn't ask you that."

"I felt like I had no choice."

"You act like I threw you out."

"That's not what I mean."

"What then? Look at me."

"It's complicated."

"You're making it complicated."

"No, Annie. It's complicated. Trust me."

"Why should I trust you about anything?"

He finally meets her eyes.

"Why are you here?"

He leans into the sofa and blows air from his lips. Then he bends forward with elbows on knees until his face is only inches from hers. He's about to say something, then seems to think better of it and says something else. "I made a mistake." He sets his mug on the coffee table and touches her face with his warm hand.

"I shouldn't be here," he says, and she thinks, *That's* your mistake? *Coming here?* And then he leans all the way toward her and kisses her softly on the cheek. His lips don't leave and she slides hers toward his, wanting nothing more than to feel him on her mouth. "I don't want you to get sick," he whispers and turns slightly away and squeezes her hair and works his fingers up the back of her head, removing her hair band so that her hair falls free. He always liked her hair down. "Let it go," he'd say and she'd let it whip her eyes raw in an ocean breeze just to see what she could of his smile, those white, sexy-crooked teeth, his full lips edging between her choppy strings of hair.

So many pleasures rush in that she couldn't stop herself if she tried. And yet Tess is there like a worm, twisting inside. Annie wants to tell her she deserves this for snatching him away. She deserves every little detail of what is happening here, whispered in her ear for the rest of her life.

There's no stopping something this long in the coming, and she kisses his face and draws in the smell of him and feels her whole body pull him into her as if on its own. He comes down off the sofa and begins unbuttoning her shirt, and even though she's waited all these months for this day to come she can't wait a moment longer and so she helps him with the buttons and her jeans and before she knows it they are stripped of clothes and his eyes are taking in every part of her. He's no longer the stranger on the bed.

She knows him so well. Well enough to see a look seize his eyes. A look so slight it would have gone unnoticed by someone else, but not her. Something has shifted. And the longer they gaze at one another, the more she feels a bitterness inside her chest. She wants to believe that all the waiting hasn't changed the way she feels about him, that all the months spent wanting what she finally has only makes it that much sweeter. But what about the humiliation? What about the pain? How could he have left her the way he did? Why on earth has she let him back in? The heat from the fire intensifies against her shoulder and her temples sweat and she's filled with an unbearable urge to slap him in the face.

And then she does.

It cracks like the sound of fire and he rears back, looking more hurt than angry. Then he takes her wrists and holds them on the floor next to her head. She thinks he will hit her, too, and she wants to say, "Go ahead, you son of a bitch," but then he buries his face in her neck and she's pretty sure he's crying when he slides between her legs.

The tree sparkles behind them and the snow falls all around them and she hears herself scream out so soon and he moans a bit louder and then breathes heavily against her throat as she breathes into his ear and it's over and the longer they lie there with their skin moist and sticking to one another, the more he starts to feel like a stranger again.

TWENTY-FOUR

Annie needed to find him. She called information for a Pinckney listing in the Tampa area but there was no listing, and she assumed Joshua's aunt had changed her name but then she realized his aunt probably wasn't a Pinckney at all, of course she wasn't, but instead his mother's sister. She thought of dialing variations on the last two numbers that'd been smeared away, but she knew enough to know the possible combinations were greater than one would think for just two numbers, and she gave up before she even got started.

She floundered for days, consumed by distraction—the memory of his hand lifting away, the dream that was so *real* where they kissed before he drove off in his own car. She'd paced to and from her mother's bedroom door, wanting so badly to knock, to pull her out, to ask her about swimming in a sea of strange feelings.

One week after Joshua had stood on her porch with the poinsettia, she finally got up the nerve to call the Pinckneys.

Gabe answered and she nearly hung up.

"Who is this?" he asked when she didn't say anything.

"I'm looking for Joshua. I know he doesn't live there, but I was wondering if you could give me his number in Tampa."

"Who *is* this?"

"Rebecca."

"Rebecca who?"

"Washington," she said. Rebecca was a quiet girl from school who was in a lot of Annie's classes, but she didn't know Rebecca any more than she assumed anyone else did, including Gabe.

"Hey, *Rebecca*," Gabe said. "I miss seeing that little mole on your back right above your underwear."

Annie had a mole just above her underwear. Not only did he know it was her on the phone but she realized with a sick feeling that the kids in school must have seen the mole every time she leaned forward on her desk, and she was doubly horrified.

"Come on, Annie. What'd you do? Lose the number he gave you?"

She sucked in a mouthful of air and slammed the phone down and sat on her bed staring at the poinsettia she'd made sure to water every day since Joshua gave it to her. The thought of him talking about her to Gabe made her sick to her stomach. Was he playing some game? Was this all a trick to get back at her, finally, for the beating she'd given them? Had he kept her alive that day just so he could hurt her in some other way?

She stomped outside with the poinsettia and flung it in the garbage can. Layers of anger and hurt caved in her chest. She got so worked up that the smell coming out of the can was all it took for her to lean forward and lose the fish sticks she'd eaten for dinner. Then the smell of *that* caused everything in her to escape, and she was no better than her mother on a binge, puking till it came out green. She spit the taste from her mouth and kicked dirt over the mess to hide it from possums and coons. When she turned to come back inside Calder was watching from the kitchen window, and by the time she reached the door he was there.

"You all right?"

"I was wrong about him," she said. "You were right, I was wrong."

"Wrong about who?"

"Joshua."

"What did he do?"

"He's a Pinckney," she said, and felt herself slowly rise above it all.

She brushed her teeth and closed herself up in her room and put everything she had into her guitar. For the first time in her life she felt the scope of what she knew and loved about music, and it began to feel limitless.

* * *

Within days Joshua Pinckney was slipping his hand in her pants, and every time he went away she put her own there and wished it were his.

It began the Saturday after her conversation with Gabe. Joshua got a driver's license just like in her dream. He borrowed his aunt's car and made the two-hour drive to visit Annie.

She slammed the door in his face.

He rang the bell and Calder opened it back even when Annie asked him not to. "Stay the hell away from my sister, Joshua Pinckney," Calder said, and she felt good about him being able to say that.

Then she heard Joshua around the corner from where she stood. "I'm sorry. Did I do something wrong?"

"We don't have enough time to go over all the things you've done wrong," Calder said.

"I just want to talk to Annie."

"Well, that's not going to happen."

It was quiet and Annie assumed Joshua was staring Calder down and she suddenly feared they would break into a fight over her; and so she stepped out from the corner and said, "I don't think we have anything to talk about"; and the breeze lifted his aftershave to her nose and she'd meant for everything to end right there, to close the door and walk away but she stood a second too long staring at his mouth on the verge of speaking. He licked his lips and swallowed, and when she looked into his eyes it felt like they were seeing all the way inside her to the place that ached.

"What did Gabe say to you?" he asked.

"What do you want with me?"

"Gabe's an idiot. If he said something that hurt you, tell me."

"It's got nothing to do with Gabe," Calder said. "My sister wants you to leave."

"Do you?" Joshua asked Annie.

"Yes." She held the corner of her bottom lip between her teeth and darted her eyes toward the car.

"I'm sorry." He hesitated, looked around as if confused.

"Leave," Calder said.

Joshua glanced from Annie to Calder. "All right." He wasn't angry. "I'll go." He started to leave and then he stopped and said, "Listen, Calder. I just want to say one thing. I don't expect you to forgive me for all the stupid things I used to do. I didn't understand things the way I understand them now. I'm not making excuses. I'm just saying I know that I was cruel and not a little dense and I made both your lives miserable and I'm sorry as a person can be for that."

More than anything it was embarrassing. He was acting like a grown-up. Annie didn't know what to say.

"My life was a living hell back then," Joshua continued. "It's changed now, but back then I didn't know any better than to take it out on you two, and I'll have to live with having been that sorry bastard, no better than my own father, for as long as I live."

It was quiet for too long. Just when Annie couldn't stand it any longer, Calder held out his hand and shook Joshua's the way Joshua had shaken Annie's in Lukeman's that day.

Annie was sure they were all thinking the same thing— Annie's and Calder's lives were now the ones that had become the living hell. They'd become the angry kids, the dirty kids, the suspicious kids, kids angry at a world that'd left them behind.

The handshake dissolved without words, and Joshua gave a curt smile but it wasn't directed at Annie. He turned and headed for the car. Calder walked off into the house, and Annie stood abandoned in the doorway.

By the time Joshua opened the car door she was at his side.

"Is this a game?" she asked.

He let go of the car door and inched close enough for her to see the honey-colored tips of his lashes.

"I just want to hear it from you," she said. "That this isn't some kind of game, your coming around like this."

His Adam's apple bobbed. "I understand. OK. I don't blame you for asking that." He blushed and it caused her stomach to stir.

"After everything I've done I don't expect you to believe me. I mean, after everything *you've* done I don't exactly understand it either," he said, scratching the scar near his eye. "But

I like you, Annie Walsh. I like you a lot. That's why I'm here. That's why I gave you my number and waited every day for you to call."

"There was water in the plant. The number got smeared away."

He slapped his forehead and laughed.

"Since when have you liked me?"

The smile slowly disappeared from his face. "Since the day in the grove."

"Oh," she said. "Oh," as he leaned in and kissed her gently on the mouth. He let go, slightly, and then he kissed her again with more intention. She had no idea that a kiss could travel throughout a whole body like that. The tip of his tongue found hers and hers found his and she leaned into him for support, but touching only made it feel more like she was falling. *Falling off the edge of the world.*

They stopped to catch a breath, and he closed the car door, and she searched the windows of the house for Calder or her mother and felt a warm thrill at finding neither.

They held hands through the loblolly pines that filled the whole forest with the scent of gin. There were turkeys in the scrub and sometimes hunters who shot them, and there were bobcats and cackling birds so big they shook the branches when they lifted into flight, but they saw none of these things. Annie showed him where she often sat and played her guitar inside a natural cove created between the scrub. They sat down and he told her why he used to run away, about his father and the beatings. She told him about her own father, how she missed him more as time went by, and then her mother disappearing in her own way and how Annie felt like a runaway herself, taking care of everything on her own. He said when he was younger he used to dream about razing his whole farm to the ground and starting over with a place that was so clear and real inside his head that he could still see the seams of wooden beams laced together in the corners. He said he still thought a lot about building things from the ground up, and she said that was exactly how she felt about music, making something out of nothing at all.

"That reminds me," he said. "I brought you something."

"It's not another poinsettia, is it?"

He grinned and reached into his pocket and pulled out a pen. It was a real pen, shiny and silver with a cap that made a pleasing click when he snapped it open to show her the sleek black tip inside.

"It's for writing your songs."

The sun slanted through the trees as if all of nature was shining a light on them, and it was there on the soft bed of needles, swallowed in the scent of gin, that everything good she'd lost came flooding back to her in waves.

TWENTY-FIVE

When Calder picks up the phone and the screen comes on, the face looking back at him is familiar; but it still takes a moment to sink in, partly because the face has aged over the decades since he's last seen it, but mostly because it's so out of context. He can find no reason in the short span of time he has to think for why Joshua Pinckney should be holding that phone to his ear and smiling that unassuming smile of his through this screen.

"Calder?"

The Haldol doesn't stop Calder's shoulder from pumping, or his body from shooting up behind his chair. He grips the chair back and draws in a heavy breath. Ms. Thompson has warned him to stay cool. He takes another breath and nods his head and lowers himself back into the chair. "What the hell," he says into the phone.

"Believe me, I'm as surprised to be sitting here as you are."

Calder's eyes get carried away in a fit of blinking, and suddenly he hears Joshua from back in the days when he was still Josh. *You jerking around like that cause you're a retard or what?*

"Well," Joshua says. "You mind if we talk a little?"

Calder blinks without end.

"I want to talk to you. Do you mind?"

"Yes. No. I don't know."

Joshua turns away. He turns back. "It's important."

Calder bangs his knees together to keep his eyes still. He has trouble looking Joshua in the eye and so he focuses on his expensive-looking shirt, a dress shirt, the color of sage. Small pearly buttons shine beneath the lights. Calder finally glances up into his face. There's no question that he's changed. When Calder describes him to Annie he'll say that it's more of a feeling than a look. An air coming off. You get the feeling he's a traveled man. A man who's been through plenty and come out the other side. "I guess I couldn't hardly let you leave at this point without finding out why you're here," Calder says.

Joshua grins. "How are you, Calder?"

Calder laughs. "Everyone that comes here asks me that. You all know the answer but you ask it anyway. I'm fine. Just fine."

"Well."

"For a man who's about to be put to death for something he didn't do. That's the part I usually don't say."

"You're getting a little ahead of yourself. They haven't even had a trial yet."

"No. But I don't see them out arresting anybody else."

Joshua looks as if he's just been struck with an ice cream headache.

"You know, your brother is part of the reason I'm in here. He felt the need to exaggerate what I'd told him about Magnus."

"I know. That's why I came. One of the reasons I came."

Seeing Joshua causes the grit of the place, the gray walls and stale odors to rise up into Calder's face. Who would have thought there'd come a day when Calder would be behind bars and his visitor, a clean-cut Pinckney? He feels the same kind of mixed-up shame and gratitude he felt twenty-four years ago when Joshua apologized to him on the front porch.

"We need to talk," Joshua says, and stares as if the rest will come through his eyes.

Calder notices for the first time that Joshua's accent has changed. "Where are you living these days? You don't sound like a Pinckney anymore."

"I'll take that as a compliment."

"Feel free."

"I've been all over, but right now I'm back here."

"All over, like where?"

"The world. The last place was out West, Seattle."

"I hear it rains like hell out there."

"In winter, yeah," he says a little defensively, though Calder can't think of a reason why he should. "I don't know if you know this but it's snowing outside right now. In the Sunshine State. We've got several inches on the ground."

Calder does know. He's seen it from the small window in his cell and heard the guards talking about how their trucks handled on the way to work. "Merry Christmas," Calder says. "Who'd have ever thought?"

Joshua doesn't crack a smile. "Like I said, I need to talk to you about Gabe."

"Shoot."

"He has a big mouth."

"I know you didn't come here to tell me what I already know."

"Why'd you ever give him a job, Calder?"

"I felt sorry for him. I gave you another chance. I figured I could give him one, too."

"He's not like me."

"You married?"

"What? No. I was. It only lasted a year. Why?"

"Just making conversation. Never mind. Am I going to have to pull it out of you or are you going to tell me what it is you've come to say?"

"Gabe was protecting me, Calder. That's why he exaggerated what you told him about Magnus."

"Protecting you from what?"

Joshua clamps his mouth shut. The muscles in his jaw flex and release. "I don't know if I should say it right here, right now. I need to meet with your lawyer. In fact, I need to get one of my own."

Calder feels the weight of something mysterious bearing down on him. It's the mud on Annie's hand all over again. He can't follow what's happening; he only knows deep down that it's bad. Really, really bad. "What'd you do?"

"I didn't do anything," Joshua whispers. "But I guarantee it's not going to make you feel a whole lot better when I tell you who did."

TWENTY-SIX

It was late spring and blood lilies bloomed along the south side of the house where Annie waited every weekend to catch the first glimpse of Joshua's little red car coming down Lakeview Drive, a cloud of dust trailing behind as he sped above the limit. The thought of him going away in the fall to a private school in Tallahassee became the weight behind every tear, every laugh, every hungry, greedy kiss. It'd be too far for him to visit on weekends. The best they could do would be holidays—Thanksgiving, Christmas, and Easter when he came home to his aunt in Tampa. Three times total inside a whole school year.

Annie never asked him not to go, as badly as she wished he'd stay. She knew enough to know that this school was the best chance he had of shaping a life for himself. It would make all the difference where college was concerned considering his earlier years of schooling were worse than none at all when you saw how it looked on paper. He wanted to go to college as badly as she wanted to play music.

The woods were now full of mosquitoes leaving knots the size of grapes on their skin, so they traded the woods for long drives in the air-conditioned car. When traffic was light they parked on small service roads along Highway 217 and groped in a clumsy frenzy, kissing until their lips were red and tender.

One time they went to Disney World and couldn't stop kissing, even with families swarming in packs and galloping costumed characters in between. They made fun of people standing in lines, though they stood in a few themselves, indoors where it was cool and dark and they could rub against each other unnoticed in the crowd. They rode the Pirates of the Caribbean twice. The line was long and so was the ride and they kissed until Annie thought she would burst with longing.

When they came out the second time, a father was bent over jerking the arm of his blond-headed son near the exit. The boy's orange push-pop melted down his arm as he held it up into the sun, away from his father. "I'm sick and tired of this bullshit," the man growled through his teeth. Then he got down in the boy's face. "I should have never brought you here in the first place, you little shit."

Everyone stopped to stare. A clean-cut man with four kids scattered around his legs stepped forward and gently told the man to take it easy. Joshua squeezed Annie's hand. His back stiffened, and his free hand slowly curled into a fist. The angry father told the man to mind his own business and dragged his son away by the hand. The crowd dissolved, but the agonized expression on Joshua's face remained.

The ride home was quiet. Joshua asked if she wouldn't mind leaving the radio off, and Annie rode with her head against the window. It wasn't until they reached the driveway that she sat up and quickly caught her breath to speak.

Uncle Calder's truck was parked in a crooked skid near the porch. He hadn't been to their house in years. Annie immediately thought the worst. Something terrible had happened to her mother.

She found Uncle Calder standing with his back pressed into her mother's closed bedroom door, his chin dropped, his chest heaving with anger and tears. When he looked up he cried even harder at how Annie had grown. "I wouldn't have recognized you on the street," he said, and slid to the floor where he wept some more. It was clear he'd been drinking.

Calder crouched next to him. "There's some fresh coffee in the kitchen. Why don't we go in there and have a cup?"

"I just want her back," Uncle Calder said. He said it again, and then he screamed until his face grew purple. "He's been gone for four fucking years, Miriam!" He hammered his fist into the door.

"What's going on?" Annie shouted. Joshua took hold of her hand, a fresh wave of anguish in his eyes. "Do you want me to go?" he whispered.

"No. Please stay."

Her mother wasn't saying anything from inside the bedroom.

"Mom?" Annie yelled.

"Go away. All of you!" she said.

Calder took Annie by the elbow and motioned for Joshua to follow him into the kitchen.

They stood around the table for a moment until Calder finally spoke through all the blinking.

"He's in love with her," he whispered. "It's not just because he's drunk. He told her there had been nothing wrong with loving two men at the same time. He said Kearney would have wanted them to be happy."

Annie took a seat at the table. The weight of her hips sank into the wood. Joshua slid into the chair next to her. Uncle Calder continued to sob down the hall. "Please, Miriam," he cried. "It's not fair. Stop punishing me like this. We've all been punished enough."

"My God," Annie said, looking at Calder. His eyes skipped between her and Joshua.

"They had an affair," Calder said.

Annie covered her eyes. Joshua rubbed her back.

"Before Mom locked herself in her room she screamed at him to go away. She said it was all their fault that Daddy was gone. She called it punishment for doing what they did behind his back."

Annie's mouth had fallen open. She closed it, waited for him to finish.

"From the way they were talking it must have gone on the entire time she was married to Daddy."

Annie stood without thinking, without any real awareness of what she was doing, only of the heat burning in her hands and eyes. She ran down the hall and banged on her mother's door above Uncle Calder's head. She tried the knob but it was locked. "Open the door!" she screamed. Uncle Calder wept with his head down. He looked up and said, "No, squirt. Please. Leave her alone."

Her mother wailed the same way she'd done the day Annie's father died.

Annie finally understood why her mother hadn't wanted Uncle Calder in their house. "Why did you come here? Get out!" Annie screamed. "Get out of our house."

Joshua and Calder froze in the hall behind her. Only Calder's eyes blinked.

Uncle Calder clambered to his feet and stumbled past the boys. He patted Calder's shoulder and Calder laid his hand atop his uncle's as he passed.

"He can't drive home like that," Joshua said.

"He's not staying here," Annie said.

"I can give him a ride."

Annie nodded, but she was already back to thinking of Joshua leaving her in the fall, and in that moment she didn't want him near her, she didn't want to be so attached. She closed herself up in the bathroom, put the toilet seat down, and sat there, numb.

Then all the feelings caught up with her at once. She screamed into a bath towel that clearly needed to be washed. The whole bathroom needed to be cleaned. She could smell the mold from the tub as she choked back tears.

Calder rapped lightly on the door and came in and sat on the edge of the tub, facing her. They stared at the pink floor mat, brown from their dusty summer feet.

"Joshua took him home," Calder finally said. "I told him I'd stay here with you."

Annie nodded at the mat. She was pleased that Calder and Joshua got along. They seemed to genuinely like one another, and as she sat there thinking about that she felt a little better knowing how far people could come, how much they could change for the better.

Her mother never did come out of her room.

Calder and Annie waited for Joshua in the steely light of the television set. Back-to-back episodes of *M.A.S.H.* flickered into the otherwise murky den.

When he finally returned he appeared exhausted, emotionally and physically, looking around the kitchen as if for his bearings. He still had to drive two hours to get home.

All the feelings she'd had of non-attachment disappeared. She threw her arms around his neck and kissed him, something she'd never done in front of Calder. From the corner of her eye she saw Calder turn away. She stepped back from Joshua. "How'd it go?"

"I helped him to his bed and took off his shoes. He was out by the time I shut the door. Does he always drink like that?"

Annie and Calder looked at one another. They didn't know. They hadn't the slightest idea about anything.

Weeks later their mother announced that they were going to start visiting Uncle Calder on the weekends, the same way she'd announced they had to go to church years before. And just like church, only Annie and Calder would be doing the visiting. It was as if her mother and uncle had just gotten divorced.

TWENTY-SEVEN

They rustle awkwardly into their clothes.

"Still snowing," Owen says.

"Yes." Annie closes the final button on her blouse. She shakes her hair behind her shoulders and scours the floor for her hair band.

They end up at the kitchen table, a splotch of red still visible on Owen's cheek.

He opens his mouth and scratches his whiskers. He slides his hand across the table toward her then pulls back. Annie crosses her arms and makes a point of saying nothing. She will wait until he fills the silence with his version of the truth.

He rises from the table and starts another pot of coffee. "Do you mind?"

"Not at all."

He waits at the counter, watching the snow through the kitchen window. Annie watches too. The live oak appears drawn inside all the white. The deep brown lines of bark like shadows, as if the snow-covered branches were the living thing.

When the coffee is done Owen fills a cup and slides it toward Annie.

"I don't know if I can stay," he says, and the air itself seems to break in two.

Annie's throat feels brittle. She's overcome with a sudden thirst. She stops herself from swallowing the hot coffee in gulps. "Yes, well. No one asked you to."

"That's true, I just thought—"

"What? You thought what?"

"Annie."

"Say it."

"I'm about to become a father."

The room turns into a kind of melting fun house, the tree lights swirling in a liquidy stream in the corner of one eye, the white tree coiling upward in the other, until she blinks away the moisture gathering against her will. For a moment she's paralyzed, even her mouth, because there's plenty to say to this, a million possibilities to choose from, but not one of them forms a word.

"I'm sorry," he says, and it isn't until he lets go of her arm that she realizes he was touching her.

Something has died in the center of her, hollowed out and blown away like powdery chalk. She starts to say his name but can't. It's no longer in the place she keeps it. She looks intently into his eyes, trying to imagine the two of them in the future. It's possible to get past this. They could make this work. She will be a stepmother and together they'll help raise this child, not unlike the one they might have raised of their own. But she cannot see any of it.

"Congratulations," she hears her voice say. "You must be thrilled."

"I tried to tell you earlier. It's complicated. I didn't plan this." He puts his hands on his hips and sighs as if he's about to tackle a big project. "This isn't easy. I mean, a baby, a girl, she doesn't deserve—"

"A girl."

"Tess said she was on the pill. Maybe she was. Those things happen."

"Yes."

"The truth is I always imagined it happening with you and I just, I have such mixed feelings."

"You need to go home."

"Annie."

"I'll get the security guys to pick up a can of gas for you. I'll make you a sandwich for the trip."

"Please. Just wait."

"I want you out of here."

"I understand. I really do."

"You have no idea. You can't possibly understand."

"Annie, it's me. Come on. Let's talk this through." He slides his hand across the table for her to take. She doesn't even look at it.

"When is your baby due?"

He withdraws his hand, takes a deep breath, and coughs into his fist. His eyes burn into hers. "About two weeks."

She calculates months, allowing the truth to slowly dawn on her. "So, not only were you fucking her for three months before you left me, but the woman who is now your wife could go into labor at any moment and you're hundreds of miles away fucking *me*."

"I know it looks bad," His fists slide across the table toward her. "It looks completely wrong. But you've got to believe me when I tell you that I love you. I don't love Tess, I never did, I just—"

"Couldn't pass up a good fuck?"

"It wasn't that."

"Were there others?"

"Please."

"Tell me."

"No!"

"Fuck you."

"Come on, Annie."

"Christmas is tomorrow. You're such a shit."

"It's not as simple as that."

"You need to leave."

"Just let me explain about Tess. It was a stupid affair, I admit. But I was going to stop seeing her. She actually made me realize what I had with you, and I was about to tell her it was over when she told me she was pregnant."

"Oh, that's such a cliché, Owen. Really. Come on."

"It's true."

"So why are you here? What the hell am I supposed to do with the mess you've dragged in here? Do you have any idea how ruined I was before you added this on top of everything else? You left me a goddamn *letter*!"

He raises his hand to explain at the same rate the blood of embarrassment flushes his face. The mark of her hand fades in all the red.

She cuts him off. "Did it ever occur to you that staying away at this point would have been the best thing? I was getting over you, Owen. I really was. As hard as it's been, I felt the heartache in my chest beginning to lift, and now you show up like you've got some right to me. Some right to pile it all back on. Did you think I've been doing nothing but waiting for you to come home?"

Of course she's been doing exactly that, and he senses it; surely he must sense that he has her exactly where he wants her.

She jumps up and hurls her coffee cup through the living room at the tree. Coffee trails her arm and across the table. It trails the floor and into the lights. It splashes the wooden ornaments and she doesn't care that he was just a boy when he made them.

"Get out of here."

Owen slowly rises from his chair. "Annie. I don't want to go. Please. Just hear me out."

"Does your wife have this number?"

"What?"

"Did you give her my number?"

"No. Why?"

"She can't even call if she needs you?"

"I didn't think—"

"What if she goes into labor?"

"I'll deal with that, Annie. It's none of your business."

"You didn't *think*? It's none of my *business*? Were you always this stupid, Owen? Were you always so dumb and callous, or did you turn into this toward the end?" Her voice crawls up her throat as she tries not to cry. "Because I have to say I'm sick at the thought that I ever loved you. I can't believe I let you touch me."

The hurt is clear in his face.

"You're not thinking straight. I don't blame you. I guarantee when you calm down you're going to see things differently."

"You don't even know the half of it. It has taken me six fucking months to even *begin* calming down."

"I'm sorry."

"I was pregnant."

"*What?*"

"I was pregnant when you left me."

Owen looks around the room as if for a baby. "*What?*"

She holds her hand up to say, "Enough."

Owen drops back into the chair and covers his face, and if there's anything that ought to make him sorry for the rest of his life this ought to do it.

"Jesus, Annie."

"It doesn't matter."

"Did you have an abortion?"

Annie laughs. "I was coming home from the store with the pregnancy test while you were driving off into the sunset with your girlfriend."

He drops his hands from his face.

"You need to leave," she says.

"What happened?" He pleads with his eyes. Then he coughs so hard she can't tell if this is what causes his eyes to run, but she doesn't care because the sound of the phlegm in his throat brings her to within an inch of hating him.

"Fine. If you won't leave, then I will." She throws on her jacket and boots and looks for her purse while Owen follows her around the house. "Please," he says. "I'm begging you to stay and talk to me." His tone grows more maniacal the longer he speaks. He's like a crazy boyfriend heading her off in every room. "Annie. No. Please. Tell me what happened to the baby." He's pretending to stay calm, but it's clear he wants to grab her by the throat. She holds her keys between her fingers in her pocket. She will claw his eyes out before he knows what hit him.

"If you don't get out of my way that little girl of yours is going to grow up with a blind daddy."

He steps aside.

She plucks her purse off the coat rack. "Good choice. Now call your wife and tell her you're on your way."

"I can't. Even if I wanted to. I can't drive a Miata in snow."

She steps outside to the wind sweeping waves of white into the air as far as she can see. The snow has blotted out the entire world beyond her driveway.

"Fine. Fine! But just how am I supposed to get back home?" Owen says, and for the first time in months Annie hears the makings of a song.

She slams the door but doesn't move. She knows if she turns around and goes back inside she will find him right where she left him. If she goes back in she might not say the thing she needs to say.

But there is nowhere to go and she doesn't want to stare any longer at the lump beneath the willow tree. She turns and goes inside. Finding him exactly as she knew she would somehow robs her of her anger. "Sit down," she says.

He doesn't move.

"Go ahead," she says. "Don't look at me like that."

He moves to the sofa and reluctantly takes a seat.

She's in control now. He's no longer calling the shots. He doesn't get to decide who goes and who gets left behind, whose heart gets broken and who carries on, who lives alone, becomes a parent, or never gets the chance.

"Go back to her, Owen."

"Annie."

"You made the choice once, you can make it again."

"I wasn't thinking straight."

"You're not thinking straight now."

"What are you talking about?"

"You can love two people at the same time."

"But I don't," he says, and she sees a flicker of doubt in his eyes. He pulls his earlobe then quickly drops his hand.

She sits in the chair across from him. The fire has died out. Her heavy breathing is the only sound in the room. She drops her hand down the side of the chair and loosely plucks the low E on her guitar. "I read somewhere that a lot of men panic just before their babies are born. Some even kill their wives."

"Good God, Annie."

"It's true."

"I'm not panicking."

"You should be. You're here with all this snow between you and your wife. Your child could come at any moment."

"It's not that."

"What is it?"

"I don't know."

"Sure you do. We used to joke that we'd get married if we ever had the time. But it doesn't take time, does it? You proved that with Tess."

"That was different."

"You're right. But not in the way you think."

He turns his head to the side, and then he looks at the floor and bobs his heel nervously. "Do you remember the time we snuck naked into Cypress Springs?" he says.

Annie lifts her chin to think.

"The park ranger came and threw us out."

"Sort of."

"We were kissing in the water. Your legs were wrapped around my waist. You told me you loved me. I don't know why it had such an effect on me. You were just being playful, but I swear I've never felt more love for anyone in my life than I felt for you in that moment. Not before and not since."

Annie nods at the floor.

"It was like a bullet to the heart. Powerful as that. I started to tell you, but then the ranger came and we had to go. After that it seemed too contrived or something. I don't know. Misplaced. Too out of context to bring it up and have it matter the way it should."

Annie shakes her head. "Sorry. I don't really remember."

"We could see clear past our feet to the limestone."

"I lost the baby three days after you left."

The red in his face drains away. He stands and paces a wide circle into the kitchen and back with a hand rubbing the back of his neck. "I'm sorry, Annie. *Jesus Christ*. If I could just say more than that. It's not enough. That was my fault just as sure as I'm standing here."

"I thought so, too."

He kicks one of his own ornaments across the floor.

"Then again, those things happen," she says. "We have no way of knowing either way."

"We can change what's about to happen here, Annie. Here and now. We can decide what the future looks like. Don't send me away."

"I'm sorry," she says.

"What have you got to be sorry for?"

"For letting you in. I'm sorry for opening the gate. And I'm sorry to your wife."

This seems to hit Owen harder than anything else she's said here today.

"Go back, Owen."

"Annie." His chin quivers.

She can still smell him on her hands. "It's your second chance," she says, recalling in detail the morning at the spring.

TWENTY-EIGHT

The summer before Joshua left, he and Annie discovered places along country roads they'd never been down before. Wentzville Springs had more than anywhere else. One time they wandered into a small museum where they couldn't take their eyes off an old cornflower-blue dress that hung next to a washboard once used to scrub it clean. There was nothing else on that corner of the wall, and the glaring omission, it seemed, was the woman, gone from the dress for a hundred years. Joshua said it was one of the saddest sights he'd ever seen. Annie thought so, too. Before they left he bought her a postcard with the photo of the dress on it. He said she could write something on the back and send it to him in the fall, or she could just keep it, to remember him by, to remember this day. He was always giving her things to remember him by, as if she would ever forget.

Another time they came across a fish house along the St. John's River where they sat and watched gators slip from the banks into the water like giant duffels of lead. Snakes hung from trees in view of the outdoor patio. Everything smelled like fried catfish, and they gorged on cornbread with butter and honey and had their Cokes refilled every time the waitress rushed by.

It was on the way home, with their bellies full of cornbread, that they had their first real fight.

"'Lovely Rita' was not on the *Sergeant Pepper's* album," Annie said.

"Yes it was."

"It was *not*. How would you know?"

"I'm not stupid," he said.

"No one said that."

"It doesn't take a rocket scientist to know things like that," he said.

"Oh, so *I'm* the stupid one?"

"I didn't say that."

"And you're the rocket scientist?" Annie said.

"I didn't say that!"

"You didn't have to. You're the one going off to a fancy private school and then college, not me, and it doesn't take a rocket scientist to figure out who's going to end up where ten years from now."

Joshua stopped the car.

She felt miserable and childish and unbearably sad. He held her face in his hands and said, "Promise me you'll write."

"I promise," she said, though she wasn't sure which he meant, write to him or keep writing music.

He kissed her long and hard. He stopped long enough to say, "I love every inch of you, Annie Walsh." And she smiled and said, "You would know," and kissed his neck because that got him every time.

The last day of their summer, the last moment before he drove off, Calder came outside to say good-bye. The two of them hugged one another and got teary-eyed, and Annie had to turn away and wipe her already soaking face. "So we'll see you at Thanksgiving, right?" Calder said.

Joshua nodded.

Calder touched Annie's arm and went inside. It was late and way past the time Joshua told his aunt he'd be getting on the road.

They couldn't keep from holding hands. Every time they let go they found themselves attached seconds later.

Joshua pulled her against him, and she could feel him shaking with tears. She was doing the same, and they held on like that until they settled down and he whispered in her ear, "I love you, Annie Walsh. I know we're young and people say these things never work out, but I swear I'll never love anyone the way I love you. Remember that when you're closed up in your bedroom writing sad songs."

Then he held her away from him and stared into her eyes. She didn't wonder if anyone else could ever love her the way he did. What she wondered was whether anyone else would ever look at her the way he looked at her, like the world mattered just because she was in it.

When he drove away the pain in her chest nearly doubled her over. But even when his letters came and she read them till she had them memorized and she'd sit in class and stare out the window dizzily rereading them inside her head to the point that she was failing that first term, even then she knew the seams that had held them together would slowly come apart.

Thanksgiving came, and they rushed into each other's arms in the driveway, but the feel of him was different. He was mannerly and quiet and she couldn't imagine what his days were like, but every now and then she got a glimpse that seemed to embarrass him. He'd say something about having been in the middle of studying for a test on the classics when so-and-so wouldn't stop talking about how much he loved the Greeks, and then he'd look over and see the glazed look in her eyes and fall silent.

Christmas was more of the same. Their letters began to sound like they were meant for someone else. His aunt had gotten a promotion, which was helping with the expenses at school, and he'd held on to straight A's the entire term and was so excited to see where all this was going to lead because already he was thinking he'd become an architect, and what did she think of that? She'd missed school again, she told him, because she couldn't stand to get out of bed to go sit in a classroom that bored her to tears, but in the meantime she'd written another song that she was fairly happy with and yes, it was sad just like all the others.

They officially ended it, oddly, in spring when orange blossoms drenched the air and a drought had kept away the mosquitoes so that if they'd wanted to, they could've spent hours alone in the woods. But the end was like a crea-ture growing day by day, inevitably coming into its size. A part of Annie was glad to be rid of it, to no longer need to live with the anticipation, the doom. She was sure he was thinking the same thing though he never said so and neither did she.

"Should we keep in touch?" he asked.

"Don't you think that'll just make it harder?"

"I don't know."

"Me neither."

Several short letters were exchanged, and then they finally lost touch for good. The last time she ever saw him was over a decade later in, of all places, Lukeman's Grocery.

It was fall, and the weather had turned cool and clear and everyone seemed to have an extra bounce to his step.

And then Annie read in the paper that Mr. Lukeman had hung himself, and the blue sky took on a deep, faraway melancholy that prompted her to phone her mother without thinking. His wife had discovered him with another man, her mother explained, and shortly after confronting him she found him hanging in the garage. "Why," her mother posed, "would anyone *choose* to take his own life?"

Annie drove the long way round past Lakewood Elementary wondering if Mrs. Brinkman was still alive, past Peterson's Peach grove that was now called Gruger's and the stretch of land that used to be a cattle field but was now full of concrete culs de sac. She barely recognized the acres that were once filled with piney woods and the scrub that had formed a cove she once sat in. Once lay in. It was now an apartment complex, and in front of that, a strip mall with a dry cleaner, pizza parlor, and a pet store. Lukeman's Grocery, however, looked exactly the same with its green awning and red faux brick and tar-filled railroad ties to park against.

Annie wore a jean jacket and her favorite silk scarf that shimmered the color of lapis in the sun. She wandered inside to the smell of cinnamon sticks on the counter and green produce in wooden barrels straight ahead. They still carried Tab in the cooler and Polaroid film on the wall behind the register.

She heard his voice immediately and thought she must be imagining it. She dipped her head around the aisle and heard it again. "I didn't even know they still made Quisp cereal."

He was a grown man of twenty-seven and sharply dressed, and he would have taken her breath away if it weren't for the fact that he was holding the hand of a woman who looked, she had to admit, a little like Annie.

He turned in Annie's direction, and she walked right up and said, "You were right. 'Lovely Rita' *was* on the *Sergeant Pepper's* album."

Joshua let go of the woman's hand and his mouth fell open. The woman smiled nervously between them.

He wrapped his arms around Annie and it felt like no time at all had gone by since they'd stood in her driveway, twelve years before. "How are you?" he said, letting go, his eyes searching her face and hair as if to make sure it was really her. "You look great," he said. The woman next to him gently took his hand back and he turned to her. "This is Annie Walsh, Melinda. Annie, this is Melinda, my fiancée."

She didn't know why she hadn't expected this. People go on with their lives. She'd gone on with hers, if one called a series of dead-end relationships moving on. She looked at Melinda's ring. A gold band with a cluster of diamonds. Annie was sure Melinda had picked it out herself. Annie would've chosen something simpler. A solitaire set in white gold.

"Congratulations," she said with her best smile. "When's the big date?"

"Sometime mid-December. We still have to pick the day. Joshua loves that time of year around here."

Joshua quickly looked away, and Annie felt the blood pool in her face.

"I know what you mean. The light is really great, isn't it?" she said.

He took a deep breath. "We're on our way to see my mother. My father passed away a few years back, did you know?"

She'd known how he'd felt about his father. "I heard. I'm sorry," she said. It was an awkward condolence. But maybe his feelings had changed for his father over the years. She had no way of knowing. She wanted to say that they were both fatherless now, but it sounded stupid and cruel, even inside her own head.

"Why don't you two catch up?" Melinda said. "I need to grab a few things."

They were alone again in the produce aisle.

"I've settled back in Tampa, for now," he said.

"Nice."

"I travel quite a bit for work, though."

"Me too," she said with a smile.

"Still singing."

"Still singing. Still writing sad songs." She didn't tell him that she still wrote them with the same silver pen he'd given her years ago. She could practically see the memories spinning in his head the way he searched her face. "I'm playing a lot of mid-size venues," she said. "Things have really taken off, just lately, in fact. I'm booked a lot up in Gainesville and Athens. College towns, you know."

"I saw you play once," he blurted.

"What? Where? *When?*"

"At The Grinder in Tampa a couple of years back."

"You're kidding!"

"You were amazing."

"Why didn't you come up to me?"

He looked at the lettuce. "You were there with someone. You seemed happy. I didn't want to interfere."

For the life of her she couldn't remember who she was even dating two years ago the night she played The Grinder.

Melinda was pretending to search for crackers on a shelf. Her back was turned, and Annie reached for Joshua's hand and he squeezed hers in return. "Joshua."

"She's a great woman, Annie."

"I'm happy for you."

"I'm an architect. At least I did that," he said, as if to make up for something else he *should* have done but didn't.

"I'm not surprised."

"What's happening with you? With your life?" He squeezed her hand as if she were about to let go. She wasn't. He glanced at her empty ring finger and she thought she detected a look of relief.

"Well, the music, like I said, it's good. It's a long road but it feels like it was paved for me."

This made him smile. "And all the rest?"

"I have no children, no marriage plans if that's what you're asking."

They both looked at Melinda still searching the shelves.

"I don't know if I'll ever get married," she said, though she didn't know why she said this. She hadn't actually believed it. She hadn't ever subscribed to the thought at all.

They were still holding hands when Annie saw Melinda coming. She pulled her hand away, and Joshua hugged her tightly and whispered, "I'm always hoping I'll see you here," and then there was Melinda standing at his side, looking confident as could be, and Annie had to give her credit for being such a good sport.

"They didn't have what I was looking for," she said.

"Well. It was good seeing you," Joshua said.

Annie nodded and told Melinda it was nice meeting her and wished them both the best of luck.

Melinda gave a jaunty kind of wave. Joshua checked the air with two fingers and Annie smiled as if he were taking her picture.

She thought about how happy they must look to other people. Crossing the parking lot beneath the sun, their hands locked and swinging. As they drove off she busied herself with her own pretend shopping. Then she walked outside to an empty blue sky and a day as cool and perfect as any day she could have hoped for. She sat behind the wheel of her car and stared a good long while across the road at a gull on a broken steeple. A substitute, she thought, for what was meant to be in its place.

TWENTY-NINE

Annie shouldn't be driving in this weather. Government buildings closed early, a twenty-car pileup on the interstate has left traffic at a standstill in both directions, and power lines have already begun to snap. People all across the state are being warned to stay home and here she is, roaming snowy streets with practically the whole county to herself. She passes housing developments with yards of swarming children and their armies of lopsided snowmen. She passes empty strip malls, car dealers with glittering flags and balloons, the only thing moving on the lot. But it isn't until she reaches the winding back roads of Wentzville Springs in the middle of a pine forest cloaked in snow that she feels she's exactly where she's supposed to be.

She's afraid to blink for fear of finding out it's an illusion, an exquisite hoax painted on a life-size backdrop, a North Pole theme park drawn up overnight. But it is none of these. The white peaks towering above are so real she can almost smell the frozen pine coming through the vent of the car. She opens her window and breathes as deeply as her lungs will allow. Clean, frozen pine.

The Land Cruiser is about to run out of gas so she pulls into what looks like an abandoned station. If it's open she'll pay a fortune for full-service only, and that's fine. She feels like spending everything she has just so she can start over with money Owen hasn't helped her earn.

A red, round pump stands alone in the center of the concrete drive. The vending machine is empty. A single can of motor oil is placed in the window next to a handwritten sign that reads OPeN. Annie scoots the car forward over the bell and stops. For a moment nothing happens. She's about to drive off when an old woman with a crude underbite appears in the doorway as if she's just been retrieved from a fairytale. She smiles with a genuine lack of teeth and swings her arm as she scampers around, moving quickly at her business of filling Annie's tank. When she's finished she appears at the car window with her hand held out. She's wearing a headscarf as plain and brown as butcher paper. Annie includes a twenty-dollar tip in the pile of cash.

"Isn't there a fish house this way somewhere?" Annie asks.

"Used to be years ago," the woman says. Her lower jaw strains her *s*'s into a hiss. She points up the forested road with a thick, yellowed fingernail. "It's the Bull Creek now," she says. "Best barbequed grouper in the state of Florida."

"Thank you," Annie says.

"It's *Frank's* place," the woman adds with a hiss.

The Bull Creek parking lot is packed with trucks and SUVs. Maybe it's the same place, maybe it isn't. The air smells of burning logs and mesquite and charcoal, weighted by the sounds of laughter and loud voices drifting from inside the tavern.

Annie opens the door to a room full of men holding beers and women passing around plates of food like a picnic or a family reunion. Christmas lights are strung in all the windows. Babies, a set of dark-haired twins, pass between women in red and green holiday dresses while a man's voice rises above the others to say that Bill Greene is destined to be a justice of the peace. A circle of men clang their beer bottles at the center. "Here, here," they say, and drink up around an enormous stone fireplace roaring with heat.

Annie stands in the doorway feeling as if she's crashing someone's party.

The place certainly looks like something out of the past. Everything made of knotty pine, the acrid smell of old beer, jars of pickles and boiled eggs and raw peanuts on the counter. The green-lit jukebox glows near the pool table situated under an array of muted light from a stained-glass shade. Otis Redding is singing "White Christmas" from all corners of the room with more sex and soul and yearning than anyone has ever put into that song. A small, makeshift stage lines the back wall, and she imagines the excitement of a local band playing live for the first time.

A thickset man with peppered gray hair crosses the room toward her. His baggy carpenter pants and surf shop sweatshirt make him appear younger than he is, or else the thin creases around his eyes and across his forehead make him appear older. She guesses he's the age her father would have been had he lived.

He introduces himself as Frank, and as he shows her to a table in the back, a smoky layer of citrus drifts off the grill behind the end of the bar. She assumes it's the grouper. "Do you marinate it in orange juice?" she asks, and slips off her jacket and lays it across the extra seat at her table.

Frank grins.

"Grapefruit?" she asks.

Frank places his hands on the hips of his baggy pants, and with a kind-looking grin that produces two dimples he says, "As much as I'd like to tell you I'm afraid I can't."

She smiles and turns to the happy crowd. She understands the rules of privacy. An hour has gone by since she left Owen in her living room, and she wouldn't care to tell another living soul about what went on there for as long as she lives.

"One beer, coming up," Frank says without asking. Her face must say it all and she likes that he can read it. He's got a familiar way about him, like a cousin, an uncle, someone who gets a kick out of you for no reason at all.

He starts to hand her a menu. "I'll have the grouper," she says, and leans into her chair and rubs her hands together. Frank smiles. "On the double, Captain," he says, and steps behind the bar.

A newspaper lies folded on the empty table next to her. The giant red headline reads: *WHITE CHRISTMAS LEAVES FARMERS IN THE RED*. Beneath it are several shots of ice-coated oranges like candies dipped in frosting. Annie flips it over. In the bottom right corner a smaller headline reads: *Prosecutors Seek Death Penalty in Jørgenson Case*. Calder's mug shot stares back at her. Seeing it causes an ache in her chest, and she rubs it like a bout of heartburn until it fades. His tangled hair is thrown around as if he has just emerged from a convertible. His eyes are bloodshot and one lid appears to be closing, and she imagines Calder struggling to keep still for the camera. Next to him is the picture of Hal's roadside bar, its white, clapboard siding and gravel parking lot. She skims the article. *Brother of singer/songwriter Annie Walsh...could have only been committed by someone with a great deal of strength...apparently crushing the large man's skull against the wall of the roadside bar...The coroner's office believes a heavy metal tool of some kind was used in the crime.*

She flips the paper and tosses it back where she found it.

Frank sets the foamy beer in front of her and she swallows big, uneasy gulps like a child forcing medicine down her throat. Heat rises to her face and hands. She watches as people laugh and lean into one other with ease, people who don't seem to have a care about anything or even have a life outside of the one they are experiencing right here.

She has a perfect view through the double glass doors to the patio out back. Animals have tracked through the snow. Birds, raccoons. There's a post to tie up dogs and a dish for water and a small bed of wood chips under the eave for them to lie on, and she knows right away that she likes this man, Frank. Forest surrounds the patio on three sides, and she scoots her chair to better see the trees draped in snowy moss.

She drinks down the last of her beer. After the second one her whole body feels dreamlike and snug, her hips softening into the wooden chair. If not for Frank arriving with the grouper, she may have fallen asleep.

"Does a river run out back there?" she asks.

"The St. John's," he says. "Can't see it for the trees."

"You wouldn't happen to have any cornbread would you?"

"Coming up," he says, and hurries off to the sound of a kitchen bell.

The grouper gently breaks apart in her mouth, a heavenly melt of buttery pepper and citrus and smoke, and all she wants is to linger in the sounds of people laughing, Aretha Franklin now crooning on the jukebox. But the beer seems to have doused her brain, and a memory she had buried long ago floats to the surface.

Her mother, young and smiling from her blue oversized chair in the corner near the floor lamp with the chain switch. She looks up from the big book in her lap and offers Annie bits of odd information the way she did so often in those years. She tells her how years ago women were diagnosed with things like *bad humors, hysteria,* and *nostalgia.* Doctors ordered them to sit outdoors in the sun. The cure was fresh air and sunshine. Fresh air and sunshine is something her family has had nearly every day of their lives. "It's like insurance," her father says, walking into the room with a greasy car part in his hands. Calder follows behind with some tools. "We're so full of it," her father continues, "we can save some up inside ourselves for when hurricane season sets in." Her mother smiles and says, "According to this, nothing of the mind is ever going to ail us." She laughs so peacefully and flashes her bright white teeth at her father and the two of them lean in for a small kiss inside the pale yellow cone of the light.

But this is not the way it happened. This is not the real memory. This is the one Annie made up.

All her life she's managed to switch that afternoon around inside her head, turning Uncle Calder into her father. Uncle Calder was the one she'd seen leaning in to kiss her mother. Her father had come in later with the car parts, with Calder trailing behind, and her mother *did* say the part about sunshine and fresh air and her father *did* say the part about insurance. But there had been no kiss, at least not between her parents. Uncle Calder, who'd been working on the car with them, was the one who'd walked in and kissed her mother after her father had come and gone. And Annie wasn't sitting there when the kiss happened either. She'd just stepped around the doorway, and when she saw what was happening she held her breath and slipped away and somehow flipped the whole incident inside her head to the thing that made more sense. Her father was the man who'd kissed her mother. He was the only man her mother would kiss.

The beer has gone right through her. It feels a little like floating as she makes her way to the bathroom. Her hands reach in front of her, her mother's hands, slender and veiny, searching for something to hold on to. The men tip their hats as she drifts past. Old country boys.

A plate of warm cornbread steams on the table when she returns with a weighty ache behind her eyes. Why on earth did Uncle Calder go after the one person it was clear he wasn't supposed to have? And why would her mother cheat on a man who loved her as much as Annie's father did? Why should she cheat on her father at all when she loved him so much that losing him nearly killed her, too?

No wonder Annie didn't confront Owen that morning at the table. No wonder she made him eggs Benedict and pretended everything was fine. She'd gotten a head start on denial, on keeping her mouth shut, on twisting reality the day she witnessed her mother and uncle kissing beneath the lamplight.

She thinks of Owen's hands between his knees, his foot bobbing on the floor. Doubt trickles in. Maybe she was wrong to tell him to leave. She was just reacting to the news. Maybe it's not as bad as it seems once she's had a chance to think it through.

She takes a deep breath and turns to the forest floor filled with giant Elephant Ears like downy hearts springing in all directions. The trees above are twisted and tangled, one into the other, a woven canopy of earthy brown and green and white. She feels weepy and misplaced, a woman suffering from nostalgia, a woman years removed from everyone and everything that has ever offered her life a sense of purpose.

Thin tears slide so quickly she's unable to catch them with a swipe of her hand before they reach her mouth. The salty taste shakes something loose in her shoulders. Her mouth falls open and she doesn't know if she's laughing or crying. She leans forward and then throws her head back at the ceiling and groans.

If he's still there when she gets back she'll know she was wrong about him. If he's there she will ask him to stay.

"Unrequited love's a bore," she quietly sings. "Yeah, and I've got it pretty bad. But for someone you adore, it's a pleasure to be sad." The lyrics keep rolling off her tongue until Frank scrapes his grill with a metal spatula and Annie turns, startled by the sharp sound of metal on metal. His eyes fix on her, giving the feeling he's been watching, listening to her sing. She covers her mouth, embarrassed.

Frank flips the fish with his tongs. "The Mamas and the Papas," he says, pointing his tongs at her. "'Glad to Be Unhappy.' Haven't heard that one in years."

"You've got sharp ears, mister." She feels a wave of drunkenness. It's late morning on Christmas Eve and she's drunk in a tavern in the middle of nowhere.

Frank smiles at her.

She gawks at the gap between his teeth.

"You've got a pretty voice, young lady."

She shrugs, feeling a momentary jolt of sobriety.

"You do that for a living?" he asks.

Something tight rises in her chest.

The thing is, he won't be there when she gets home. He's already rushing home to Tess, his heart banging around in his chest over all the stupid things he's done, over just how close he came to losing everything.

For a moment they don't speak. The conversation seems to have nowhere to go.

Then suddenly it's as if she's listening while her mouth jabbers on. "I have a record. It sold pretty well. *Selling* pretty well, I guess I should say."

"What's the name of it?"

"You know what's *really* funny? My favorite song off that album is called 'Falling Off the Edge of the World.'"

"That's you? Wait a minute." Frank lays the tongs aside. "That's you? Singing that song?"

She nods and her head feels wobbly, loose on her neck. "It's funny because my boyfriend who ran off and left me for someone else, twice now, I'm pretty sure, twice now for the same woman, it's complicated, don't even try to figure it out," she waves her hand around, "but that's beside the point, what I'm saying is this guy always thought that song was about him. It's not about him." She shakes her head and everything moves in slow motion.

"You're Annie Walsh?"

"Shh."

"I'll be damned. It's not every day I get a celebrity in here."

"A celebrity. No. I'm no celebrity, Frank."

He crosses over and shakes her hand. His palm is dry and coarse and he shakes and shakes the way Joshua did and Annie gets weepy again and pulls her hand away. "I thought it ended so well. I thought we did a good job, the way we walked away like that. Like real grown-ups."

"If you're talking about love, it never ends well. Not as far as I can tell."

"You made a rhyme."

"It's a pleasure to meet you, Miss Walsh."

"I don't normally drink," she says. "Just so you know." She needs to catch her breath. "I don't drink."

Frank pulls out the extra chair and joins her. "I suppose with your brother. I mean, if I was you I'd have another," he says, and quickly catches himself with a small laugh. "Apparently you bring out the poet in me."

She's conscious not to look sloppy when she laughs.

"Can I get you anything else?" He rises as if needing to get back to work.

She burps the taste of grouper, and even the burp tastes good. She shakes her head.

"Coffee? I've got some fresh brewed back there."

"Yes. Coffee. I'll have coffee," she says, remembering her cup sailing at the Christmas tree. It seems funny to her now.

She looks over at the makeshift stage. There's a microphone and a stool in the center. "After that I'd like to sing a song, if you don't mind."

Frank stands there in silence.

Annie's palms sweat and she rubs them down her thighs but they don't feel dry. "Is that not all right?"

"That's more than all right, Miss Walsh."

"You wouldn't happen to have a guitar back there some-where would you?"

"No, but I know where to get one."

"And a violin. I need someone who can play the violin."

Frank rests his hands on his hips. "You're looking at him."

"Seriously?"

"Cracker born and bred. But it's a fiddle, if you don't mind."

"How about that. You know any Dylan?"

"How on earth did you stroll in here today?"

"Simple twist of fate, I guess."

"That's corny as hell," he says.

"Way more where that came from, Mr. Rhyme Maker."

"I have no doubt," he says with his dimpled smile. He looks around for someone in the crowd. "Hey, Bill," he yells. "You mind running home to get your guitar for this lady here?"

Bill stands like a man used to filling favors. His cap reads *Inspected by Allison*. He glances at Annie and then he pulls the keys from the front pocket of his jeans. "It'll take me a few minutes with the snow."

"My place is right next door," Frank says to Annie. "I'll go grab that *violin*."

PART FOUR

THIRTY

The railroad tracks are covered in snow. For the first time in Uncle Calder's life he looks down from the window to find them gone. He throws back two orange pills and drinks from the tumbler of ice water in his hand. He's unusually tired, his stomach alternately sour, hungry, and tight. He feels unsteady, a little drunk, though he hasn't had a drink in weeks.

He burps the bitter taste of medication and thinks to lie down but can't. He's supposed to visit Calder in little over an hour. The blue Christmas lights blinking in the corner remind him of the boy's eyes.

But now he's fallen into heavy thought at the window. He's beaten the odds, lived past eighty without ever having married. Bachelorhood should have shaved ten years off his life, but he's already passed the average lifespan of the American male. "Do you have some lady friend who keeps you going like this, Mr. Walsh?" they ask down at Florida Geriatrics Research, Inc., and he wonders if loving a woman, even one who breaks your heart, has a way of keeping a man going for another day.

He recalls her hands. Someone should have turned those hands into a painting. A sculpture. Slender, porcelain-looking fingers fastening her copper hair to a pin. When she laughed it caught like wildfire around her. That should have been on film. He could have watched reruns of it every day of his life.

Who could resist that mouth? Those lips? That copper hair falling around her shoulders when she laughed?

"What kind of food do you eat?" the researchers ask him. *Cantaloupe and green beans and swamp cabbage.* "How much exercise are you getting?" *With my stairs, plenty.* "How often do you urinate?" *When I drink sweet tea, plenty.* "Would you mind stepping up on the scale?" Red and white blood pressure caplets, orange painkillers for the lower back, ammonia-smelling shampoo for hair loss, and little yellow pills for erections. He was just telling someone this the other day, listing off all the medication he takes. Annie. Annie was here in his living room. He didn't tell her about the one for erections.

He glances at the Rollator in the corner. A glint of gold flickers from the Purple Heart beneath the lamp on the end table. He is, and always has been, a sturdy, steady man.

He rests his forehead against the cold window and wonders what it would feel like to smash his skull through the glass and then stand there, breathing in snow through the shards.

He tightens his grip on the tumbler in his hand and the cold feels good inside his aching fist. It's possible that the tiniest bones might actually be broken. He'll need to stay away from the researchers a while longer. They'll want to know all about his hands, want to take x-rays and feel along the brittle bones of his fingers with the firmness of their own.

Anguish is what he feels. A word that still reminds him of Kearney's death. He thinks of how he'd stumbled through the days afterward, knocked around by pinballs of torment he couldn't foresee. An old customer asking for Kearney; the look on her face when he told her Kearney had passed was all it took to splay the tender hole in his chest. A cedar birdhouse propped in the window display at the hardware store had him choked up by the time he asked for nails. An Irish joke on the radio caught him unaware and he laughed before jolting back to the fact that there was no one in the world he could tell it to.

But the one thing he never could have imagined was Miriam turning him away. They'd never needed to fight over money or children or housework, the usual domestic spats he assumed had been reserved for Kearney. The only anger he'd ever felt toward her before she turned him away was of his own doing. He'd lured her away from his brother with nothing more than his own vanity, a trumped up manly flirtation designed specifically for her, and a part of him hated her for being so easy to penetrate, for taking the bait, for causing him to fall so helplessly in love with her.

And then Kearney died and he should have stepped in and redeemed them both, but instead Miriam's eyes went hollow. They were no longer bright and quick to drink him in when he got her alone. He would never again watch as her lids floated when he entered her, and then flung back open when she came. They were eyes that never wanted to see him again. She said she couldn't bear the thought of tainting Kearney's *memory*. It was not enough that in life they had to protect him from their love affair, but now they would have to protect the man's *ghost*. "What if he can look down and see the two of us in his bed?" she'd asked, as if through a fever dream. "We shouldn't even be in the same room together." She was convinced that an all-knowing Kearney would put two and two together and figure out what had gone on while he was alive and spend the rest of eternity writhing in devastation from the betrayal of the ones he loved most.

Uncle Calder tried to reason with her. "This is not some class you're teaching on Shakespeare, Miriam. For Christ's sake, think of the kids. They're hurting, too, you know."

"It's the kids I'm thinking of most," she said, but instead of seeing Miriam loved for the rest of her days, instead of watching his kids play ball and fish and star in school plays, Kearney got to look down from heaven and watch Miriam lose herself in hardnosed misery while his kids fended for themselves, and with that kind of logic he got to watch Uncle Calder masturbate to a photo of Miriam at the beach.

He pulls his forehead away from the window and kicks his foot into the wall, spilling water to his wrist. He's angry. So heated so fast. It's happening all over again.

He pitches his tumbler to the floor and grabs the Rollator. With a two-fisted grip he hurls the Prime 3 Deluxe Edition against the window with an enormous crash. The yellowed plastic shade tears from the rod, and he beats it until the shade and rod and jagged glass have all plunged outside into the snow. Then he wedges the Rollator into the sill and all it takes is a small shove for it to fly into the air.

The room swells with cold.

That Dane's accent had been distinct. Not more than three bar stools down from Uncle Calder. There was no mistaking that the man was from somewhere else. He had a handsome, big baby face he would clearly never outgrow. His fists were pink and meaty as grapefruits. Couldn't be the same Dane, Uncle Calder thought. Not the man whose wife Calder was in love with. Then Uncle Calder ordered another beer and got to thinking about Kearney up there orchestrating the whole thing.

The Dane had a lady hanging all over him. A breast slipped out of her low-cut blouse, and without warning the Dane tucked it back in. Sally was the woman's name. "Where is he, Sally?" he asked more than once. "You just made up this skinny landscaper to get me jealous."

Uncle Calder sat up straight and wished he had a hearing aid.

"You'll see," Sally said. She took on a playful, sassy tone. "I've seen him with her. He'll show up here and order a Coca-Cola and you can ask him about the way he looks at her. Like there's no one else in the room."

The Dane turned his head away and knocked back the rest of his drink. He reached down and pulled his sock securely over what Uncle Calder could see was a knife with a pewter handle. Their eyes locked.

"What are you looking at?" the Dane asked.

"Not a thing." Uncle Calder peered down the other end of the bar and fingered the rim of his beer.

Sally wiggled her way onto the stool between them.

Moments later the Dane leaned forward and studied Uncle Calder with lazy, drunken eyes. "What's your name?" he asked.

Uncle Calder hesitated. "Kearney," he said. "What's yours?"

"Magnus." He offered his hand around Sally's back and they shook.

"Are you waiting on someone?" the Dane asked.

Uncle Calder had to laugh. "I'm waiting on someone. But I don't think she's ever going to show."

The Dane seemed to consider this. He looked at Sally fixing her hair in the mirror strung with red Christmas lights behind the bar. "I know what you mean."

"You'll see," she said.

Uncle Calder slid off the stool and slowly wound through the people lining up for drinks. He dropped two coins in the pay phone across the room. It rang until Calder's voice mail picked up.

He hung up and returned to the stool and ordered another beer. He sipped it slower than the first. With every medication he was prescribed, he was warned to stay away from alcohol. The list of side effects was long and varied. Some were simply *unknown*.

Bing Crosby sang "White Christmas," his voice slinking out of speakers in the corners of the room. Somebody must have turned up the heat. Everywhere Uncle Calder went people were fussing with thermostats, trying to deal with the cold. The Dane's forehead glistened. He wiped it with a beer napkin until the napkin was limp.

Uncle Calder's own head sweated and he swiped it with his hand.

"Do you have a wife?" the Dane asked him.

"No. I sure don't."

"I have a wife."

"Well," Uncle Calder said.

"She doesn't care for me."

"I'm sorry to hear that."

"It's my fault," the Dane said.

"Is that right."

"Because I think she is a bitch."

Sally burst out laughing.

Uncle Calder flushed with anger.

"I hate this place," the Dane said. "What is wrong with you people? The water smells like sulfur."

The Dane continued to wipe his pink face with a napkin that was now the size of a gumball. He called for another whiskey, knocked it back, and then held his hand to his chest and belched. From the way he stared he seemed worried that more than air was about to come up and Uncle Calder almost felt sorry for him, so easy was it to imagine him as a sick little boy whose face would never grow up and whose mother would baby him accordingly.

The Dane slid off the stool and staggered across the room and banged his way out the door.

Sally slapped her hand on the counter when the bartender refused her another drink. The place was fuller now, and all eyes seemed to be on her when Uncle Calder slid off his own stool and strolled past a red-haired man he thought he recognized in a booth. From the side he looked a lot like that boy Annie used to run with when they were teenagers. But not so much that Uncle Calder was sure it was him.

"Just one more?" Sally argued. The bartender refused. She called him a motherfucker and he was asking her to leave when Uncle Calder picked up the Rollator he'd parked in the corner and weaved out into the night.

He found the Dane laughing in the dark parking lot behind the bar. Puffs of steam rose from his mouth in the cold. His rear end leaned against the side of the building, his head bowing forward beneath the small bathroom windows at his back. A light came on in the bathroom and after a moment went out again. Uncle Calder dragged the Rollator behind him through the gravel. "What do you say, Hans Christian?" he asked.

Someone turned the music up inside. "Rocking around the Christmas Tree" breached the walls. The Dane staggered upright and seemed to be focusing in the dark. He pointed to the Rollator. "You're old," he spit out. He held his hand against the wall and dropped his head like he was going to be sick.

The bathroom light went on again, and the man's skin in the dim light was as pale and smooth as the underbelly of a shark.

"I guess I am," Uncle Calder said.

The man looked deep into the ground. He tensed up, clearly on the verge of getting sick. He belched but nothing came. "What do you want, Kearney?" he said through the thickness of his accent.

"You ought to get your life straight," Uncle Calder said. He wasn't planning on hurting the man.

"Who are you?"

"It'll all go by a whole lot faster than you think, and then what'll you have to show for it?"

The Dane gagged and still nothing came. "Get away from me," he said.

"Nothing. Except a trail of hurt."

The Dane reached for the knife in his sock. He swung it sloppily in the air as if he were only playing.

Uncle Calder reared back. "There's a whole lot of other women out there to choose from, you know."

The Dane seemed to consider this. "Kearney," he said. "I choose them all the time."

Here's your chance, he heard the real Kearney say from on high, *to put things right*.

"Let your wife go then."

The Dane shook his head at the ground. "She belongs to *me*," the Dane said. "What is it you say here, till death do we part?"

And that's when the anger shot up faster than a freight train.

The Dane must have felt the heat coming off Uncle Calder. He seemed to think it was funny. He laughed so hard he barely made a sound. He poked the knife into the air like jabbing holes in a sheet.

"Put the knife down, boy."

The Dane jabbed harder.

"I wouldn't do that," Uncle Calder said.

"I wouldn't do that," the Dane mocked him with a whiney little voice. "No wonder this woman you're waiting for is never going to show. You're a coward. Listen to you. Don't you know how to stand up to people?"

Uncle Calder stepped forward.

"Forget it," the man said with a laugh. "Don't listen to me. You're a good man, Kearney. You're the best." He tossed the knife to the ground and came forward with an outreached hand.

That was the last thing the big Dane ever did.

Snow blows through the open space where the glass used to be. The arms of his brown sweater are covered in flakes. Hunger, tightness pulls in his chest.

Calder could be his own child. Wasn't this the real truth Miriam didn't want Kearney to discover? That his only son wasn't even his? Of course, a boy could take after his uncle. But there was so much likeness. The hands, the feet, the voice, the height. And worst of all, the need for a woman who belonged to someone else.

There's a bang on the door. "Mr. Walsh? Is everything all right?" The woman from downstairs. Whatshername.

"Everything's fine," he whispers.

"I heard a loud crash. Something fell out of your window. Are you all right?"

The blue tree lights blink and blink and blink. His body feels heavy, the insides of his feet pooled with blood. How long has he been standing here? He slowly crosses the room and falls into the sofa and taps the quartz face of his watch. He's supposed to see Calder in forty-five minutes. He could close his eyes for twenty minutes with no harm done. He just doesn't want to forget.

"I'm going to call someone! If you can hear me I'm calling someone, all right?"

He thinks to write something to Miriam. A line in a Christmas card, something. He's never had the chance to write her anything. In the beginning Kearney might have found it, but even after Kearney was gone Miriam would have thrown away, unopened, anything he tried to send. Still, he wants to tell her before it's too late. He reaches down and tears off a large corner of the newspaper and with the pencil he uses for crosswords he writes, *Miriam, I never stopped*, but then the pencil begins to feel as if it's made of something softer, a blanket, a napkin, a silk glove sliding from his fingers.

Sometimes when he takes the red pills and the white pills and the orange pills all on the same day he has trouble remembering things. Sometimes his chest feels like a hot ray of light.

But now he sees the other man, big as life, the one he'd actually known as a boy. He pulled into the parking lot as if by a gravity feed. He must have been meeting his redheaded brother inside, that man in the booth who looked so much like him. This one here was the real deal, Annie's old boyfriend, the one who'd driven him home that night, the night he got drunk and tried one last time to convince Miriam she was wrong. And all these years later he was moving out of the shadows, a grown man but so easy to recognize with the spark of that boy still in him. "Mr. Walsh!" he yelled, cutting through the fog inside Uncle Calder's head.

"Jesus. What have you *done?*" the boy who was now a man said.

What happened? What had he seen?

Uncle Calder doesn't know. All he thinks he knows is that at some point the Pinckney boy lifted the Rollator off the Dane's head. There was a wet, sucking sound, and the boy turned and nearly threw up against the arm he'd raised to his mouth. The knife lay on the ground reflecting the bathroom light before the light went out again. The boy grabbed Uncle Calder by the elbow and led him to his car with the Rollator. "Are you drunk? Can you drive yourself home?" he asked, and it was like a dream, how everything had come around.

"He would have killed my boy," Uncle Calder said. "You understand? If it weren't for me the two of them would never be together."

"Who?" the boy asked.

But then he was home, tugging the chain beneath the ceiling fan. How to turn it on? How to turn it off?

THIRTY-ONE

Christmas Eve and the Haldol takes hold like a warm gel beneath Calder's skin. He's thickheaded and dry-mouthed, his concentration fractured, but his body is finally still, which seems a miracle, considering.

It's only a matter of time now. He could walk out of here tomorrow. It's possible. Anything is possible. What starts out one way ends up another, and who better to tell him that than Joshua Pinckney?

"Just tell me if it was a man," Calder insisted yesterday.

Joshua finally nodded yes.

Calder turned away and nearly wept with relief. He thought of the different shades of white in Sidsel's hair, her fingernails smooth as frosted glass, her full lips always ready for a kiss. "All right," he said. "What are the initials?"

Joshua shook his head. "I'd rather not say."

"Why not?"

"I just don't...Trust me. They're the same as somebody else's."

"Whose?"

"Never mind. You'll find out soon enough."

"I need to know now, Joshua," Calder said, fighting off the urge to blink. "Look at me. I. Need. To. Know. *Now.*"

Joshua rubbed his face, struggling. He took a deep breath. "Remember that time in the spring when Annie and I went to Disney World?"

Calder narrowed his eyes. "No."

"Remember?"

"No.

"Sure you do. We came home and someone was at your house. Someone who wasn't normally allowed to be there. He'd come to see your mother and I had to take him home."

Calder leaned back in his chair with the realization. "What are you talking about? That doesn't make any sense."

"I'll spare you the details, Calder. I came up on him right after it happened. He didn't seem in his right mind if that makes a difference."

"I don't understand."

Joshua appeared pained at the memory. He didn't meet Calder's eyes when he spoke. "He said, 'He would have killed my boy. If it weren't for me the two of them would never be together.'"

Calder dropped the phone in his lap. At some point he held it up to his ear and said good-bye. At some point he hung up and walked back to his cell with a guard because that's the way it is always done. All he knows for sure is that all night long he's watched snow falling past the iron mesh of his window in a state of disbelief.

THIRTY-TWO

Bill returns with a Gibson. Frank with his fiddle. He dims the tavern lights even more than they already are and flips on a single light above the stage. "This here's a pretty little lady who felt like singing us a song," he says into the mic.

The place settles to near silence when Annie hops on stage. The jukebox cuts off, and Annie's close enough to hear the firewood pop behind the sooty screen. She hasn't sung a note in months, and here she is about to make a fool of herself in front of all these good people who, only moments ago, were full of such holiday cheer but are now shifting in their chairs, waiting for something that clearly better be good.

Then a loud burst throws everything into black. Voices rumble in a mix of groan and delight. The fireplace gives off the only light in the room. Long, shadowy heads stretch against the ceiling where everyone seems to be searching for the missing light. For a moment there's only the crackle and hiss of burning wood.

Annie doesn't move. The stage is dark, and she's sure to trip and tumble to the floor.

"Don't panic, folks," Frank says and is quickly groping his way across the room. "Storm's knocked the power off is all." Others join him and before long, a dozen or more candle flames tremble across tables. Flashlights pulled from the trunks of cars shine beams onto plates of half-eaten meals and empty beer glasses.

Annie waits on her stool, not knowing what to do.

Frank moves through the crowd with a kerosene lamp like a nineteenth-century ghost. He places it on the stage near Annie's feet and his gap-tooth smile, lit from beneath his chin, is both spooky and hysterical.

"You ready?" he asks.

"To sing?"

"No. Shovel snow. Of course, sing."

"As I'll ever be tonight," she says, convinced she's about to make an idiot out of herself.

It takes a while for her to tune Bill's guitar, and this stirs a few jokes into the quiet about him singing so far off-key that it's actually tuned about right.

The snow has stopped falling and the moon has come out. From the corner of her eye a clean swath of snow shimmers across the patio.

The fire weakens and a young, aproned woman from the kitchen plops another log onto the charred wood. Embers smolder among the ash and rise up the chimney, and the fire gains strength.

Annie feels like a child pushing herself to rise through the air on a swing. She pulls the air to the bottom of her lungs and lifts her chin, taking one last look at the trembling candles, and suddenly her voice emerges from deep inside her chest.

She sings about the evening sky going dark, and the sound of her voice is warm and thick and bigger than the room. She sings about a tingle in her bones.

When Frank draws the bow across the violin she nearly weeps at the sound. Her voice continues on, as if without her, her mind as big and empty as the spring-blue sky.

"He woke up and she was gone," she sings. "He didn't see nothing but the dawn. He got out of bed and put his clothes back on, and pushed back the blind, found a note she'd left behind, to which he just could not relate, all about a simple twist of fate."

It isn't until the end when the crowd stands in near darkness and claps for her that the gravity of what has just happened sinks in. Frank pats her back and leans into her with a huge grin.

"You got another one in you?" he asks, and she tells him that yes, she believes she does.

THIRTY-THREE

Owen looks around the kitchen one last time. What he's looking for is food. His appetite has suddenly swelled. He's like a teenager scrounging and stuffing, first a blueberry muffin, then a banana and a glass of juice, and after that another muffin while he scrambles some eggs; and it's while he's on the phone with the airlines that he rakes the eggs, along with a piece of buttered toast, into his mouth.

"Let me see," the woman says. "It doesn't look good."

No matter, he feels light and airy as if the egg has turned him into a soufflé, rising and light, even after cramming in all this food. It's not so much the fact that he's going home that makes him feel so buoyant, but rather the sense of direction he feels. A hum, a call, *this way, now.*

"The next one leaves in two hours," the woman says. "Though there might be some delay."

He hasn't understood until now that it wasn't so much that he needed to come back for Annie, not really, though a part of him did, and probably always will. What he needed to come back for, truly needed, was for her to tell him to leave.

"I'll take it."

He hangs up and calls for a taxi. A driver finally agrees to meet him at the turnoff to Annie's road, a mile down from her driveway.

Then he calls Tess with his eyes squeezed shut. He doesn't open them until he hears her voice.

"It's already started," she says.

"What?"

"They're not close yet but it's happening."

"What? Right now? You're in labor right *now*?"

"My water broke when I leaned down to plug in the lights on the tree. We're going to have a Christmas baby."

"There's a flight in two hours. It only takes half an hour to fly home, but I've got to get to the airport. I've got to leave right now."

"You need to hurry!"

"Don't let her come before I get there."

"Ach!" she says. "I'm having another one." Her voice squeezes out.

"Hold on. Can you make it stop? Is there anyway to make it stop?"

Her teeth seem to be chattering. "There. OK. It's all right." She seems to catch her breath. "Did you see Calder? Is everything all right?"

He can't believe she's asking this now. He promises not to hate himself for what he's done. What good would it do Tess, what good would it do Caroline? "Yes. I did. And it's all right. It's fine. Don't worry. I'll tell you all about it when I get home."

And then he adds, "I love you, Tess."

There's a pause on her end of the phone. Maybe she's looking at the ceiling the way she did when he first laid eyes on her, studying and thinking things through. It's clear that she knows more than she's letting on. She's always known more than he gives her credit for. She understands the meaning of every little nuance in his face. *You've gone there again, haven't you? And look, now you are back.* It's only in her sleep that she gets a reprieve. "Tess?"

"I love you, too," she says.

Owen throws on his coat and runs coughing down the snowy driveway with the pills clanging in his pocket. The cold air irritates his chest, though not as much as yesterday. Something shifts at his back and he turns to see the storm has knocked out the power in the house. Airports have generators. It will be all right.

When he reaches the gate he sees a man in a long camel coat holding a poinsettia on the other side. He's talking to the security guard. He doesn't look like he's from here. Something in the way he holds himself, the gesture of his hands, the self-assured laugh he shares with the other man.

The two men fall silent when Owen approaches. The man in the camel coat nods, the guard does not, and Owen looks away at the exhaust on the Suburban melting a dirty hole in the snow.

The man hands the guard the poinsettia. "Tell her it hasn't been watered so the card tucked inside is nice and dry."

Owen looks in the distance for the taxi. He waits as the guard places the poinsettia on the hood of his Suburban and opens the gate just far enough to let Owen out, and there is no good farewell spoken here, just the clang of the iron behind him and the crunch of his shoes in the snow.

Owen walks past the Miata. He will have to hire someone to drive it to Destin when the snow melts.

Twenty feet down the road the man in the camel coat, the man from who knows where, pulls up beside him in a Land Rover. "Can I give you a ride?"

Owen decides he's a reporter from New York. Maybe L.A. He wants to get Owen in the car so he can ask him questions about Annie and Calder. Owen looks down the road for the taxi. There's still no sign. What if he doesn't show? His socks are already wet inside his shoes.

"The airport?" Owen says.

"Hop in."

The two of them pull away in silence. Any moment the man is going to start asking questions.

Minutes go by, then several more, and all the man does is whistle.

Owen is so grateful for the ride that he decides to tell the man whatever he wants to know. But they are on the freeway and the man still hasn't asked him anything.

Owen looks out at the stream of white fields and snow-covered roofs. It reminds him of the beach at home. "My wife is about to have a baby," he says.

The man nods at the road in front of him. "Are you going to or coming from the scene of that?"

Owen laughs. "Going to. I live in Destin."

The man smiles and nods again. "Congratulations. A boy or a girl?"

"Girl."

"Got a name picked out?"

"Caroline."

"Pretty name."

"It *is* a pretty name."

They ride again in silence. They are nearly at the terminal when Owen says, "Why didn't you ask me anything?"

"About what?"

"Aren't you a reporter?"

"What makes you think I'm a reporter?"

"Well. For one, you just answered my question with a question."

"Are you Annie Walsh's boyfriend?" the man asks.

"No." Owen slowly shakes his head and looks out the window. Not anymore, he thinks, and sits with the feeling.

"She married?"

"No. She's never been married."

The man nods slowly as he winds the car into the terminal. "Well. It looks like we ran out of time for more questions," he says.

THIRTY-FOUR

"There you are," Calder says, as if they're still kids playing a game of hide-and-go-seek and he has just found her behind a tree.

"Orange is not your color," Annie tells him through the video screen. He looks as if he's aged several years since she saw him on her porch.

He glances at his shirt and smiles with more delight than a person ought to have locked up in a place like this on Christmas day.

"And not exactly festive," he says, running his hand through his floppy hair.

"Merry Christmas," Annie says.

"Merry Christmas."

"Sidsel's coming over for dinner," she says. "In fact, she's making the dinner herself. She insisted. Mom's coming, too."

Calder sucks in a sharp breath and leans into the back of his chair. "All the women I love gathered around one table."

"She's lovely, Calder. I'm a little in love with her myself."

"You see?"

"I do."

Calder leans into the screen and places his hand against it.

"I'm sorry," Annie says, and raises her own hand to the glass.

"For what?"

"Everything. This. You in here. Me not coming to see you before now."

"There's something I need to tell you."

Annie sits on her free hand and braces herself. *Don't let it make a difference*, she thinks, *you love him either way*.

"It's all right," he finally says. "Something's come up to get me out of here."

It takes a moment for the words to register.

"What are you saying?"

"I'll be out before you know it."

"How?"

"You'll find out soon enough, I promise," he says with a flicker of trouble in his eyes.

"Tell me."

"I can't. Besides. It's Christmas. Let's talk about something else."

"Calder."

"You'll just have to trust me."

"You'll just have to tell me," she says.

"I don't want to ruin today."

"Telling me how you're about to get out of here is going to *ruin* the day?"

"Yes," he says, with a seriousness she hardly recognizes. "Trust me, Annie. Please. I don't want you to worry. I don't want you to think I'm going to be in here for life. Or worse. I'm not. It's going to be all right."

"When you say 'something's come up,' does that mean they found the person who did this?"

"I can't talk about it right now."

Annie takes a deep breath and decides to back off. She understands there isn't a whole lot he can say over the phone like this. Then she changes her mind. If he didn't do it, then who called him from Hal's and why?

"Fine. Just one question. Who called you from Hal's that night?"

"What?"

"From inside Hal's. Who called you from the payphone?"

Calder looks stricken. "Who told you that?"

"Sidsel. But I'm sure it's common knowledge by now."

"I don't know," Calder says, looking away.

"Well? Who was it? If you had nothing to do with it, and I believe you when you say that, then why was someone calling you from there?"

Calder leans back in his chair and blinks softly, the way anyone might when they are thinking something through.

Something doesn't feel right. There's a faraway look in his eyes. Maybe it's just the medication, but there's a distance, and it seems to be widening.

"You're lying," she says.

"No. What? I'm not."

"Who called you then? Why won't you tell me?"

"Because I don't know."

"That doesn't sound very likely, Calder. You're lying about something. Is it because we're on the phone like this?"

"No. Yes."

"Come on. Which is it?"

"I can't tell you. I haven't thought this through. I need to wait."

"Thought what through? Wait for what?"

"Can't you just take it on face value that it's going to be all right? Stop interrogating me!"

It can't be easy. She knows this. Being locked up in here for such a terrible crime. And yet his anger still feels misdirected. Something in his tone is off-key, as if he's upset that he's about to be set free.

"It's Christmas," he says, with a sigh. "Can't we talk about something else?

Annie nearly laughs. "What else is there to talk about?"

"You."

"Me."

"Yes. You."

"You're not going to try something stupid, are you?" Annie says. "To get out of here?"

"What, like escape?"

"Well, I guess not, if you're blurting it out like that over this phone."

He laughs. "No. I don't have a way of filing myself through the concrete walls. Now let's talk about something else. Have you had any visitors lately?"

How does he know? She feels a sense of betrayal rise up. The two of them on one side, Annie on the other. She tries pushing it away.

"As a matter of fact."

Calder gets a big grin on his face. "How'd it go?"

"I sent him home and hope to never see him again."

"What? Why'd you do that?"

She thinks of how she felt when she'd opened the door last night to find Owen gone again. He'd left the tree lights on and the ornaments were still there, along with the broken cup on the floor. She didn't even call out his name. She knew the feeling in the air. Vacant. Eternal. Only this time was different. This time it allowed her to breathe.

Calder chews the inside of his cheek.

"He's about to become a father. Did you know that?" Annie says.

"*What?* No. I didn't even think he was married."

"But you're the one who told Mom he got married."

Calder stares with a look of complete confusion. "Who are we talking about here?"

"I'm talking about Owen. Who are you talking about?"

Calder leans back in his chair and laughs. He leans forward and shakes his head. "You saw *Owen*. Where the hell did you see *Owen?*"

"My house. What do you mean? You knew he was coming to see me."

"Not a clue."

"Then why'd you ask if I'd had any visitors lately?"

Calder shrugs. "Just making conversation."

Annie lifts her eyebrow. "Who are you making it with, me or Mr. Haldol?"

He brushes the whole thing away with his hand. "So what else is going on?" he asks. "I'm serious. I want to know what you've been up to."

She realizes that this is what he craves. Normalcy. Stories of the every day. Gossip. She starts slowly by telling him about the Bull Creek Tavern, how the reason she looks like hell is because she was out most of the night singing until her voice gave way. Cigar smoke lingers in her hair even though she's showered, and as she tells him this she sees a shift in his eyes, his joy popping back to the surface. She tells him how snow looks under a magnifying glass and how it really does smell like new upholstery the way Daddy told them, but she saves Detour for another time.

And then she comes back around to Owen. "I don't know what I was thinking, wasting all those months. I can't tell you how good it felt to get out and sing last night. I felt like I was twenty years old. Like everything was new to me, everything still out there and me on the verge of discovering it."

Calder gets a huge grin on his face and rocks back and forth like a child about to burst with a secret.

"What? That was corny, wasn't it," she says.

"No. It's not that."

"What are you grinning at?"

"Remember the *what if* game we used to play?"

"Talk about ruining the day," she says.

"No, no. Listen. I've got one for you."

"I'm not sure I want to hear it."

"I'm pretty sure you do."

"All right. Go on. Let's hear it."

"OK. Let's see. Oh, here's a good one. What if *Joshua* had never left?"

The fluorescent lights buzz above her head. They're suddenly the only thing she hears.

"What?"

"Wait," he says. "How about this one? What if Joshua was the one who came back?"

THIRTY-FIVE

Sunday morning and the house smells of cooked bacon and coffee and warm buttered biscuits. Her mother stirs the gravy with a wooden spoon. She bends down to check the biscuits and croissants in the oven, recipes given to her by Sidsel, whose café her mother has insisted on running for the last two years. She calls her recent burst of energy nothing more than a second wind, but they all know she was desperate for something to keep her busy. She was desperate not to make the same mistake again.

Strands of gray hair pepper the red in her part. Her skin seems to have fallen, just a little, along her jaw. She looks older than she did two years ago, though nowhere near her sixty-five years.

Dragonflies float past the window. The summer sun glares through the live oak into the kitchen where Annie works at the sink.

"They ought to be here by now," her mother says.

Annie slices open a cantaloupe, picks up a large spoon, and gouges the seeds into the compost. "They're coming, don't worry. It takes a while to get through customs." She's been to see Calder and Sidsel twice since they moved to Denmark two years ago. The second time was a stop she made while she and Joshua were visiting Ireland.

She lets go of the melon and pats her mother's arm. "They'll be here."

They finally decided to move back. Calder asked that everyone wait for them at home. This is how he imagined his homecoming, here in Annie's house, the smell of home-cooked food and the quiet of the country. She thinks he also wanted to have a few minutes to recover after arriving back in Florida for the first time since he got out of jail. The judge had been right about one thing. The minute Calder was set free he took off with Sidsel to Denmark.

Annie and her mother work side by side in silence. Behind them her father's long farm table, the one he'd left unfinished, gleams beneath a vase filled with red amaryllises from Annie's garden. Two years ago she'd found the tapered legs and table-top leaning in the back of Uncle Calder's garage beneath a dusty moving blanket. Annie and Joshua turned her shed into a workshop and set to work on the Tiger Maple. Now, its rich, undulating grain tempts everyone who sees it to reach out and stroke it like a fur.

In the living room the puppies have worked themselves into a frenzy, thin ribs thumping against the hardwood floor, growls from pulling and chewing what Annie hopes are the toys she bought for them and not the rugs, the drapes, her socks and underwear from the basket in the bedroom. Joshua is no help at all. He comes down from Washington, D.C., twice a month, and even though he's only been here for three days this trip he's somehow managed to spoil them.

Her mother flips on the radio to the country oldies station Annie likes to set it to these days. The kitchen fills with slide guitars and violins, the melancholy notes of love and loss. Annie can almost hear the old percolator gurgling next to the golden radio in their kitchen all those years ago. The radio was always on in those days, just like her father. *Did I ever tell y'all about the time old Weaver's cable pulley went missing off his tow truck...*

"Frank will be in soon," her mother says. "He's just about done checking on Mrs. Lanie's blueberries. The crows are in there again so he's setting up another plastic owl to scare them off. This one better have teeth."

Annie wonders if the old songs have made her mother think of her lost husband, and in turn, made her think of Frank. They've been flirting ever since she came to hear Annie sing last year at the Bull Creek Tavern. Frank has since gotten braces to fix the gap in his teeth, and Annie suspects they're doing a lot more than flirting, though her mother is too private to say. Annie's schedule is busy these days with the release of her new CD—*How Am I Supposed to Get Back Home?* The single "Backstory" may turn out to be her biggest hit yet. She has concerts as far away as Prague, but every chance she gets she still pops into the Bull Creek unannounced and sings a few songs with Frank.

She looks out the side window at Mrs. Lanie's new farm. The woman decided to take the future into her own hands and razed the dead tangelo grove and corn and everything else that once grew there, including the grass. She replaced it all with mature crops that can sustain the "new winters," as they're calling them. Blueberries, avocados, squash, and macadamia nuts. She's already making a fortune off the macadamia nuts alone, much to the delight of her daughter Abigail who has no idea that all the property and its proceeds are being left to the children's home in Mrs. Lanie's will, so long as it remains a farm. If anyone tries otherwise, the ownership transfers to Annie.

"Turn it up," her mother says with a hot cookie sheet in her mitts. Emmylou Harris is singing, "Why can't I forget the past, start loving someone new, instead of having sweet dreams about you?"

Annie stares at her, surprised she wants to hear this.

Her mother smiles. "Remember when your father said that that could be you someday on the radio?"

She must see the look on Annie's face. She rubs Annie's shoulder and smiles a little more weakly this time. She turns back to the food on the counter.

Annie wonders if she's thinking of Uncle Calder, now buried near her father, separated only by the plot reserved for her mother. And that piece of paper they'd found on his chest with *Miriam, I never stopped* scribbled across a corner. They all knew what it was he meant to say, and it must have taken a good year before her mother could hear his name without tearing up. Annie doesn't think her mother needed a note to tell her what she already knew. For all any of them know, he is somewhere with her father, the two of them loving her still.

The puppies begin yelping at the door, scrambling against the oval glass as if their lives depend on alerting everyone to the fact that someone has arrived.

Annie rushes to the door to see Declan's animated face in the cab of Calder's truck. His curly hair rises above the dash, his chubby hands lift into the air then smack down against the front of his car seat as if he is riding a rollercoaster. The last time she saw him he was a red-faced infant with silky threads of blond hair, his mouth like a bird's squawking for food.

Sidsel turns to Declan and laughs, apparently moved by something he's done, some sound, maybe a word her son has spoken, or perhaps it's nothing aside from the sheer pleasure of having him there that causes her to reach for his hand and blow a kiss inside his palm. He falls into a fit of laughter so deep that by the time he rises from the truck he's purple-faced and limp, at the mercy of his own sense of humor.

Annie's chest swells at the sight of her brother. He looks so much like Uncle Calder. Her mother must see it, too, as she rushes out the door with her arms spread. His long gait, and the thing with the hair, Annie realizes only now—his hand running through his floppy hair—is Uncle Calder made over.

She stays put, allowing her mother to embrace the three of them at once. As they come closer to the porch Annie sees her mother in Declan's face.

She picks up the male puppy inside the front door, the one she's giving to Calder and his family. Joshua holds the girl she's keeping for herself. They kiss the velvety blond knots on the tops of their heads. The puppies squirm in their arms, and for a split second, Annie allows herself to wonder what might have been had Joshua not gone to meet Gabe at Hal's that evening.

Joshua sets the puppy down and pulls her into him as if reading her mind.

"I love every inch of you, Annie Walsh," he whispers.

"You would know," she says.

It's Sunday. This is what Declan will remember when he's grown. Days just like this, with music layered through the smell of cooked meat and bread and cake, the nuts and berries growing outside the door, his parents laughing around a farm table, quarreling over the facts of one another's stories with his Auntie Annie and Uncle Joshua and Granny and Frank and the dogs, these dogs, and all the others to come, wrestling across the floor.

ACKNOWLEDGMENTS

Thank you, Kathleen Concannon, David Ciminello, Rachel Hoffman, Patricia Kullberg, Monica Spoelstra Metz, and Linda Sladek, for years of insight and encouragement.

Thank you, Rima Karami, Jessica Donnell, Stephanie Sutherland, Laurie Creed Holst, Stefin McCargar, and Melissa Crisp, for all the hopes, wishes, and dreams on my behalf.

Thank you, Dylan and Liam, for making me laugh, ponder, and try harder to get everything right.

And thank you, Andrew, for making this, and so much more, possible.

ABOUT THE AUTHOR

Photograph by Andrew Reed, 2011

Deborah Reed comes from a long line of storytellers and musicians and finds creative inspiration in the composition of alt-country, folk, and homespun goods. She currently resides in the Pacific Northwest, where she also writes suspense fiction under the name of Audrey Braun.